FRESH START AT BRAMBLE COTTAGE

A heartwarming grumpy/sunshine romance with a seaside setting and a HEA guaranteed

SUSANNE McCARTHY

Choc Lit
A JOFFE BOOKS COMPANY

Choc Lit
A Joffe Books company
www.choc-lit.com

First published in Great Britain in 2024

Cover art by Jarmila Takač

ISBN: 978-1781897041

To my husband Geoff.
Who, in his younger days, bore a striking resemblance
to one of the main characters in this book —
down to the Devon accent!

CHAPTER ONE

"*At the next junction, turn right.*"

"You've got to be kidding me! I'm not driving up there."

"*Turn right.*"

"Oh, shut up, you silly bitch. Have you seen it? It's just a track. It's all potholes and mud."

"*Turn right.*"

"If you don't shut up I'll swap you for Stephen Fry." Vicky threw up her hands in exasperation. "Oh, Lord, I've really lost it now! I'm sitting here arguing with my satnav."

"*Turn right.*"

"Okay, okay, I'm turning right."

This was going to be tricky. Potholes and mud were the least of it — there were deep ruts in the lane as well, as if something heavy had regularly been driven over it, and it sloped steeply uphill. Her nippy little hatchback was a city-bred car — it wasn't accustomed to coping with that kind of thing.

"If this goes pear-shaped," she snarled at the annoying gizmo sitting on her dashboard, "I'm never speaking to you again."

Satisfied, the satnav lapsed into smug silence.

At least the ruts suggested that the lane led to somewhere. According to the naggy voice of the satnav, it led to Bramble Cottage, which was where she wanted to get to.

"Ah, well — here we go."

Keeping her fingers crossed that the underneath didn't bash on the ruts, she eased her foot on the accelerator and the car edged forward reluctantly. Replacing a dinted catalytic converter would be a nightmare inconvenience at the moment.

Jolting and squelching, she managed to inch the car up the slope. The lane might be rubbish, but the view was spectacular — gently rolling hills of lush green grass, squared off with thick flowering hedges and stands of trees. And off to the left, the shining blue of the sea.

When she was little, she had come down here every summer with her parents to stay with Aunt Molly for a couple of weeks. Well, Great-Aunt Molly to be more accurate — Dad's aunt. After he died, they had gradually lost contact with her, except for birthday and Christmas cards — always with a five-pound note tucked inside.

After her mum had married again, holidays had become Spain or Greece — much more exciting than South Devon, and you could always rely on the sun.

But now she was remembering how much she had loved Bramble Cottage. And Sturcombe, the little seaside village just down the hill. And Aunt Molly, with her soft white curls and the sweet scent of roses that had always clung to her.

And now the cottage was hers . . .

She had reached the crown of the slope, still with her foot on the accelerator — and squeaked in alarm, the tyres slithering on the mud as she braked too sharply. The lane ahead was blocked by a herd of black-and-white cows, ambling slowly down the hill.

To make matters worse, the mud had been churned up by the cows' hooves. She was helpless to stop the slide — and those swaying black-and-white rumps weren't going to shift out of the way.

There was only one place to go. She swung the wheel and with a graunch — which sounded expensive — the car tipped into the ditch at the side of the lane.

A large black-and-white head turned towards her, the wide pink nose so close that the side window was misted with warm cow breath. A pair of liquid brown eyes gazed at her in mild curiosity, then the animal turned away and strolled after her sisters.

"*In five hundred yards, you will have reached your destination.*"

"Thank you for nothing."

She reached out and jabbed the 'off' button on the sat-nav, and for good measure slid the thing out of its bracket and tucked it away in the glove compartment. Then she surveyed her situation.

Not good. The car was tipped at an angle of around thirty degrees, one front wheel in the ditch, both back wheels off the ground. She wasn't going to be able to simply reverse out.

With a sigh she switched off the ignition and sat back, closing her eyes. *Okay, serves you right for not taking out that rescue service membership.* Now she was stuck with trying to find a local garage — which could be a problem. She had no idea where the nearest one was.

But those cows were heading somewhere — further down the hill, and through a gate in a long stone wall.

A farmyard. And where there was a farmyard there was likely to be a nice big tractor. Maybe the farmer would be willing to tow her out of the ditch.

A vague memory stirred in her brain of running up the lane from Aunt Molly's to visit the calves, or sitting at the big scrubbed wooden table in the farmhouse kitchen eating home-baked scones still warm from the oven.

Her memory of the farmer was even more vague. A nice, jolly dairy farmer with a ruddy face and a warm South Devon accent, who'd called her 'my luvver' and given her a glass of milk fresh from the cows.

Though with the luck she was having today her recollection was likely to be well off. He'd probably turn out to be a grumpy old man with a face like a prune and droopy corduroy trousers held up with a bit of frayed rope.

Well, whatever, she needed to ask for help, even if she got her head bitten off for it. Hoisting her bag onto her shoulder, she pushed open the car door.

It was awkward to struggle out of the car — the angle of tilt meant that the door kept swinging shut again. But she managed it — only to land both feet in a deep muddy puddle that swamped her shoes and didn't want to let go.

"Damn, damn, damn!"

Leaning against the car for support she managed to drag one foot out still with its shoe, but the other resisted all attempts. In the end, she had to slide her foot free and then reach down into the cold puddle to extract the shoe — leaving her with a wet, muddy hand as well as two wet, muddy feet. And nothing to dry it on except her jeans.

The cows at least had reached their destination, turning into the farmyard ahead, followed by a pair of sleek black-and-white collies. One of them ignored her, the other spared her a single look in passing. A look that Vicky had no difficulty in recognising as utter contempt.

It was only fifty yards or so to the gate. In spite of the discomfort of her squelchy feet, she had to stop and gaze in delight. Yes, it was just as she remembered it.

On one side of the wide yard stood a long, low farmhouse, built of the local grey stone, with a grey-slate roof and dormer windows along the upper floor. Bright geraniums and aubretia tumbled out of window boxes and large pots on each side of the red-painted front door.

The second side was stables, which seemed to be mostly used as garages and storerooms, and on the third was a large steel-roofed barn. And, yes, there was indeed a tractor in the yard — large, green and muddy.

The cows were filing into the barn, ushered by the busy collies. She followed — and stood gazing around in surprise. This certainly wasn't the Old MacDonald's Farm she had painted into her childhood memories. It was all concrete floors and stainless-steel rails and festoons of rubber piping, starkly lit by strip lights in the high roof.

The air was sharp with the smell of industrial-strength disinfectant mingling with the pungent aroma of cow dung. One row of cows were plodding into their places in the stalls like obedient schoolchildren, as the row on the other side plodded out at the far end.

The two collies had trotted off after the cows that were leaving, presumably to return to their field, and a small, scruffy brown-and-white terrier was snuffling busily around a pile of feed sacks in the corner.

A lanky teenager was shovelling dung into a wheelbarrow. Two men were working their way along the rows of stalls. The one on the right, checking the rubber pipes, looked to be in his late twenties, with a pleasant face and ginger hair that stood up like a brush.

The other . . .

Scrub the jolly cartoon farmer. This one was a hunk — at least from the back. She'd guess at over six feet tall, with wide shoulders and thick, curling dark hair. And the way he was moving with brisk efficiency along the row of cows suggested that he was rather less than middle-aged.

"Excuse me." She stepped forward. "I'm sorry to bother you."

"Huh?" He glanced over his shoulder.

"I've had a bit of an accident. My car's in the ditch, just up the lane. I wondered if you could help me?"

He shook his head. "Sorry — You've picked a bad time. I'll be busy here for a while."

"I didn't mean right now." She tried a friendly smile but didn't get one in response. "I can see you're busy. But could you help me when you've finished? Or is there a garage I could call?"

"There's a couple, but you'd probably have to wait even longer. Weekends they tend to be kept occupied up on the moor."

"Oh . . ."

He had come to the end of the row and turned to the steel water-trough in the middle of the barn to wash his hands. "I'll be another half hour, if you want to wait that long."

"I don't seem to have much choice," she conceded wryly. "Thank you."

"Sit down, then."

"Thank you . . ." He'd already gone, striding down to the far end of the milking shed. There had been no 'my luvver', no answering smile. He looked as if he didn't know how.

But he certainly was a hunk. His eyes were dark beneath dark, level brows. The hard line of his jaw was shaded by a hint of stubble, and in the open collar of his plaid cotton shirt she had caught a glimpse of rough, curling hair at the base of his throat.

He was wearing brown oilskin dungarees — hardly the most elegant of garments, but they did nothing to detract from his hunkiness. There was something uncompromisingly male about him. It was in the easy confidence in the way he moved, the air of someone completely comfortable in his own skin.

She couldn't say that he had been impressed in return — the cool glance that had flickered over her had registered nothing but indifference. She really couldn't blame him for that. She must look as if she'd dropped in from another planet, in her slim-fit designer jeans and the flat scarlet pumps she wore for driving. Both caked in mud.

She probably had a couple of smears of mud on her face, too. And her hair, which her stepsister frequently disparaged as 'not-quite blonde', had fallen from the neat twist on the top of her head to tumble untidily over her shoulders.

Not that she was bothered what he thought of her — no matter how good-looking he was. She was only here for a few days — a week at most — to clear out Molly's things and check out any repairs or renovations needed at the cottage before she put it on the market.

Then she'd be off back to London, to her career and her fiancé. And this guy wouldn't figure in her memories at all.

She glanced around, but there was nowhere to sit except for a bale of hay. Well, that would have to do. The brown-and-white terrier came to sniff around her feet and jump up with his paws on her knees to say hello.

At least someone was friendly.

She stroked his soft head and tickled behind his ears, and his tongue lolled out, his warm brown eyes conveying pure ecstasy. Then he was off, back to sniffing and snuffling around the feed sacks — probably looking for rats. A new group of cows were ambling in from outside, ushered by the efficient collies into the stainless-steel pens. Vicky watched, fascinated, as the farmer worked his way steadily along the line, wiping their swollen pink udders with some brown liquid and fitting the rubber tubes. It was almost like a well-coordinated dance.

The shed was warm, and she was growing accustomed to the smell. The contented mooing of the cows and the rhythmic click and clang of the milking machinery spun a strange melody, a lullaby . . .

* * *

"Okay, are you ready to go?"

Vicky sat up sharply, startled awake. She hadn't intended to fall asleep. Had she been sleeping with her mouth open? Or worse, snoring?

"Oh . . . yes, right. Thank you."

She scrambled to her feet as he walked away. The mud had dried around her shoes, making them even more uncomfortable than when they had been wet, but there was nothing she could do about that now.

She followed him as he strode across the farmyard. He walked with an easy, athletic stride, the little terrier scrambling around his feet. The dungarees had gone . . . and what was she doing, admiring his butt in those well-worn jeans?

He swung himself up into the cab, the dog jumping up behind him, and held his hand out to her. She regarded the height of the cab with some misgiving.

7

"Jump up." Yes, he could smile. "Unless you'd prefer to walk?"

"No . . . um . . . okay — thank you very much."

She put her hand in his and found herself hauled bodily up into the cab. There was a narrow seat next to the driver's seat — but the dog was sitting on it, a look of smug possession on his furry little face.

The farmer laughed and clicked his tongue. "Come, Rufus."

Instantly the dog scrambled up and disposed himself around those wide shoulders, gazing alertly out of the windscreen, ready to give directions.

The farmer brushed a hand over the seat, though it had little effect. "I'm afraid it's a bit mucky."

"That's okay — these jeans are probably beyond salvation already." The little dog turned his head to study her with those quick dark eyes. She tickled one floppy brown ear. "He's a cute little thing."

The farmer laughed dryly. "Don't let him hear you say that. He thinks he's a Great Dane."

So — he had a sense of humour after all? Vicky laughed too. "You're probably glad he isn't if he makes a habit of sitting on your shoulders."

"Oh, that's far from being his only bad habit." He tickled the little dog under the chin, inducing a look of sheer bliss. "Bring any more half-dead rats into the house, Rufty Tufty, and you're for the dog pound, you horrible mutt."

Clearly the mutt wasn't remotely intimidated by the threat, turning his head to lap his long pink tongue up his master's cheek.

"I'm Tom, by the way." He fired up the tractor's ignition and it rumbled into life like some giant Transformers monster.

"Vicky. Thank you for your help. I hope I'm not keeping you from your work."

"No — only from my tea."

"Oh . . . I'm sorry . . ."

"No problem. This won't take long."

He turned the tractor out of the farm gate and up the lane. The ride was bumpy and she had to cling to the sides of her seat to stop herself being thrown around.

"How did you end up in the ditch?"

"I had to swerve to avoid your cows."

"You mean you didn't see them until the last minute?" He arched one dark eyebrow in lazy amusement. "They're pretty big."

"I know." She smiled wryly. "But it was muddy and the tyres wouldn't grip. I slid pretty much the whole way down the slope."

"What were you doing on the lane anyway?" His arm brushed against hers as he changed gear — and yes, those muscles were as hard as they looked. "It's just a farm track — cars hardly ever use it."

"It leads to Bramble Cottage, doesn't it?"

"It does. But if that's where you're heading why did you turn off down Haytor Avenue? You'd have been better to keep on the main road and take the next left down Church Road."

"I was following my satnav."

"Ah. Your satnav." She couldn't see it, but she suspected that he had rolled his eyes. "Anyway, why are you going to Bramble Cottage?"

"I just inherited it from my Aunt Molly."

"Molly was your aunt?" His voice had suddenly chilled. "Funny, I didn't know she had any family. I must have missed your visits. Regular, were they?"

"No . . ." She'd been feeling a bit guilty about that since she had found out about the will. She had been Molly's only living relative — she should have at least made some kind of effort to check that she was okay.

And now her aunt had left her the cottage and all its contents, as well as the contents of her bank account. "I haven't been down for a long time. We . . . more or less lost contact after my dad died."

9

"Really? And yet she was here all the time. You wouldn't have had to hire a private detective to find her."

His sarcasm put her on the defensive. "It wasn't my fault," she protested awkwardly. Her conscience bit back. *Yes, it was.*

He returned her only a brief, withering glance.

Fortunately they had reached the car. He manoeuvred the tractor behind it, jumped down and took a rope from the back. She watched as he stooped beside the back of the car and clicked off a plastic panel from the bumper.

"Oh . . . I never knew what that was for."

"Well, you know now." Any trace of friendliness was gone. With swift efficiency he threaded the rope through the tow loop and tied it in a secure knot. "Right. Take off the handbrake and turn on the ignition."

She did as he instructed. He climbed up into the tractor again and put it in gear. The tow rope tightened and, bit by bit, the car was dragged clear of the ditch. It bounced and jolted back onto all four wheels.

Anxiously she looked around it. The front nearside wheel didn't look right.

"It's out of alignment," Tom advised grimly. "You'll need to get it fixed before you try to drive it anywhere."

"You said I'd have difficulty getting a garage to come out."

"I'll give you a number. Ring them first thing in the morning — you can probably catch them before the tourists on the moors start flapping. I'll tow it down to Molly's for you."

"Oh." She was slightly surprised at the offer, after his earlier disapproval. "Thank you. Thank you very much."

"I need the towing hook."

"The . . . towing hook?"

"It's probably in the boot, under the spare wheel."

"Oh . . . right . . ."

She opened the boot, fumbling clumsily to remove the screw holding the spare wheel in place. With an impatient grunt he moved her aside — it was the most fleeting touch, but it sent an odd little shimmer of heat over her skin.

Steady girl — what was that about? Just because he had hard muscles and sexy eyes. And a judgemental attitude.

He swiftly unfastened the screw and lifted the wheel out, and located the metal hook in the tray beneath. In a few moments he had re-tied the tow rope and returned to the tractor.

It looked worryingly as if there wouldn't be room to turn the big machine around and get it past the stranded car, but she shouldn't have underestimated him. He bounced the thick wheel over the ditch on the opposite side of the lane, and eased round to the front of the car.

Rufus jumped up and wrapped himself across his shoulders again, and he held out his hand to help her up into the cab. Sitting beside him again, she was all too aware of the raw male power in those wide shoulders, the strength in his hands on the steering wheel.

She clenched her fists in her lap, the diamond ring on her finger digging into her palm. Okay, she could acknowledge that he was an attractive man — just thinking that wasn't being disloyal to Jeremy. But he clearly didn't like her.

Besides, there'd probably be a farmer's wife in the farmhouse on the far side of the yard.

They passed the entrance to the farm. The lad was hosing down the muddy yard, supervised by the two collies who lay side by side in the entrance to the barn. Rufus didn't even deign to glance in their direction.

A little further on they rounded a slight bend in the lane, and the cottage came into view.

It was a lot smaller than she remembered. It was tucked into a dip, with a rough patch of lawn running down to the front door. Built of the same grey stone as the farmhouse, it didn't look as neglected as she had feared. The grey-slate roof tiles and square brick chimney looked sound.

An overgrown hedge bordered the frontage. Tom manoeuvred the car into the gateway so that it was clear of the lane. "It'll be okay there until the garage can come and pick it up." He held out his hand. "Give me your phone and I'll put Barry's number in for you."

"Thank you."

He keyed a number into her phone and handed it back to her. She jumped down from the cab, and Rufus scrambled down after her and set off to explore the patch of lawn.

Tom unfastened the tow rope and coiled it up, tossing it into the back of the tractor, then stood and studied the cottage, his thumbs in the pockets of his jeans.

"What are you planning to do with it?" It wasn't friendly curiosity in his voice — there was more than a hint of suspicion.

"I don't know yet — that's why I came down to look at it for myself." She strolled slowly down the gravel drive, pausing to tug at a flourishing weed. "It's probably going to need a major renovation project."

"And then?"

"Well — sell it, I suppose."

"Why not sell it as it is, so someone local could afford it and do it up themselves?" he suggested.

"There's a greater profit margin if you sell it after it's been renovated." Uh-oh — she sounded just like Jeremy.

"And of course that would be the most important consideration."

She turned sharply, stung. "That's not fair. You don't know me — you don't know anything about me." She drew in a steadying breath. "Look, I appreciate your help with the car, but I'm not going to discuss my business with you."

"Fine. Have a nice day." And without another word he turned his back on her and whistled to Rufus, scooped him up and deposited him in the cab of the tractor, then swung up into the driver's seat. Putting the machine into reverse he drove away up the lane to the farm.

CHAPTER TWO

Vicky felt a small stab of guilt as she walked down the over-grown path to the cottage. Aunt Molly had always been very proud of her garden. Tom had been right to be critical of her. She ought to have made more of an effort to keep in contact over the years, especially recently, when Molly would have been in her late eighties, her nineties, and may have needed help.

Not that she would have accepted help easily. The old lady she remembered from more than sixteen years ago had been fiercely independent, and she didn't imagine that she would have changed much.

The solicitor in London who had read her the will had given her the key. Pulling it from her bag, she climbed the three stone steps to the front door. The wrought-iron railing beside them was pitted with rust in places, and the terracotta and blue-glazed flowerpots on each step were spilling over with rather bedraggled geraniums in bright reds and pinks.

She hesitated for a moment before opening the door. It felt a little weird to be back here now, as a grown-up. To think that she owned the cottage now — that Aunt Molly wouldn't be there in her kitchen, ready to greet the family with a beaming smile, a 'nice cup of tea' and a plate of warm scones with thick Devon cream.

The key clicked in the lock and turned easily. She pushed the door open and stepped into the kitchen.

It was much as she remembered — whitewashed walls, oak beams in the ceiling, a wood-burning stove in the inglenook fireplace. There was a faint smell of stale drains, but hopefully that was just because the place had stood empty for a while, not a warning of anything serious.

A stripped pine table stood in the middle of the room, with four wooden chairs around it. Half a dozen pots of dead herbs lined the windowsill above the big white butler sink, and the blue paint on the cupboard doors was scuffed and faded — the hinges on a couple of them had come loose, leaving the doors hanging at a slightly drunken angle.

Pausing on the doorstep to ease off her muddy shoes, she set off to explore. Beyond the kitchen was a narrow passageway. To her right a flight of stairs twisted tightly up to the first floor. She opened the door to her left. Yes — Molly's sewing room.

More memories flooded back. Molly's old sewing machine stood on a wooden table against one wall. A wicker basket held all her paraphernalia — scissors, tape measure, pincushion, marking chalk. There was a cardboard box full of fabric remnants, and several biscuit tins — a treasure trove of buttons and cotton reels. Vicky used to play with them on rare rainy days, sitting on the floor and sorting them by colour or size.

Next she moved to the room at the end of the passageway — the sitting room. Longer than it was wide, with windows on each side, it was a cosy room, the walls papered in a gold-coloured Regency stripe, the floor covered in a green-and-gold carpet over dark oak floorboards.

A heavy walnut sideboard stood at the back of the room. A recliner armchair and a battered old sofa upholstered in a flowery chintz faced a huge stone inglenook fireplace at the near end. She could just visualise one of those big leather chesterfields, as big as a divan, with a pile of cushions and pillows, in that place.

She smiled at the memory of how Molly had always filled the fireplace with vases of flowers in the summer. Now the vases stood empty and rather sad, just a few withered petals scattered on the stones around them. It would be nice to bring in some roses from the garden later . . .

Stupid. Impatiently she shook her head. She was letting herself imagine what she would do if she stayed — but she wouldn't be staying.

A pair of French windows opened onto the back garden. The key was in the lock, so she opened them and stepped outside. Like the front garden it was overgrown, but there was something charming in the way nature in her exuberance had taken over.

At the far end was what looked like a vegetable garden — a frame of bamboo canes for growing runner beans, rows of potatoes, cabbages and rhubarb showing lush greenery in spite of the tangle of weeds fighting them for space. In one corner stood an old apple tree smothered in delicate pale pink blossom.

Closer to the cottage, dog violets and cow parsley, and vivid red campion thrust their colourful heads up through the long grass. The air was filled with their fragrance and the happy twitter of birds, the hum of busy bumblebees, and the twinkling flash of butterfly wings.

She stood for a moment, just breathing it in. So different from London, with its acres of hard grey pavements, looming concrete office blocks, and rows and rows of narrow brick houses. If she had worn a corset, this must be what it would feel like to take it off . . .

Her phone buzzed, cutting through the moment. Reluctantly she pulled it from her bag.

"Hello." Jeremy's clear, well-modulated tones. "Are you there yet?"

"Yes — I got here about ten minutes ago." She chose not to tell him about running the car into the ditch, nor her enigmatic neighbour.

"What sort of state is it in?"

15

"Not too bad. As we thought, the kitchen will need to be replaced and I expect several of the windows too. And the garden is a bit overgrown." She would enjoy getting stuck in to tidying it up a bit — the apartment she shared with Jeremy was very smart and very convenient, but she had always regretted the lack of a garden.

"Okay. Send me photographs of any work that needs to be done and I'll check that you're not being overcharged. Don't forget to get three quotations."

She rolled her eyes. "I won't."

"By the way, has the valuation on the Eastman Road property been completed yet?"

"It's in the file."

"Ah — good. Well, I'll see you in a few days then. Goodbye."

"Goodbye, Jeremy . . . I love you."

"Same here. Goodbye."

She smiled wryly as she closed the call. 'Same here' was about as close as Jeremy could get to saying anything romantic. Well, that was okay — she was used to him.

She had been working for him for four years in the estate-agent office he managed — one of the chain owned by his mother. Dating him for two years, engaged for six months, due to marry him next summer. His mother was already looking at suitable venues. She had the contacts to get a good deal.

She tucked the phone back into her bag and climbed the stairs to the first floor. The stair carpet was a bit threadbare — that would need to be replaced. Jeremy would no doubt tell her that she ought to be recording her notes. If she was valuing the place for sale she would, but she didn't want to start thinking like that. Not yet.

Up here there were more signs of problems that would need fixing. An ominous dark stain in the corner of the ceiling suggested a leaky roof — or possibly just a loose gutter. Several of the wooden window frames on the side exposed to the sea were going to need more than just a lick of paint.

The bathroom was a festival of Edwardian plumbing, with an enamel roll-top bath — unfortunately badly chipped, but it could possibly be repaired. Those kinds of baths were popular with buyers. But the sink wasn't worth bothering with, and the toilet cistern was hanging precariously from one bracket high on the wall.

There were two small bedrooms — neither of them looked as if they had been used for years. The smallest was the one she had slept in when she was little. There was no furniture. A windowpane was cracked, there was another mouldy stain on the wall, and the bare floorboards were thick with dust.

In the slightly larger of the two, the only furniture was a double bed with a bare mattress, a heavy old wardrobe, empty, and a rather battered chest of drawers — also empty. Again there was thick dust everywhere.

That left only Molly's room. Vicky hesitated as she opened the door — she had rarely been in here before. More than any of the others it seemed to hold Molly's spirit.

This was the room where she had slept, had brushed her hair while sitting at that dressing table, had delicately dabbed the rose-scented perfume she had always worn onto her wrist and throat — its fragrance still lingered in the air.

Auntie Molly . . . A single tear spilled from the corner of her eye and tracked down her cheek. Impatiently she brushed it away. It was silly to cry — it had been so long since she had even seen her; she had been just a child.

It was a lovely room, if a bit too pink for her own taste. Delicately feminine, with dainty rosebud wallpaper and a lace-trimmed bedcover that matched the curtains. The carpet was a dusty pink, a pink-shaded lamp stood on the bedside table, and a sheepskin rug beside the bed would welcome bare feet when you got up in the morning.

Strolling over to the walnut dressing table, she sat down on the pink-upholstered stool in front of it. Like everything else, the surface was covered with a thin film of dust.

She touched each item lightly with one fingertip — a silver-backed hair brush, a crackled-glass bowl containing potpourri, a pretty enamelled trinket dish holding hair grips, a couple of elastic bands and a pearl button.

The large triple mirror reflected back her own image and the room behind her. She propped her elbow on the dressing table and dropped her chin into her cupped hand. More than forty years Aunt Molly had lived here, according to the solicitor.

Why had she chosen this little village on the pretty South Devon coast? Had she been happy here for all those years? She knew almost nothing about her . . .

As she gazed at the reflection of the room, something caught her eye — something that seemed jarringly out of place. A painting in a plain dark wooden frame, about eighteen inches high, on the wall opposite the bed. She didn't recall that she had ever noticed it before.

It was a portrait — sort of. Weird, slightly exaggerated, slightly surreal. The eyes were large and luminous, the lips full and red. But . . . the features were sharply angular, the skin had the colour and texture of driftwood. And the hair looked as if it was made from shavings of mahogany.

But even more weirdly, it was of Aunt Molly. A much younger Molly, but unmistakeably her.

Vicky stood for a moment, staring at it. It was certainly strange, and yet . . . as you looked at it, it became oddly beautiful. There was no signature, just a small symbol in the bottom left-hand corner — an M perhaps, or two Ns. Even a pair of rabbit's ears.

Who had painted it, and when? It wasn't at all the sort of thing she could have imagined Aunt Molly liking. But then it must have been painted years ago — in spite of the distortion it looked as if she had been maybe in her thirties.

Bemused, she shook her head and turned to go back downstairs to the kitchen. She was tired after her long drive from London, and hungry. She had brought some groceries, so she could make herself something to eat.

But first she needed to make up the bed in the spare room — she couldn't quite face sleeping in Molly's room. It would feel like she was . . . intruding, somehow.

She had brought her own bedding, on the advice of Jeremy's mother: 'Her sheets will probably be those awful nylon things that old people like. And anyway they won't be aired.'

* * *

Sunshine pouring in through a gap in the curtains, and the sweet-throated song of a thrush, brought Vicky gently awake. She lay for a long moment, just breathing slowly. No thunder of traffic from the Shepherds Bush Road a few hundred yards away, no splashing from the bathroom where Jeremy would be showering and shaving.

Peace.

With a luxurious stretch she tossed aside the duvet, rolled out of bed and crossed to the window. The garden looked lovely in the soft early morning light. She could still trace the outline of overgrown flowerbeds, where a few brave rose bushes and japonicas were holding on.

The wooden fence looked as if it was going to need some urgent repairs. Beyond, a long field rolled down to a stand of trees, and over their leafy tops she could glimpse the vivid blue of the sea.

A surge of excitement rose inside her, just as when she had been seven years old and couldn't wait to run down to the beach to build a sandcastle, to paddle in the waves, to lick a delicious ice-cream cornet — somehow ice cream had never tasted so good at home.

But before she could do that, she needed to ring the garage and get her car sorted out.

Barry from the garage was a little doubtful at first. "Ah, now, I don't know if I can come out today, my luvver. We get pretty busy on weekends up on the moor, see, what with all the tourists. I might be able to get out to you tomorrow, but Tuesday's more likely."

"Oh." That was a disappointment, though not entirely a surprise. "Tom said you'd probably be very busy."

"Tom?"

"Yes. He has the farm just up the lane from me. He pulled the car out of the ditch for me."

"Oh, *Tom*. Why didn't you say he's a friend of yours? I'll be there in about half an hour."

"Thank you." She raised her eyebrows in surprise as she closed the call. Apparently she had said the magic word — 'Tom'. Well, she wasn't going to complain — at least she was getting her car fixed.

* * *

True to his word, Barry arrived forty minutes later, reversing a red tow truck down the lane. Vicky grabbed her car keys and hurried out to meet him.

"Morning, my luvver. Let's have a look at this car of yours, then."

"Thank you for coming."

"No problem — anything for a friend of Tom's."

"Er . . . yes." She rolled her eyes as Barry bent to examine the front wheel.

"You've given that a good knock. Ran into a ditch, you say? How'd that happen?"

"I skidded trying to avoid the cows."

He laughed. "What were you doing on that bit of lane? It's just an old farm track."

"I was following my satnav."

He laughed. "Oh, your satnav." He appeared to share Tom's opinion on that. "You'd have done better to have stuck on the main road a bit further and turned down Church Road instead."

"Yes — so Tom told me."

"Ah well, let's get this thing loaded up, then."

"Will it take you long to fix it?"

He sucked his teeth. "Hmm . . . That's going to depend on how much damage there is. Could be just a matter of aligning the wheel, but if you've done in the steering or the suspension . . . Might be tomorrow, so long as we've got the parts."

"That's great — thank you very much."

She stood for a moment watching as her little car was hooked up to the tow truck and trundled off up the lane. Then she turned and strolled back into the cottage. She could make a start on listing the work that needed to be done — or she could take a walk down to the beach. Get a feel for the location.

She remembered it from when she was little, but those memories might not be reliable. As Jeremy's mother had pointed out, access to a good beach would be a big selling point for someone looking for a holiday home.

Swinging her bag onto her shoulder, she checked that she had her door keys and set off.

At the corner where the lane reached the road down to the village — the road she should have taken instead of the earlier turning and that stupid rutted lane — she paused and looked back at the cottage, nestled in the fold of the hill, sheltered by a small copse of leafy beech and ancient oak trees.

Yes, it would make a perfect holiday home.

She felt her heart grow heavier as she gazed at it. It was stupid, but she didn't want to part with it. Unfortunately she had no choice — there was going to be a hefty bill for the inheritance tax, which she would have to pay within six months or it would start to accrue a very unhealthy rate of interest.

And anyway, how could she spend more than a few weeks of the year down here? Even if she could persuade Jeremy to take his quota of annual leave, it would be even more difficult to persuade him to come to Devon instead of jetting off to somewhere with fascinating architecture and lots of high culture.

In truth, she didn't just want the cottage as a holiday home — she wanted to live here. But that was even more stupid. There was the small matter of money to live on. A job. The nearest estate agent was probably in Exeter or Plymouth

— even if she wanted to continue with that career. Which she wasn't sure she did.

With an impatient sigh she shook her head. Dreams were all very well, but they rarely came true in the real world. Reluctantly she turned away and walked on down the hill.

It was a pleasant ten-minute stroll past a row of cottages with neat gardens. Past the church, past a few shops — a small convenience store, a hairdresser, and a shop that sold second-hand furniture and household items. That one might be useful when she began clearing out Molly's cottage.

On the other side of the road were several large Victorian houses, most of them converted to bed-and-breakfast establishments, with names like 'Sunny Dene' and 'Bay View'.

On past the clock tower and the memorial garden, with its neat lawn and colourful flowerbeds and spiky dwarf palm trees, and down to the rather grandly named Esplanade.

A wave of nostalgia flowed through her. It had changed little in sixteen years. The amusement arcade on the corner, the chip shop, the shop selling rather tacky souvenirs and trinkets — did anyone actually buy that stuff these days?

And of course the beach shop, with its stands of post-cards, and nets of brightly coloured beach balls swinging in the breeze, wire baskets of frisbees and paddleboards and buckets and spades ranged along the pavement outside.

But it was the beach that drew her. The sand was a red-dish-gold, large-grained crunching beneath her feet as she stepped from the sloping ramp down from the Esplanade.

Though it was still only early May it was busy — excited children building sandcastles and digging long canals from the sea to fill the moats, just as she'd done all those years ago, while their parents watched benignly from deckchairs or stretched out on towels.

But the true owners of the beach were the seagulls, flashes of white against the blue sky, shrieking as they swooped over the waves, strutting arrogantly about on the sand, snatching discarded crisp packets or unguarded sausage rolls.

The tide was almost out, leaving a long stretch of damp sand glistening in the sunshine, lapped by lazy frills of white foam. The sea was a vivid blue. Far out in the bay a white sail scudded westward, while on the hazy horizon she could just see the grey shape of a large ship — whether an ocean liner or a cargo ship she couldn't tell.

To her right, where the beach ended in a jumble of rocks, a slope of reddish sandstone covered in scrubby bushes climbed to the elegant facade of the Carleton Hotel. It had been one of their holiday treats when she was little — tea and scones on the wide stone terrace overlooking the bay.

How had the place fared over the years? Had it been taken over by one of the big hotel chains, rendered anonymous in the name of maximising corporate profit? Or had it slid into a state of dignified neglect, struggling to attract guests in the teeth of competition from cheaper holidays in Spain or Greece?

She strolled along, past the row of gaily painted beach huts — miniature homes-from-home for the families clustered at their doors, with their picnics and crossword magazines. On the far side of the bay, half a dozen rows of white caravans curved around the rising ground.

The soft breeze from the sea was ruffling her hair and she could taste salt on her lips. She closed her eyes for a moment, breathing in the pure, clear air, the tang of damp seaweed, listening to the soft, sleepy whisper of the waves.

The sun was warm on her shoulders. Maybe she should have thought to bring some sun cream with her? Never mind — that little shop on Church Road that she'd passed on the way down probably sold some. She could pick up some milk while she was there.

* * *

The shop was small, but seemed to stock the whole gamut from groceries to newspapers and washing powder, several shelves of pharmacy goods and even a post-office counter.

The selection of sun creams wasn't extensive but they had her second favourite brand. She took a basket and picked out a few other items — milk, eggs, a bunch of bananas — and took them to the counter.

"Good afternoon." The ruddy-faced woman behind the counter beamed in friendly welcome as she began ringing up her purchases.

"Hello." Vicky smiled back — it was rare to get such a pleasant greeting in her local supermarket back home. "It's lovely weather."

"Oh, ah, 'tis that. Are you enjoying your holiday?"

"I'm not actually on holiday." She fished in her bag for her purse. "I've come down to see about my Aunt Molly's cottage."

"Molly? That's six pounds twenty-eight, please. You mean Molly Marston?"

"That's right. She was my aunt — well, great-aunt."

"Well I never!" The shopkeeper chuckled. "Ah, she was a one, old Molly. The way she used to race around on that old motorbike and sidecar of hers."

"Oh, heavens, yes! I remember that." Vicky laughed. "I was always begging to have a ride in the sidecar, but Mum wouldn't let me."

"I never knew she had any family."

"No, well . . . we used to come down for a few weeks every summer when I was little, but I'm afraid we rather lost contact with her after my dad died."

The shopkeeper nodded. "It happens . . ."

A door slammed open and from a back room behind the counter a teenage girl slouched out, not lifting her eyes from her phone as she steered on autopilot towards the shop doorway. Long brown hair framed a face that would have been pretty if it hadn't worn such a sulky expression.

"Bethany?" The shopkeeper's voice was sharp with impatience. "Where are you going? Have you finished all your homework?"

The only response was a grunt.

The shopkeeper sighed and shook her head, turning back to Vicky. "Kids!" An awkward laugh. "So she's left it to you then, the cottage? We all wondered who it would go to."

"Yes." Vicky smiled to herself as she tucked her shopping into her bag. She'd always thought it was just a cliché that in a small village like this everyone knew everyone else's business, but it seemed to be true!

Someone else had come into the shop and was wandering down the back aisle, but the shopkeeper was still intent on gathering as much news as she could for the village grapevine. "So you're going to be moving in, then?"

"Of course she isn't."

Vicky turned sharply as a cold voice spoke behind her. Tom.

"She's a city girl. Why would she want to bury herself down here among us country bumpkins? She can't wait to sell it off to some London dude who'll come down for Easter and three weeks in the summer."

The shopkeeper's smile faded. "You're going to sell it?"

"You know how much people will pay for a nice little cottage down here." His voice was heavily laced with sarcasm. "Who wouldn't sell it? And after all, that's just what we need around here, isn't it, Brenda? Another place standing empty for most of the year. Or maybe a holiday rental. Certainly nothing that anyone around here could afford."

"Yeah." A glare that could crack rocks. "Like we don't have enough of those."

Vicky felt her cheeks flame scarlet. Clearly the friendly welcome had been rescinded. Well, why should she care? She'd be back in London in a few days. Tilting up her chin with all the dignity she could muster she picked up the rest of her shopping and stalked out of the shop.

She had started to walk up the hill, but stopped and turned back. As Tom came out of the shop, she confronted him.

"What did you do that for?" she demanded. "I was having a nice friendly conversation, until you came along and put your oar in."

"So?" A cold sneer curled his hard mouth. "Why would you want to make friends? You'll only be here long enough to flog Molly's cottage for as much as you can get."

"That's beside the point. And it's not Molly's cottage now — it's mine. I can do what I like with it."

Oh Lord, where had that come from? She sounded just like the grasping bitch he clearly believed her to be. But he was way over the line. How dare he speak to her like that?

He didn't even bother to answer — he just stepped past her and strode off up the hill.

Huffing out a sharp breath, she set off up the hill behind his receding back. At least he was walking so fast that there was no danger of her catching up with him. She'd really like to throw something at him, but she didn't think a banana would do much damage.

CHAPTER THREE

Vicky was still fuming by the time she got home. Of all the arrogant, aggravating, infuriating men! She had wondered whether the local people might be wary of accepting her, but he had deliberately made it more difficult for her.

Okay, he had done her a favour, towing her car — well, two, counting recommending the garage. But that didn't compensate for what he had done.

She slammed around the kitchen, putting her shopping away and making herself a coffee. *Calm down* . . . After all, it didn't really matter — it wasn't as if she was going to be living here permanently.

The buzz of her phone forced her to come back down to earth. She glanced at the screen. Her mother. Oh Lord, that was all she needed right now. She drew in a long, steadying breath and made herself smile to warm her voice as she opened the call.

"Hi, Mum."

"Hello, darling. How are you?"

"Absolutely fine, Mum. How are you?"

"Oh, I'm fine, thank you. Did you have a good trip down?"

"Yes, no problem — the weather was lovely, which made it a really pleasant drive."

"And how's the house?"

"It's fine." Too many fines — was she protesting too much? "Well, it needs a fair amount of work, but it'll be fine. Which is more than can be said for the next-door neighbour." Oops — she hadn't intended to mention that.

"You mean the farm? Oh dear — are they being difficult? I remember them being quite nice. They used to let you go up and feed the calves — do you remember?"

"Um . . . yes, I think so." She frowned, delving back into distant memories. A pleasant middle-aged couple, always warm and welcoming. A cosy kitchen filled with the aroma of baking. "But that was a long time ago — I don't think they own it now. It's someone called Tom. He can't be more than early thirties."

"Tom? Oh, that could be their son. He'd be about the right age. Why is he being difficult?"

"He doesn't approve of second homes. Oh, I suppose he has a point," Vicky conceded reluctantly. "It must be hard for the local people to find anywhere to rent, let alone get on the housing ladder, when people from London come down and buy up houses that they only live in for a few months of the year."

"Well, yes, dear — but that's hardly your fault. What could you possibly do with the place if you don't sell it? You have to be sensible."

"Yes, Mum." Vicky rolled her eyes — it was fortunate that her mum hadn't figured out how to use FaceTime yet.

"What does Jeremy think about it?"

"I'm going to take some photos later to send to him."

"That's good — he'll be able to give you the best advice about what to do."

Vicky clenched her teeth to hold back what might have been too sharp a response. Her mother had always thought the world of Jeremy.

"Well, look after yourself, dear. Speak to you soon."

"Yes, Mum. Bye."

She closed the call with a sigh and put the phone down on the table. Oh, that word 'sensible' — it was her mother's mantra.

It was through being sensible that she had ended up as an estate agent. It hadn't been her dream job. She'd needed something after leaving university — a degree in medieval history wasn't exactly an open sesame for a wide range of careers.

She'd worked in a shop for a while. Then the vacancy for an administrative assistant at the Shepherd's Bush branch of Thoringtons had cropped up — it had seemed quite interesting, the money was good, and it was just a short bus ride from home. Sensible.

A year later, Charlotte Thorington, who owned the string of agencies, offered her the chance to train as a lettings agent. It was more money, and she liked the people she worked with.

Sensible.

It had cropped up again when she had started dating Jeremy. 'A nice, sensible young man,' her mother had said. 'Don't let him slip through your fingers.'

So she hadn't. But sometimes she wondered what it would be like not to be sensible. To have a dream — even a crazy one — and just go for it.

Like her vague plans to write a biography of Elizabeth Woodville, wife of King Edward IV and one of the most influential women of the Wars of the Roses.

She'd studied the period for her degree, and had been completely fascinated by Elizabeth — her renowned beauty, her secret marriage to Edward, the disappearance of her two sons — the famous Princes in the Tower.

She had made a few tentative starts on the book — though she had to agree with Jeremy that it was probably not a subject that many people would be interested in reading about. Still, she really wanted to write it, even if it was only for her own pleasure and never got published.

Putting those thoughts aside, she made herself some lunch. This afternoon she would go round the cottage to identify all the work that needed to be done to make the place saleable.

It was likely to be a long list, and some of the items could be pretty expensive — repairs to the roof, replacing all the windows with double-glazed units. Central heating, a new kitchen, a new bathroom . . .

Maybe Tom had been right, she reflected with a sigh. Maybe she could try selling it as it stood, let the purchasers do it up themselves.

But something about the place had got her hooked. She could see how it could be, with careful renovations that would make it more convenient without losing its comfortable cottagey charm.

In the sitting room she'd have one of the walls taken back to the natural brick, the wooden floor sanded and polished. The kitchen . . . Stone tiles on the floor, white walls, good lighting. Cream-painted shaker-style cabinets with granite worktops, a new white porcelain Belfast sink, and a big range-style cooker in the inglenook — cherry red, with brass fittings. Modern, but with a nod to traditional style.

Although that might run up a bit too expensive — maybe she'd have to compromise a little. Cheaper tiles, laminate worktops, ordinary oven. Even so it was going to cost a lot. But she could take out a loan against the value of the cottage and pay it back when the place was sold. Even after paying the inheritance tax she would still have a good amount left.

Together with what Jeremy could get for the sale of his flat it would give them a chance to buy a really decent property in London. A dream property in Twickenham or even Hampstead, with a garden . . .

A dream . . .

But weren't dreams meant to leave you fizzing with excitement? A house in Hampstead would probably be many people's dream. But there was no fizz — just a dull acknowledgement that it was the sensible thing to do.

* * *

It was almost nine o'clock when Vicky woke — she hadn't bothered to set her alarm. She hadn't slept so well in ages — it must have been the fresh sea air. But she had work to do — this morning she was planning to spend a couple of hours sorting through the kitchen cupboards.

Most of the stuff in the pantry would have to be thrown away — the potatoes had sprouted, the cabbage was a soggy brown mess. A lot of the packages were well past their sell-by dates — only the tins were usable, though she wasn't keen on oxtail soup or baked beans.

The pots and pans, cutlery and crockery could go to the charity shop down the hill — she'd keep enough to cook with while she was here. There was a nice big Pyrex casserole dish she would take home with her, plus a couple of vases and a blue-glass water jug.

She had finished her lunch and was washing up her plate when her phone buzzed. Barry from the garage.

"Miss Marston? I've got your car fixed. But I won't be able to fetch it out to you for a couple of days, I'm afraid — too busy up on the moors, see? But if you can get in on the bus, or get a lift, it's all yours."

"Oh, that's great — thank you. I'll get the bus."

* * *

'I'll get the bus' had proved to be easier said than done. For someone who lived close to one of London's busiest thoroughfares, buses were something that appeared whenever you looked up.

Here in the wilds of South Devon it was different, as she had discovered when she had checked the website of the local bus company. It had been a wise move to check — the only bus that came close ran only once an hour.

Trudging up the road to the bus stop, she was grateful that at least she'd be able to drive back from town instead of having to hang around for the bus . . .

A silver-grey SUV pulled up beside her, and the passenger door was opened. "Hi — jump in."

Tom.

She tilted up her chin, trying for as much dignity as she could muster. "No, thank you."

He arched one dark eyebrow. "Well, if you'd prefer to spend an hour or more bouncing around in an old bone-shaker that stinks of diesel while it winds its way around the countryside, that's up to you. I can get you there in fifteen minutes."

"How do you know where I'm going?"

"Where else would you be going? Anyway, I'd like to apologise for yesterday. I was out of line — I shouldn't have said what I did." Oh boy — that smile. It transformed the rather austere lines of his face, and Vicky felt her heartbeat accelerate alarmingly.

"Oh . . . well . . . um . . . thank you. I appreciate that. And . . . um . . . I wanted to thank you for recommending Barry."

"No problem." He patted the passenger seat. "Jump in."

With a murmured, "Thank you," she climbed in beside him. "This won't take you out of your way?"

"Not at all — I have stuff to do in town."

They reached the top of the hill and turned onto the main A road into town. The car was a manual transmission, and she found herself fascinated as she watched his hands work smoothly up through the gears or rest lightly on the steering wheel.

Strong hands, with long fingers and short-clipped nails. Strong wrists, with a smattering of that same dark, curling hair she had glimpsed at his throat . . .

Quickly she snatched her gaze away and turned it instead to studying the interior of the car. It looked quite new, and top of the range, with dark grey leather seats and a very futuristic technology touch-screen on the dashboard.

Clearly dairy-farming was more lucrative than she would have guessed.

"I suppose you have to get back for milking?" she asked brightly.

"Not till five o'clock."

She was absently twiddling the diamond ring on her finger. To stop herself fidgeting with it she folded her hands together in her lap. "How many cows do you have to milk?"

Again a raised eyebrow, suggesting that he was amused by her attempts to make polite conversation. "We've got a hundred and forty in milk at the moment. Plus we have twenty-four in calf and twenty-seven young heifers waiting to join the milking herd."

"That sounds like a lot."

"We're a medium-size operation," he responded genially. "Some of the bigger farms have over a thousand head."

"Wow! That must take some milking."

"They'd be a lot more mechanised than we are. We prefer to keep to a manageable size — we can know all the animals individually, keep a close eye on their health. And we're organic, so we get a slightly better profit margin."

She liked the sound of that. "Have your family always owned the farm?"

"Depends how far you want to go back. The old enrolment records show it's been ours for over three hundred years."

Her eyes widened. "That is a long time."

"It is." There was a distinct note of pride in his voice. "My dad's the tenth generation of Cullens to work the land."

"And now it's yours?"

He shook his head. "My dad's. And he's certainly not ready to retire just yet."

"Oh?" She slanted him an enquiring look. "I didn't see him when I was up there the other day."

"He and my mum have gone to Australia to visit her sister."

Her eyes danced, daring to tease him. "And they've left you in charge?"

"Pretty much. But I've got Bill to keep me in line — he's the stockman. You saw him on Saturday — ginger hair, big feet."

She laughed. "And who was the young lad who was there?"

"That's Wayne. He's doing an apprenticeship with us."

"Ah — is that why he gets all the mucky jobs?"

"It's like anywhere — you start from the bottom."

"Did you?"

"Of course. My dad never gave me a pass. I was mucking out from when I was six."

Vicky smiled to herself. "I remember your dad, from when I was little. He used to let me feed the calves. They were so sweet, all big brown eyes and soft pink tongues, licking at your hand. He let me name some of them, too."

His eyes glinted with genuine humour. "Were you responsible for sticking one of them with the label Horatia?"

"Probably." Oops — there went her crazy heartbeat again. "I wanted to call one Horatio — one of my favourite books when I was little was about a hippo called Horatio. But your dad told me there weren't any boy calves. It was only later that I realised that was because they would all have . . . gone off to be slaughtered." She was silent for a moment, remembering how that had made her cry. "I remember you, too. You pulled my hair once."

"Did I? Yes, you're probably right. Teenage boys can be pretty obnoxious."

"But then you stood up for me when some boys kicked over my sandcastle down on the beach." She smiled at the memory. "You hit one of them and they all ran away."

He laughed. "I remember you. You were a little scrap of a thing, always chattering and asking questions. You'd have been . . . what, twelve years old the last time you came down?"

"I was eleven."

"Why did you stop coming?"

"My dad got ill, then he died." She sighed sadly. "I suppose my mum didn't want to come down here anymore — too many reminders. Then she met my stepdad, and we started going abroad instead — Spain, Greece. We more or less lost contact with Aunt Molly, though she used to send me a birthday card every year, with a five-pound note in it. I suppose when I grew up I should have made more of an effort to come and see her, but . . ." She shrugged. "Well . . ."

His attention was diverted for a moment as he overtook a caravan. "To be honest, I doubt there was much you could have done for her. My mum kept an eye on her, but she was very independent, right up to the last. And I suppose it would be a long way to come to visit someone you barely knew."

She glanced up at him, surprised. "Well, yes. Though it's no excuse, I suppose — especially now she's left me her cottage. I had no idea she was going to do that." She was silent for a moment. "The solicitor who contacted me about the will said she died in her sleep."

"That's right. Her heart just gave up." He smiled. "It was a good way to go in the end. Very peaceful."

"And she'd had what I suppose you'd call a good innings. She was well into her nineties."

He nodded, slanting her a questioning look. "Are you still planning to sell the cottage?"

"Yes." Her mouth quirked wryly. "I don't really have much alternative. I'll have quite a hefty inheritance-tax bill to pay. And anyway, I can't really live in it myself. My job's in London, and . . ."

"Your fiancé?"

"Yes."

"He wouldn't want to move down here?"

The very thought of that made her laugh.

"Well, if you're still planning to fix it up, you'll need a builder you can rely on."

"Is there one you can recommend?"

"Yes. His name's Dan — I'll give you his number. He might be busy for a while though."

"Thank you." She glanced up at him. "You don't mind now — about me selling it? Even if it ends up being a second home?"crooked smile. "I'm being philosophical. There's no point being fractious about it." They had come to a roundabout. He turned left and a short distance further on pulled over onto the forecourt of a garage. "Here you are."

She could see her little hatchback parked in the alley beside the service centre. She unfastened her seat belt and opened the passenger door, and turned to Tom. "Thanks for the lift."

"No problem." Again that heart-bumping smile. "See you around."

* * *

Vicky stood at the open French windows, watching as the dusk settled quietly over the garden. The bees and the butterflies had gone, but the birds had discovered to their delight that their feeder had been replenished and were making the most of the feast.

A few stars were already twinkling as the sky deepened to a soft cobalt blue — with no streetlights to compete, they seemed so much brighter than in London.

When she was little she had always been sad to leave Aunt Molly's cottage — she'd cry as the car had pulled away from the lane. She was going to feel the same now — even, she suspected, including the tears.

Telling herself to be sensible wasn't going to help . . .

The ping of her phone intruded rudely on the moment. A text message. Jayde — her stepsister. Probably just to tell her about the fabulous night out she was having at the latest trendy nightclub, or possibly a new man.

Her mouth quirked into a wry smile as she clicked on the phone and read the message.

hows hunky neighbour (Punctuated with a wow emoji.)

She rolled her eyes. Typical Jayde. She typed in a reply: *not hunky pain in butt* (Angry emoji.)

The response came back at once: *not hunky* (Quiz emoji.) *check this* (Triple wow emojis.)

There was a link to a website. Vicky clicked on it warily. A news report, with a picture of Tom — in a dinner jacket, no less! It was some kind of awards ceremony — and he was winning an award for an organic feed company, Cullen Organic Mill.

He certainly scrubbed up well, she was forced to acknowledge. The dinner jacket was immaculately tailored over his wide shoulders but couldn't quite disguise that aura of dynamic male power; the neat clip of his hair couldn't quite control that tendency to curl.

not bad she acknowledged in her reply to Jayde. *still a pain coming 2 c 4 myself*

That was all she needed! Quickly she typed, *wouldnt like it place a mess* (Zany emoji.) *nothing to do*

The prompt reply. *1 check out hunk 2 work on tan ok but dont say i didnt warn u*

* * *

Did the sun really always shine in South Devon? That was how Vicky remembered it from her childhood, and it seemed to be proving true. The sky was a glorious vivid blue, tempting her to walk down to the beach again.

Okay — that could be her reward for getting the cupboards and shelves in the living room sorted out. But first she opened the French windows wide to let in the warm, fragrant breeze.

On the rose bushes the buds were just beginning to open, soft shades of white and pinks and yellows. She had planned to bring some in to fill the vases in the fireplace, as Aunt Molly had done.

There must be a pair of secateurs somewhere — probably in one of the kitchen drawers. A quick hunt found them — second drawer down, among a load of other utensils. They were a little stiff, but they would do the job.

Fifteen minutes later she had a lovely display, set off with a couple of fronds from a small juniper that had been hiding behind a rather straggly mahonia. Perfect. She sat back on her heels, breathing in the sweet fragrance. No wonder Aunt Molly had loved the flowers so much.

There was a 1960s-style radiogram in the alcove beside the fireplace, and next to it a rack of old vinyl LP records — Etta James, Billie Holiday, Edith Piaf. Switching it on, she chose the Etta James one and slid it carefully from its cover and placed it on the turntable.

Piano music filled the room, and that rich, smoky voice singing of love. This must have been one of Aunt Molly's favourites — had she listened to it in the evenings, lazing in her recliner, her eyes closed, a cup of tea or maybe a glass of wine in her hand?

She left it playing while she got to work. There wasn't much of interest in the sideboard — a box full of old post-cards and Christmas cards, a lidless Tupperware container with a jumble of paperclips, elastic bands and dried up Biros. A nice carved chess set in a wooden box. Her 'good' china.

Next she turned to the bookshelves. There were a lot of books, some of them in French. Of course . . . she had forgotten that Aunt Molly had lived in France as a child.

One of them had a pretty cover of vine leaves. *Les Vrilles de la Vigne* — a collection of short stories by Colette. As she flicked through it, a piece of paper slipped out and fluttered to the floor. Thin paper, pale blue, folded in half. With lines of beautiful handwriting — written in fountain pen and proper ink, not Biro. A poem.

I never loved till I met you,
My heart was never touched with gold.
Now my heart will be ever true
Though years may pass and we grow old.

Love is the light between the leaves
Love is the birds that soar in bliss
Love is the stars and the summer breeze
Love is the silence in a kiss.

Roses have thorns and love has tears.
Should I be first to say goodbye

My love will last beyond the years.
Love and roses never die.

Oh . . . A lump rose to her throat. It was signed with the same rabbit's ears as the portrait in Molly's bedroom. A lover? Who had he been? Why was there no other trace of him in the cottage? Had he left her? But how could he, after writing a poem like that?

Her mother had never mentioned him — but maybe she didn't know. It had probably been a long time ago, when Molly was young.

She tucked the poem back into the book and put it aside. The rest of the books she packed into a couple of cardboard boxes — though she wasn't sure if the charity shop would want them. The rubbish went into a black bin bag to go to the waste-disposal centre.

After all that hard work, she felt that she had earned her treat — which meant the little café along the Esplanade, on the corner next to the gift shop. It had been her favourite place for tea and cream scones when she was little.

It seemed pointless to drive down to the seafront and try to find a parking space, so she left the car at the cottage and walked down the hill.

The café was picture-postcard pretty. The window frame was painted ice-cream pink, the sign above it bearing the legend *Cupcake Café* in blue and pink, with three dancing cupcakes in case anyone missed the point.

There were a few tables on the pavement outside, with families eating pasties and iced cupcakes, and drinking coffee. A small spaniel came to sniff at her ankles and she bent to tickle his ear.

Inside, the café was very much as she remembered it, though it had clearly been spruced up since then. A cool black-and-white tiled floor; Formica-topped tables and white painted chairs; pale blue walls hung with colourful framed 1950s-style posters: *Welcome to Sturcombe*.

At the back was a counter with a glass-fronted cabinet displaying a selection of delicious-looking cakes and scones, all sorts of savouries, and the famous cupcakes.

There were fifteen tables, most of them full. A young woman of about her own age, with a mass of short dark curls, was serving one of the tables. She glanced round with a slightly distracted smile as Vicky walked in.

"Hi. I'll be with you in a tick. Have a seat."

Vicky settled down at a table, watching the people strolling along the Esplanade — children kicking their scooters along, mums and dads in sandals and cotton shorts and T-shirts, pushing buggies.

But it was the view beyond that captivated her — all that vast expanse of shimmering blue, stretching out far beyond the distant horizon. It seemed to go on to the end of the world . . .

The young woman came bustling over, pad in hand. "What can I get you?" she asked.

"I'll have a cream tea, please. Those scones look delicious — are they home-made?"

"Of course." A beam of pride. "I make them myself."

Something about her tugged at Vicky's memory. "Are you . . . Excuse me, but are you Debbie Rowley?"

"Yes, I am — well, Debbie Gowan, now. Sort of." The young woman looked puzzled. "I'm sorry, I don't think . . ."

"I'm Vicky — Vicky Marston. I used to come down to stay with my Aunt Molly in the summers when I was little, and we used to play together on the beach. I'm not surprised you don't remember me, though — it was years ago."

"Vicky? Oh my Lord! Yes, I do remember. Goodness, it must be . . . what, fifteen years!"

"Sixteen. And you're married now?"

Debbie glanced away. "Divorced."

"Oh." *Oops.* "But you're running the café?"

That brought the smile back. "My mum still owns it. She's poorly at the moment — she's had a bout of pneumonia and the doctor says she needs to stay in bed for another week."

"Oh, that's a shame. Wish her well for me."

"I will. Oh — excuse me . . ." More customers had come in, two children running to the counter to gaze wide-eyed at the selection of goodies on display.

"Sure. See you in a minute."

Vicky propped her elbow on the table, rested her chin on her fist and gazed out of the window again. When she was little it had been the beach and the shallows that had excited her. Now it was the bay, and the open sea.

There was something so serene about all that wide space — a sense that she could breathe. Even though she had lived in London all her life, sometimes she dreamed of escape. She hated the traffic, the uncaring crowds, the relentless rush and bustle.

If she could stay here . . . To wake in the mornings to green grass and butterflies, to walk down to the sea whenever she wanted, to watch the dusk roll in over the fields and the stars come out in the dark velvet sky.

Into her mind drifted an image of her next-door neighbour — of those dark, mesmerising eyes, that smile . . .

No! Where had that come from? Wishing she could stay here had nothing whatsoever to do with Tom Cullen. She didn't even like him — and he didn't seem to like her very much. And it definitely wasn't him that she had dreamed about last night.

Unconsciously she twisted the diamond ring on her finger. Anyway, she was engaged to Jeremy. If she had dreamed about her neighbour at all, it was only because he was so annoying.

"Here you go."

"Ah — thank you." She smiled up at her old friend as she set a tray down on the table. Debbie had always been quite shy, Vicky recalled, but there seemed to be something almost . . . melancholy about her now.

Because of her divorce? Had it been quite recent, still painful? She didn't like to ask. Instead she gestured towards the window. "I'd forgotten about this view. You're so lucky to live here."

"Yes, I suppose I am." Debbie glanced out of the window. "I'm so used to it that I don't really notice it most of the time, but every now and then I look out and I have to smile. But it must be fun living in London. I went there once, on a school trip. We went to the British Museum, and an art gallery — I can't remember which one."

"Well, yes, I suppose it is quite fun. There are a lot of things to do. But it doesn't compare to this. I'd swap all the theatres and museums for this any time."

"I suppose . . . oh, sorry — excuse me."

Her phone had buzzed, and she pulled it from the pocket of her apron as she hurried back behind the counter to answer the call. She was speaking quietly, but Vicky could hear the agitation in her voice.

"What do you mean, you can't? Oh, please, Alan, it'll only take a few minutes. You know I can't leave the café, with Mum still poorly." A pause as the other person spoke. "No, of course she can't — the doctor said she has to stay in bed." Another pause. "I know. I'm sorry. If you can't, you can't . . . Yes, I understand . . ."

Debbie had turned her back on the café but Vicky didn't miss the movement of her hand, which seemed to brush over her eyes as she put the phone back in her pocket.

Vicky frowned thoughtfully as she sliced her scone in half and spread it with a generous layer of thick Devon cream, topping it with a smear of raspberry jam and biting into it. It really was delicious — the cream lush, the scone still warm, melting in her mouth.

Clearly Debbie had a problem. Could she ask? Maybe there was something she could do to help.

The café was still busy. Some of the tables had emptied but were quickly filled by newcomers. Debbie seemed to be rushed off her feet, though somehow she kept smiling. At last there was a lull, and she came over to Vicky's table.

"It's so nice to see you again. Are you staying at Molly's cottage?"

Vicky nodded. "She's left it to me."

"Oh, lovely!" Debbie's soft brown eyes lit up. "So you'll be coming down to live here, then?"

Vicky shook her head. "I wish I could, but what with the repairs and the inheritance tax I'm not going to be able to afford it."

"Oh, that's a shame." Her friend looked genuinely disappointed. "It would have been nice to have you here."

"Yes . . ." Vicky paused. "Look . . . I didn't mean to listen to your private phone call, but . . . well, I couldn't help hearing. Is there something wrong? Is there anything I can do to help?"

"Oh . . . No, it's all right, thank you." But tears were brimming in Debbie's eyes. "It's just . . . my mother usually works with me in the café, but this bout of pneumonia has really laid her up, so I'm on my own. And one of us usually goes to fetch my daughter from school. My husband — my ex-husband — has picked her up for the past couple of days, but now he says he can't."

"Something more important than his own daughter has cropped up?"

That brought a crooked smile. "Yes. Not for the first time, either."

"He sounds like a bit of a git — if you don't mind me saying so."

"Well, yes, he is." Debbie sighed, then laughed. "At least he's someone else's problem now. Do you remember Kelly-Anne Wallis?"

Vicky thought for a moment. "Mousey hair, a bit of a bully? Always eating sweets but would never share them?"

Debbie nodded. "That's her. She's glammed up since then, bleached her hair blonde."

"And now she's with your ex-husband?"

"They got married three months after our divorce — they'd been carrying on for a couple of years. Me — idiot — I had no idea. There's already a baby on the way."

Vicky laughed. "Well, if she's still the same as I remember, she'll have him on a very short leash. He won't dare step out of line."

That made Debbie smile.

"How old is your daughter?"

"She's five."

"And there's no one else who could pick her up?"

"Not really. I . . . I don't really know any of the other parents very well."

Debbie's cheeks were pink. No, she was probably too shy to mingle at the school gates.

Vicky hesitated briefly. "Look, I'd offer to go and fetch her for you, but she doesn't know me. Why don't I mind the café for a while instead, while you go? I worked in a café while I was at uni, so I know the ropes."

Debbie's soft brown eyes opened wide. "You could? I'd pay you, of course . . ."

"Oh, no — think of it as for old friendship's sake."

"Well, if you're sure — it would be an enormous help."

Vicky rose to her feet and picked up her empty plate and mug. "Just show me where everything is."

Debbie's shoulders relaxed as she led the way behind the counter. "It's really very simple. Have you ever used one of these barista coffee machines?"

"One very similar."

"And the till. All the prices are on it — it's quite self-explanatory really. The hot drinks are all under this button, this is for cold drinks. The cakes are here . . ."

The door opened and a family piled in — a mum and dad, grandmother and three children.

Vicky laughed. "Ah — my first customers!"

CHAPTER FOUR

The café was busy, but Vicky was enjoying herself — she had always enjoyed working in the little place near her digs when she had been at university. Though the view here was definitely a bonus — and so were the happy customers enjoying their holidays.

She served up every variety of coffee, served tea in pretty china teapots with matching cups and saucers, home-made scones with Devonshire cream, slices of cake, pasties, bacon baps and triangles of quiche and pizza.

She was clearing a couple of tables when Debbie returned, a little mini-me at her side — the same soft brown curls, the same wide eyes and shy gaze.

"Are you okay?" Debbie asked. "How's it gone?"

"Absolutely fine — it's been fun. We're nearly out of the coffee-and-walnut cake — it's very popular."

"There's another one in the pantry — I'll fetch it. Amy, say hello to Auntie Vicky."

"Hello." A shy voice, a small hand gripping her mother's sleeve.

"Hello, Amy." Vicky smiled warmly. "It's nice to meet you."

"Now pop up and change out of your school uniform, then you can bring your colouring book down and sit at one of the tables."

The little girl nodded solemnly and scampered through the door that led to the family's apartment upstairs.

"I'll fetch the cake."

More customers had come in, the children excited by the selection of iced cupcakes. Vicky was pouring an espresso when the door opened again. She glanced around — and almost spilled the hot coffee on her hand.

With the light behind him she couldn't be sure at first, but as he strolled into the café she felt an odd little tingle scud down her spine. *Tom.* Quickly she turned her attention back to serving up the coffees, before she felt able to turn to him, a bright smile fixed in place.

"Hello." He raised one dark eyebrow in sardonic question. "Got a new job already?"

"I'm just helping out."

"That's very kind of you." Something in his tone lacked sincerity. But she wasn't going to get into another brangle with him.

Debbie bustled through from the kitchen with the cake. "Hello, Tom. Your usual?"

"Yes, please. Make it a very special one for Bill." He winked at her. "You know how he loves your pasties."

To Vicky's surprise, Debbie blushed scarlet and turned away to fuss with putting a couple of pasties in a paper bag. What was that about? She glanced from one to the other. Of course it was none of her business if there was something between them — she really couldn't care less.

Tom grinned teasingly as Debbie handed over the bag of pasties. "I'll be sure and tell Bill you sent them with your love."

"No! I mean . . . uh . . ."

He laughed. "Okay, I'll keep schtum." As he tapped his card on the reader he leaned over the counter and dropped a kiss on her cheek. "But don't keep him waiting too long. He's liable to turn all the milk sour."

He nodded briefly to Vicky, and strolled out of the café.

So . . . Debbie and Bill? Vicky felt herself breathe again — she hadn't even realised she had stopped. Debbie and Bill . . . that was sweet. But clearly there was a problem there.

The café was beginning to quieten down a bit. Vicky cleared a few more tables, carefully loading the dishwasher as she turned that conversation over in her mind.

It seemed that Debbie's marriage had been something of a disaster — but Bill the stockman apparently held a candle for her. And just mentioning his name could make Debbie blush. Was there a chance for a happy ending there? Maybe one or both of them just needed a little nudge . . .

"Excuse me, miss, could we have another pot of tea here, please?"

* * *

"So I'm like, No! And she's like, Yeah! So I'm like, But he's got freckles. And she's like, So what? And I goes, Has he got them on his dong? And then she's like completely shot, like she didn't even know I was joking or nothing."

Vicky laughed in what she hoped were the appropriate places. Jayde had been nattering since she had picked her up from the train station. It was always difficult to follow these stream-of-consciousness monologues, delivered at machine-gun speed and frequently featuring people she'd never heard of but was apparently supposed to know.

She was fond of her stepsister, but she could be very tiring at times. Now she launched into another of her pet subjects.

"You know you really ought to lighten your hair — go proper blonde instead of that nothing colour. I could do it for you while I'm here, and film it for my channel."

"No, thanks."

"Oh, go on. I need some new content and that'd be great. That's the trouble with you — you've not got no ambition."

Vicky smiled to herself. Jayde's ambition consisted of wanting to be an 'influencer'. She was certainly working hard at it. She had her own YouTube channel, TikTok, whatever the latest thing was, and eagerly checked the number of subscribers at least half a dozen times a day.

Of course it left her no time for a boring old nine-to-five job. Fortunately her maternal grandmother seemed quite happy to subsidise her lifestyle.

But that accusation that she had no ambition — Vicky had to acknowledge that it was probably fair. The trouble was, she didn't know what she wanted to do, and so she had drifted.

Maybe her mum had been right — she should have chosen a more sensible career-orientated degree than medieval history. She hadn't fancied teaching, and her dream of being a writer seemed destined to remain just that — a dream.

"Is it much farther?" Jayde had been nosing in the contents of the glove compartment. Now she sat back and glanced out of the window. "This is like the back end of beyond. Is there anything to do in this place?"

"Not much. I did warn you. There's a pub — in fact a couple of pubs, I think. I haven't been in any of them yet. And there's the beach, of course."

Jayde rolled her eyes. "I mean *do* — like clubs and things."

"No — nothing like that." Vicky smiled to herself. "It's only quite a small village. There's a mini-golf."

Jayde sighed. "Oh, well. I'll just have to make the most of it, I suppose."

"Why did you come down, if you think it's going to be such a bore?"

"To top up my tan on the beach."

"You can do that in the back garden," Vicky pointed out.

"You get a better tan on the beach. Besides, I wanted to check out this neighbour of yours. And I need some new content for my channel. I was going to go to Ibiza, but I'm a bit low on funds at the moment. And flying's just a nightmare, what with all the queues at the airport. Anyway, I wanted a few days away. I've split up with David."

"Again?"

"This time it's for good. And I thought when he comes round looking for me and I'm not there, it'll serve him right for being such a pig."

"What did he do?"

"He was talking to Caroline Bailey at Tamsin's party — all night! And when I had a go at him about it, he said I was being stupid and she was just a friend. Well, she's not my friend, and if she wants him she can have him and good luck to her!"

She folded her mouth tightly, and for a few moments there was blessed silence in the car.

Vicky ignored the first turn-off for Sturcombe — much to the satnav's annoyance. She took the next junction and drove down the long hill towards the village. Tom's cows were grazing in the field beside the road — a couple of them lifted their heads to stare with benign disinterest at the car as it passed.

Turning into the lane, she felt a little glow of pleasure as the cottage came into view. Hers. At least for now.

Jayde was less than impressed. "Is that it?"

"Yes."

Her sister looked as if she'd swallowed a wasp. "I didn't think it would be so small."

"It's got three bedrooms," Vicky protested. "And a really nice garden."

"It's practically falling down."

"Not quite." The tyres crunched on the drive as she turned through the gate. "It does need quite a lot of work, but once that's done it'll be great."

Jayde grunted something unintelligible and opened her door — and squawked loudly as she took a step up the path, wobbling on the gravel in her precariously high heels. "Damn! If I break these heels you have to pay for them."

Vicky sighed. "Just walk carefully — you'll be okay."

"Huh!" She tottered up the path, leaving Vicky to bring her suitcase from the car.

She was no more impressed when they got inside. She gazed around the kitchen, wrinkling her nose. "It smells."

"It is a bit musty," Vicky conceded. "There were some vegetables left in the cupboard when I arrived. I've thrown them out, but the smell still sticks around. Come on, I'll show you your room. I've been sleeping in the spare room, so you can have Molly's."

That seemed to cheer her sister — until she saw the room. "You don't expect me to sleep in *here*, do you? It's hideous — all those roses! And the smell makes me want to puke. And just look at that picture — it's like the most gruesome thing I've ever seen in my life. It'll give me nightmares."

Vicky rolled her eyes behind her sister's back. "Okay — we'll swap rooms. I'll just need to change the sheets on the other bed."

Jayde didn't offer to help. Instead she wheeled her suitcase into the smaller room and began to unpack it, shoving Vicky's clothes aside to hang hers in the wardrobe.

Suddenly she paused and looked out of the window. "Is that him?"

Vicky glanced over to check. Tom was walking round the field, going to each cow in turn, stroking its neck gently and talking to it. The cows seemed to respond, rubbing their heads against his arm.

"Yes. That's him."

"Wow — how could you say he isn't, like, a hunk? Were you worried Jeremy would find out?"

"Find out what?" Hopefully her sister was too distracted to notice the slight catch in her voice. "There's nothing to find out. He's just a rather annoying neighbour."

As if he was aware of them watching him, Tom glanced up briefly at the window. Jayde waved, but he had already turned his attention back to the cows.

Jayde continued to stand there, staring at him unashamedly. "Does he ever take his T-shirt off?"

"What? No. At least I've never seen him. I suppose he takes it off in the shower."

Jayde giggled. "Ah, now there's a thought."

Vicky felt a stab of irritation. She could only hope that Jayde wouldn't embarrass her while she was here.

"I'll just take my things into the other room, then I'll make some dinner. What would you like?"

"Oh, anything. Whatever's easiest."

"You're not still on that vegan diet then?"

"Oh, no." Jayde made a dismissive gesture with her hand. "Amanda said she lost a whole stone in two weeks on it, but I don't believe a word of it. I didn't lose an ounce."

Vicky smiled to herself. She suspected that the main reason it hadn't worked was because her sister hadn't stuck to it as strictly as she wanted to believe. She was a little too fond of her wine to give it up.

* * *

"Mmm." Vicky glanced around the pub. "This is a nice place."

Jayde shrugged, her pretty face registering bored indifference. "I suppose."

"Oh, come on. It's a lot better than most of the pubs at home, all with the same sticky carpets and fake wooden beams." She pointed at the ceiling. "These are real."

The floor was wooden too, rich dark oak, uneven in places from years of wear. The bar was the same dark wood, lined with brass beer-pumps. One of the walls was rough stone, with a large inglenook fireplace — there was no fire in it at present, but a wrought-iron basket of hewn logs stood beside it waiting to be used.

"I need to sit down," Jayde complained. "My feet are killing me."

"I'm not surprised, in those shoes."

Jayde tottered over to a table in the corner, leaving Vicky to go to the bar.

The place was quite busy — mostly locals, with a scattering of holidaymakers. It wasn't difficult to tell the difference — the holidaymakers in bright well-pressed clothes, the locals rugged in well-worn denim and saggy polo shirts.

As she waited to be served, she was aware that several of the younger men — and some of the older ones — were looking her over with mild curiosity. News of her identity would have already spread. She could only wait and see if there was going to be any hostility.

She ordered two glasses of white wine and carried them back to their table. Jayde already had her phone out, checking her messages and accepted her wine without a word. As she sipped it, Vicky wondered if she even tasted it.

At least with Jayde occupied she didn't need to try to make conversation. As she sipped her own wine, she glanced at her sister across the table. Just one year apart in age, they had got on well when her mother had married Jayde's father. Both having lost a parent had helped them bond. She had enjoyed having a big sister to follow, and Jayde had enjoyed being the one to benevolently lead the way.

Then Vicky had decided to stay on at school to do her A levels and go to university. For reasons Vicky had never been able to fathom, Jayde had seemed to take that as some kind of betrayal. And gradually they had grown apart. Now it sometimes seemed as if they were from different planets.

She was just beginning to relax when Jayde abruptly put down her phone and sat up straighter.

"That's *him*!" she hissed.

"Who?" Vicky glanced towards the door. Tom. And suddenly it felt as if there was a fizz of static electricity in the air.

"Mmm." Jayde's eyes were wide. "He's even more gorgeous up close and in the flesh."

Vicky held back a sigh. Jayde in full flirting mode was a sight to behold. As Tom passed their table she flashed him a smile that could have lit up the National Grid. He hesitated, one dark eyebrow raised in question, as if wondering if he was supposed to recognise her.

Then he noticed Vicky, and the question resolved. "Good evening. Come to sample our local night life? Hope it isn't too wild for you."

"Oh, I think we can cope." Jayde slanted him one of her patented seductive gazes from beneath her lashes. "I'm Vicky's sister — Jayde." She patted the table invitingly. "Why don't you join us?"

He glanced at Vicky, then back to Jayde, an enigmatic glint in his dark eyes. "Thank you." He pulled his wallet from his pocket and peeled off a banknote, handing it to Bill, who had followed him into the pub. "Get them in, mate. And another one for you, ladies?"

"Thank you." Jayde smiled coyly. "White wine, please."

"White wine it is. Thanks, Bill." He sat down. "So you're sisters? You don't look much alike."

Jayde giggled. "Oh, we're just stepsisters really. I've come down for a few days to help Vicky with clearing out the house."

Yes — I'll believe that when I see it, Vicky reflected silently.

"That's very kind of you." Again that enigmatic glint. "What do you think of our little village?"

"I haven't had a chance to see much of it yet, but it looks very pretty."

Vicky sat watching them. She wasn't sure whether to be irritated or amused — she chose amused. Jayde's eyes were wide and glowing, her mouth a pretty pout. It was impossible to tell what Tom was thinking.

Up close and in the flesh . . . Phew — had it suddenly grown hot in here? Jayde's words about him taking off his T-shirt were running through her head. Those wide shoulders, those hard biceps beneath his sun-bronzed skin . . .

Dammit, what was she thinking? She was engaged to Jeremy — she shouldn't be drooling over another man, however attractive he was. And he *was* attractive — she couldn't deny that.

Well, okay — there was no harm in looking. Just so long as she wasn't tempted to take it further. Not that there was much chance of that, she acknowledged wryly. He wasn't remotely interested in her — all his attention was on Jayde.

Not that she was jealous, of course — even if she had been interested in Tom. Her sister never had any trouble in hooking any man who took her fancy. She was used to it.

Bill returned with their drinks. She thanked him with a smile, and he bobbed his head in shy acknowledgement as he sat down.

She studied him covertly from beneath her lashes. His shoulders were hunched, his gaze focussed on the table as if afraid that he might accidentally make eye contact.

So this was the guy who had a fancy for Debbie — the guy whose name could make her blush. She smiled wryly to herself. Given how shy they both were, they were likely to need a boot in the butt to get them to do anything about it.

She would guess that he was maybe a year or two older than her. He was almost as tall as Tom, almost as wide across the shoulders. But he was . . . wholesome, rather than attractive, with ginger hair and sandy lashes and soft ruddy cheeks.

Jayde was leaning forward, resting her arms on the table to display her cleavage to the best advantage. She was using every trick she possessed — but Vicky suspected that Tom might not be so easy to reel in.

Or was that just wishful thinking?

He turned on a smile that was all smooth charm. "So what do you do, Jayde?"

She preened, delicately sipping her wine. "I'm an influencer — on social media."

"Oh?"

"I have a YouTube channel and a blog." Her lashes fluttered. "And TikTok, Instagram — well, all of them, of course."

"Of course."

If Jayde had picked up the note of dry humour in his voice, she wasn't disturbed by it. "I vlog about beauty products mostly."

"Vlog?"

"It's what we call a video blog," Jayde explained kindly.

Vicky kept a covert watch on Tom as she sipped her wine. If he was aware that Jayde was patronising him, apparently under the impression that she was speaking to an unsophisticated country bumpkin, the only clue to his amusement was the slight lift at the corner of his mouth.

Jayde had picked up her phone, and with a few clicks she accessed her vlog. "See?" She showed him the screen. Vicky could hear her commentary — something about choosing the correct shade of lipstick.

"Ah." He nodded, a hint of amusement lurking behind his bland expression.

Jayde clearly believed he was impressed, glowing with satisfaction as she showed him another one, about applying mascara, and then a third.

"Very interesting. I'm sure you'll be a great success."

Jayde beamed with pleasure. "What do you do?" she asked as if she hadn't already done her research.

"I'm a farmer."

"Oh — with cows and things?"

"Cows mostly."

His West Country accent had thickened perceptibly, and Vicky was finding it difficult not to laugh out loud. He flicked a brief glance in her direction, sharing the moment.

"I like cows." Jayde had propped her elbow on the table and rested her chin on her hand, and was gazing at him like a starving man offered a thick juicy steak. "They have such lovely long eyelashes."

"Perhaps you should put them on your flog," Tom suggested with an innocence that was entirely bogus. "You could demonstrate how to put on mascara."

Jayde trilled with laughter. "It's *vlog*, not *flog* — video and blog put together, see?"

"Ah yes. I thought it was because you use it to flog things."

Vicky watched the interaction between the two with trepidation. Jayde could be annoyingly patronising at times. So far Tom seemed to be responding with just a touch of subtle humour — she could only hope that he wouldn't give her stepsister a harsh put-down.

She glanced at Bill across the table. He hadn't spoken since he had sat down. He had one hand wrapped around his beer-glass, gazing into it as if it held all the secrets of the universe. It wouldn't be easy to engage him in conversation, but this was a good opportunity to get to know him a little better.

"Um . . . are you from Sturcombe?" she ventured. "Were you born here?"

He glanced up at her with a nervous smile. "Yes."

Ah. Well, that's a start. Try to think of something that won't have a monosyllabic answer. "It must have been a great place to grow up. Do you live in the village?"

"No."

Damn — monosyllable again.

She tried the approach she sometimes needed with nervous clients at the estate agent — leaning forward and smiling encouragingly but not filling the silence, giving them space to speak.

"I . . . um . . ." His gaze was fixed somewhere over her left shoulder. "I live at the farm. Over the stables."

"That's convenient." She made her voice warm. "You don't have to get up so early to get to work."

He grinned, beginning to ease a little. "Well, five o'clock is still quite early, but I'm used to it."

Jayde heard that and gasped, horrified. "Five o'clock? Every day?"

Tom laughed. "That's the life of a farmer. Up at five, clean up the shed, then out to the fields with the dogs to bring in the girls. An hour or so to milk them, then it's time to clean up the shed again, shovel all the shit into the composter, feed the calves and clean out their pens. It's a good healthy life — invigorating."

Vicky suppressed a bubble of laughter. If her sister had been harbouring any designs on Tom, the picture he had painted of life on a dairy farm had thoroughly disabused her of the fantasy. Possibly deliberately.

She had suspected, listening to his conversation with Jayde, that he concealed a very dry sense of humour behind those enigmatic eyes. She could tell by the way Bill was trying to suppress a smile that he too knew that Tom was teasing.

Unfortunately Jayde was too self-absorbed to be aware of it. And however irritating her stepsister could be, Vicky didn't want her to be made to feel a fool when the penny dropped.

As Jayde was distracted by eagerly searching through her phone for another vlog to show him, she slanted him a warning glance, and shook her head. He smiled, and nodded — he understood.

He rose easily to his feet. "Another drink, ladies?"

"Oh . . . thank you." Jayde's smile was all sweetness. "White wine, please." She watched him walk to the bar, a smug smile on her face, then leaned towards Vicky. "I think he fancies me," she whispered.

Vicky managed not to roll her eyes. "You could be right."

CHAPTER FIVE

Tom finished his second pint and glanced at his watch. "Well, ladies, if you'll excuse us, us country boys need to hit the sack."

Jayde pouted prettily. "Already? But it isn't even ten o'clock yet."

"Sorry — we have a bunch of girls who are going to want to see us bright and busy in the morning."

"Oh . . . of course." But Jayde hadn't given up completely. She finished her wine in one swallow and rose to her feet. "We ought to be getting along too. It's been a long day."

Tom smiled down at her. "It's a long drive down from London."

"Oh, I came on the train." She giggled. "I don't drive — I haven't passed my test yet. I'm such a klutz — I've failed it five times."

Tom laughed as he held the door open for them. "At least it shows you're persistent."

The moon was half full, shimmering like silver on the dark sweep of the sea, and the sky was a swathe of black velvet scattered with a million diamonds. Vicky gazed around in delight. She hadn't been down to the seafront when it was dark before.

The tide was in, the waves lapping right up to the sea wall. The length of the Esplanade was strung with multi-coloured lights looped from lamp post to lamp post, their reflection pooling like jewels on the water below. The jangling Wurlitzer music from the amusement arcade on the corner drifted on the warm evening breeze.

"Oh — it's so pretty!" Jayde exclaimed. "I could stay here for ever."

"Really?" Tom arched one dark eyebrow. "Not too quiet for you?"

"Oh, no — well, maybe," she conceded in an uncharacteristic moment of self-awareness. "But it would be a great place to have a holiday home."

"No doubt." The sudden chill in his voice reminded Vicky that this was a touchy subject.

Jayde glanced around. "Where's your car?"

"No car. Why would I drive down when it's such a short distance, then have the hassle of trying to find a place to park? Come on — the walk'll do you good."

"But it's uphill."

"All the better."

And he strode off along the pavement, leaving Jayde little choice but to hurry to catch up with him, tottering on those ridiculous heels.

* * *

Vicky didn't expect her sister to be out of bed early the next morning, and she was right. She poured herself a bowl of cereal and sat down at the kitchen table to eat it. It was good to have a bit of peace — Jayde could sometimes be pretty tiring.

She hadn't slept well last night, waking hot and bothered, with the sheets all tangled and a slightly guilty feeling that it was her next-door neighbour who had been the cause of the turmoil in her dreams.

But there was no reason to feel guilty about it, she assured herself — she couldn't help what happened while she was asleep. So long as she didn't indulge those stupid fantasies while she was awake. Which she wouldn't. Definitely not.

With a small sigh she took her empty bowl over to the sink and rinsed it out. She had planned to spend some time today sorting through Molly's old clothes. She could probably get some of that done before Jayde surfaced.

She had finished emptying the wardrobe in Molly's bedroom and had made a start on the contents of the big chest of drawers when Jayde strolled in, yawning, still wearing her nightie, her hair unbrushed.

Vicky smiled to herself. "Hi. Do you want some breakfast?"

"Ugh." Jayde pulled a face. "I never eat breakfast. What are you doing?"

"Just going through Aunt Molly's things to see what to throw away and what to take to the charity shop."

"Huh." Jayde came over and peered at the contents of the drawer. "What a load of fusty old rubbish. You might as well throw it all away." She picked up a pink cardigan with tiny pearl buttons. "No one's going to want this old stuff. I'm surprised the moths haven't got at it."

"She put rose petals in the drawers. Mmm . . ." She lifted one of the jumpers to her nose. "It makes them all smell lovely."

"It's an old-lady smell. Still, I suppose she was an old lady." Jayde plumped down on the bed with a sigh. "I'm bored. It's a lovely day — can't we go down to the beach?"

"You can if you like — I want to crack on with this, at least until lunchtime. Then I'll come to the beach with you."

"Oh, all right," Jayde conceded sulkily. "I'll wait." She flopped back on the bed, her hands behind her head. "That Tom — he's really boring. All he kept going on about all the way home was his stupid cows."

Vicky dived into the contents of the drawer to hide her amusement. That had been a very clever tactic on his part to gently deter Jayde's unsubtle attempts to flirt with him.

She was finding herself actually beginning to like him. No more than that, of course — no matter how attractive he was. Anyway, there was Jeremy.

"Could you pass me a couple of those bin bags?" she asked.

Jayde grunted and rolled off the bed. "Here."

Vicky took the bags and began to tuck the clothes into them — one lot for the dump, one for the charity shop. Jayde was looking in the other drawers. She pulled open the bottom one, and gasped. "Oh, wow! Look at this."

The drawer was full of silk and satin lingerie, in soft shades of cream and buttercup yellow, pink and baby-blue, much of it extravagantly trimmed with lace.

"This is fabulous." Sulks were forgotten. "Whatever was the old duck doing with all this stuff?"

"It must be what she wore when she was young, and she kept it." Vicky pulled out a full-length wrap, with bell sleeves and a silk sash. It was so soft that it rippled through her hands like water.

"Put it on," Jayde urged. She had pulled out something for herself — a black satin petticoat with a lace front panel and shoelace straps. "I'm going to try this on." She danced off to her own bedroom with her trophy.

Vicky shrugged into the wrap and swirled in front of the cheval mirror in the corner. It was so beautiful, a delicate shade of lilac, trimmed with lace. A faint exotic fragrance clung to its folds.

Was this what Aunt Molly had worn for her lover, the poet, the painter? What sort of life had she lived, to have owned such beautiful things? They must have been expensive. The label inside was woven in pink on cream — *Fabriqué Elisa Roselli / Paris*.

"Ta dah!" Jayde came back in, posing to show off the black petticoat. "What do you think? I could wear this down the club."

Vicky eyed it doubtfully. "Well . . . I suppose . . ."

"These slip dresses are all the thing. That wrap thing's gorgeous. Are you going to keep it?"

Vicky turned to gaze at it in the mirror again. "Yes, I think I will."

"Jeremy will love it."

Vicky laughed dryly. "I don't think it would suit him."

"This is fun." Jayde dived into the drawer again and pulled out a full-length cream silk nightgown, followed by a scarlet camisole and a lace bra. "Wow — this is amazing! I wonder what else we can find? Have you looked in the attic yet?"

"Not yet."

Jayde dumped her trophies on the bed and darted out to the landing, and Vicky heard her footsteps on the narrow stairs up to the attic. A couple of thumps — she could only hope she wouldn't come through the ceiling. Then Jayde's voice, bubbling with excitement.

"Vicky — come and look at this!"

She slipped off the wrap and hurried up the steep, twisting flight to the attic.

A sharp aroma of dust and old wood attacked her nostrils, making her sneeze. A bare lightbulb swinging from the apex of the roof cast weird shadows over various bits of junk — a couple of broken chairs, a cardboard box of worn-out boots and shoes. And a pair of ancient steamer trunks.

Jayde had opened one of them and was twirling around with a giant feather fan.

"Where did all this come from? It looks like your aunt Molly led a pretty wild life when she was young." She plunged back into the trunk and pulled out a bundle of strands of beads. "What on earth is this?"

Vicky shook her head, laughing. "Heaven knows!"

They began to carefully untangle the strands. It took several minutes, and when they had finished they weren't much wiser about what it was.

"These bits look like they would be shoulder straps," Jayde mused, holding it up. "Then you've got a kind of necklace. And then this bit might go round your hips and down over your tush. But there's nothing over your boobs — it must have been worn with something else."

Vicky laughed. "I don't think so. Oh, Aunt Molly — what a girl you were! Haven't you seen that film, *Moulin Rouge*? These are the kind of costumes they wore."

"But that was just a film — not real life."

"The Moulin Rouge was a real place — *is* a real place. It's a nightclub, a cabaret, in Paris. The dancers there wear feathers and these exotic costumes, and some of them are nearly naked. It's very famous — haven't you ever heard of it?"

Jayde shrugged. "I might have done. Do you think Molly actually was a dancer there?"

"There or somewhere like it. I know she was born in France — her mother, my great-grandmother, was French. Her name was actually Meline, according to her will. And some of that stuff in the bottom drawer was from Paris."

"Wow! Let's see what else is in these trunks."

Jayde's boredom was completely forgotten. They spent several happy hours exploring the contents of the trunks, finding the most amazing exotic costumes, giggling as they tried them on and taking photographs of each other on their phones.

It was times like these, all too rare in recent years, that Vicky felt close to her sister again. She had missed that.

They had got to the bottom of the second trunk and she glanced at her watch. "Heavens, it's almost two o'clock. I'm starving. Shall we get some lunch?"

They decided to go down to Debbie's café to eat, then spend the rest of the afternoon on the beach. Jayde was persuaded to walk down. "Come on, it's not far. And it'll be a nightmare trying to find a parking space."

"Oh, okay. But I need to borrow your flip-flops. I can't walk in these sandals."

* * *

The café was busy, Debbie bustling between the tables and the counter. She greeted Vicky with her shy smile. "Hi!"

"Hi. Jayde, this is Debbie — we used to play on the beach together when we were little. Jayde's my sister."

"Lovely to meet you." Debbie turned her smile to Jayde. "What can I get you?"

"Is that quiche gluten free?"

"Oh . . . no, the pastry's made with ordinary flour. The tortilla wraps are gluten free, though."

"I'll have one of those, then. And a cappuccino — with fat-free milk."

Debbie didn't even blink. "Right. Vicky?"

"I'll have a couple of the wraps too. And a latte, please. How are you managing?"

"Well, it is busy, as you can see. But I can cope."

"How's your mum?"

"A lot better. Itching to come down, even if it's only to sit at the till." She hesitated, biting her lip. "There was something I was going to ask you — a favour. But . . ." She slanted a swift glance at Jayde.

"What is it?" Vicky prompted her.

"It's just . . . I've got a kiddies' birthday party here tomorrow. Mum was going to come down and help, but the doctor came this morning and he said she still needs to rest up for a few more days. She's been arguing about it, but I'm afraid it'll be too much for her. I was going to ask you . . . If she knows you're here she'll be okay about staying upstairs."

"I'd be happy to come down and help out for a couple of hours," Vicky insisted at once. "Of course I would."

"Are you sure? I mean . . . with your sister here?"

"No, it'll be fine. Jayde won't mind — will you?"

Her sister glanced up from checking her phone. "What's that?"

"I've promised to help Debbie with a party tomorrow."

"A party?" Jayde's eyes lit up.

"A kids' party. Tomorrow afternoon."

"Oh . . ."

"It'll only be for a couple of hours, tops. You can spend some time on the beach — you'll have a great tan by the time you go home."

"I suppose so."

Oh dear — grumpy Jayde was back. The phone claimed her attention again, and any possibility of conversation was wiped out. With a small sigh Vicky propped her chin on her hand and contented herself with gazing out at the view.

Far out in the bay a line of small yachts were scudding across the water, their white sails sparkling in the bright sunshine.

Could she find a way to stay here? Maybe once she'd sold Aunt Molly's cottage and paid off the inheritance tax and the loan for the renovations, she would have enough money left to buy a smaller place — a flat, maybe?

But what would she do for a job? Writing was her dream, but even if she could ever get something published it was unlikely to make much money. And she'd need to support herself in the meantime.

And then there was Jeremy, of course. She felt a small stab of guilt. He was her fiancé, he should be her first consideration, not . . . an afterthought.

Debbie came over with their food, and with a rather exaggerated show of reluctance Jayde turned off her phone and picked up her napkin to wrap it round her tortilla.

"Thanks, Debbie." Vicky smiled up at her friend. "These look delicious."

"Hope you enjoy them."

More customers had arrived and she hurried away. Vicky took a bite of her tortilla.

"I've been thinking about what to do with some of that better stuff of Aunt Molly's." Maybe the topic of clothes would engage Jayde's interest. "Do you think I could sell them online?"

"Some of them." Her sister shrugged. "It can be a bit time consuming if you want to sell a lot of stuff."

"Could you help me?"

"Sure." That was more of a smirk than a smile. "Fifty-fifty."

Vicky shook her head. "Thirty-seventy."

"Forty-sixty."

"Okay."

Jayde laughed in triumph. "I was going to accept thirty-seventy."

65

Vicky laughed with her. She didn't confess that she'd been going to offer fifty-fifty.

* * *

To Vicky's relief the good mood lasted through lunch and beyond. They strolled down to the beach, wriggling out of their clothes as discreetly as possible, then stretched out on their towels in their bikinis, slathering each other generously with sunscreen.

"Ah — this is perfect." Jayde sighed with contentment, lying back and closing her eyes. "Wake me in an hour so I can do my other side."

Vicky laughed. "Okay."

She pulled her book from her bag and found her place. But for once even the convoluted murder investigation by Ellis Peters' medieval monk couldn't engage her attention. She sat up, hugging her knees and gazing out over the bay.

The yachts had moved on. Now the grey shape of a large ship — a freighter or a cruise ship? — hovered on the horizon. The sky was a pure, clear blue, dusted with a few wisps of cloud like the sweepings of a careless broom.

On the beach, small children were racing around, squealing with joy, splashing in and out of the shallow wavelets at the water's edge. A couple of Labradors and an excited springer spaniel were chasing each other, barking and yapping and play-fighting.

Suddenly a small brown-and-white terrier came racing up out of the sea. A few yards up the beach he paused and shook himself vigorously, sending sparkling droplets of water in all directions. Then he spotted Vicky and hurtled towards her as if she was his dearest friend, and launched himself into her arms, panting and licking her face.

"Rufus! Get off — you're soaking me, you horrible animal!"

Jayde screeched and rolled aside, jumping to her feet. "Oh my God — get him off. He's dangerous. Where's his owner?"

"I'm sorry."

Vicky had her eyes screwed tightly shut against the assault of that excited tongue, but she knew Tom's voice.

"Rufty, here."

The dog ignored him. Vicky had fallen onto her back and he was standing on her chest, subjecting her face to a thorough wash.

"He's yours?" Jayde's tone had undergone a magical transformation as Tom strolled up.

"Yes. I'm sorry — he's only young, and he can be pretty boisterous, but he isn't dangerous."

Vicky had succeeded in wrestling the pup into her arms, laughing as he continued to wriggle wildly.

Tom grinned. "I think he likes you."

"So it seems. I just wish he wasn't quite so enthusiastic about it."

Tom scooped the little dog up — the pup's allegiance switched instantly as he tried to lick his master's face instead. "That's enough, Rufus. You're going to have to go back on your lead if you can't behave yourself."

Vicky had managed to sit up, but the sight of Tom standing there did absolutely nothing to ease the racing beat of her heart. He had been swimming. His dark hair was slicked back but still trying to curl. His body was tanned and glistening wet. A smattering of rough, dark hair covered his hard-muscled chest, and his stomach was washboard lean above the band of his black shorts.

Her mouth felt suddenly dry. This was crazy — she'd never reacted to a man on such a purely physical level before. Not even Jeremy. She could feel her cheeks flushing a heated red, and looked away quickly.

Jayde had recovered her flirtatious manner — apparently the sight of Tom's hunky body had caused her to forget that she had thought him boring. "Oh, what a cute little dog. Can I stroke him?"

"Of course. Tickle him behind the ear and he'll be your slave for life."

She reached out a tentative hand, still ready to snatch it back. "What's his name?"

"Rufus. Rufty Tufty. Go on," he urged. "He won't bite."

The little dog looked as if that was up for debate, slanting her a suspicious side-eye. She drew back, smiling uncertainly. "Yes, well . . . I'm not really used to dogs."

"You've never had a dog?"

"No."

"That's a shame." He glanced down at Vicky again. "It looks as if he's scratched you." He tucked Rufus under one arm, and reached down to touch her shoulder, where a red weal about two inches long had appeared.

"Oh . . ." An odd tingle of heat seemed to be spreading from the spot where his finger had brushed over her skin. Had she been in the sun too long? "Yes."

"I'm sorry — he usually behaves better than that but sometimes he gets a little overexcited. It looks sore."

"Oh . . ." Somehow she managed to find her voice. "No, not really."

"Even so, you'd better put something on it when you get home." That sounded like genuine concern. "Anyway, I'd better get this mutt on his lead and take him home." He rubbed his hand affectionately over the little dog's head. "Be seeing you."

"Yes . . . um . . . goodbye."

"Goodbye, Tom," Jayde put in brightly. "Are you coming down to the pub tonight?"

He shook his head. "Probably not. We've a couple of cows due to calf and it's my turn to keep an eye on them."

"Oh . . ."

"See you around, then."

Vicky watched him walk away. Behind her, Jayde sighed. "Mmm — he really is gorgeous."

"Yes . . ."

Jayde shot her a sharp glance. "You're engaged."

Vicky felt that heat in her cheeks again. "That doesn't mean I can't look, does it?" She yawned. "I think I'll have a snooze for a while."

She lay down on her towel again and closed her eyes, and tried very hard not to see the images that seemed to be engraved on her retinas — of that hard body, with its sculpted muscles and smooth sun-bronzed skin.

She absolutely would not let herself weave any steamy fantasies about him.

CHAPTER SIX

"Okay, you're going to need to replace four of the windows." Dan, the builder that Tom had recommended, glanced down at the notes he had made. About the same age as Tom, he had a reassuring air of competence about him. He had spotted things that Vicky had missed, but hadn't invented problems that weren't there. "You could think about replacing them all while you're at it."

"Oh, yes." Jayde nodded eagerly. "You might as well have them all matching."

Vicky hesitated. "I have to think about the cost . . ."

"You'll get that back when you sell the house."

"Well . . . yes. What about the roof?"

"It's basically sound, but I'd suggest replacing those chipped tiles at the back. The gutters will need to be replaced — cast iron, in keeping with the house. And I'm afraid you'll need to go for a complete rewiring."

"Right . . ." Vicky was tallying up the bill in her head. But after all, it was an investment.

"Then with the replastering and decorating, central heating and the new kitchen and bathroom . . ."

"Why not put an en suite in the main bedroom?" Jayde suggested. "Jer . . . er . . . I've heard you can get a good return for that."

Vicky shot her a sharp look. "Jeremy told you that?"

"No . . . I mean, he may have mentioned it sometime. A couple of weeks ago. When we were talking about one of those television shows about renovating old houses. You know how he likes to rant on about them."

Which was true enough — Vicky suspected that he fancied himself as one of the presenters. But there had seemed to be something oddly defensive in her sister's manner — though she couldn't imagine why.

The builder left, promising to email the quote over within a few days.

"How about a coffee?" Vicky suggested. "Then I want to make a start on bringing down some of that junk from the attic before lunch. Most of it can probably go to the skip."

"Okay." Jayde didn't sound enthused by the idea. "Well, if you're going to be all morning doing that, I think I'll have a bath."

* * *

"So he's going to email the quote in the next couple of days."

"Good." Jeremy didn't sound enthused either. "What about the others?"

"Others?"

"The quotes from the other builders. I told you to get at least three."

"Oh . . . it wasn't necessary." Vicky shifted the phone to her other hand. "This guy was recommended to me."

"By whom?" Jeremy's voice was edged with impatience. "You haven't been there long enough to know who you can trust to give you a good recommendation."

"It was the farmer — the guy who owns the farm next door."

"Huh! It's probably his cousin or something. They saw you coming."

Vicky bit back the sharp retort that rose to her lips. "He recommended the garage that fixed my car, and they were

71

very good. Anyway, there aren't that many builders in the area. This is South Devon, not London."

Jeremy grunted in annoyance. "I suppose I'll have to come down there and sort it out myself."

"You don't need to . . ." she protested quickly.

"It's most inconvenient. It's a busy time at the agency, and with you away Mother will probably have to draft in some help from one of the other offices."

"There's really no need for you to come down . . ."

"I don't want to see you let yourself get ripped off by some cowboy. I'll be there tomorrow."

He ended the call abruptly. Vicky sat staring at her phone, a niggle of irritation thinning her mouth. Did he think she was five years old? It wasn't the first time he'd spoken to her like that. Mostly she just let it go — it was easier than arguing with him.

But somehow just hearing his voice, without his forceful presence to back it up, she felt less inclined to ignore how it made her feel. Maybe it was time to assert herself a bit more. If he was like that now, before they were even married . . .

Spreading her hands flat on the table, she stared down at the diamond on her finger. It was a solitaire diamond, square cut, two carats on a plain platinum band — big enough to take someone's eye out. It must have cost a lot of money. She had always been a little nervous about wearing it in case she lost it.

To be honest, that wasn't the real reason she didn't like wearing it. Jeremy had chosen it, but she didn't like it very much — she never had. There was something . . . cold about it. With a small twist she slipped it off her finger and spread her hand on the table again, studying how it looked without the ring.

It looked okay . . .

"Are we going down to the beach then?"

Vicky slipped the ring back on her finger as her sister strolled into the kitchen. "Yes, if you like. I just need to wash up the lunch things."

"Oh — okay. Don't be long — I want to get down there while the sun's still shining."

"Maybe you could dry up then?" Vicky suggested blandly.

"I need to go and change into my bikini." But Jayde hesitated in the doorway. "Is everything all right — between you and Jeremy, I mean?"

"Of course." Vicky didn't miss the knowing glint in her sister's eyes. She drew the ring off again. "I think I might leave my ring at home. I'm afraid of losing it in the sand."

"Oh . . . of course."

* * *

If Jayde had been hoping to see Tom at the beach again she had been disappointed. But when they arrived at the Smugglers Arms that evening, he was there. The place was packed — apparently Friday night was darts night, and he was at the oche.

"Triple eighteen, double twelve, double fourteen," the umpire counted out. "Score one hundred and six."

There was applause from the spectators. "Well done, Tom!"

Vicky followed Jayde as she squeezed her way through the crowd. "White wine?" she asked.

But her sister's attention was focussed laser-like on Tom. She wriggled her way through the crush around the dart-board and placed herself right opposite where he was standing. He acknowledged her with a brief smile, then went back to his conversation with one of the other players.

A flicker of annoyance crossed Jayde's face. But she wasn't one to give up so easily. She was attracting a lot of attention from all the other guys — that red dress was tight enough to start a riot. And she was lapping it up, while covertly watching to see if it was having the intended effect on Tom.

With a small sigh Vicky eased over to the bar to order their drinks. She could only hope that her sister wouldn't get too drunk — she could be a bit embarrassing when she'd had a few too many.

"There you go, my luvver." An elderly man with twinkling blue eyes above an impressively bushy white beard stepped aside to let her through.

"Thank you." She smiled up at him. "It's busy in here tonight."

"Oh, ah — it is that."

He seemed more than willing to chat — it was a relief to find a friendly face at last. "I suppose with the summer coming it'll be even more crowded, with all the holidaymakers?"

"It certainly will." He beamed. "Season's just getting started. Once it starts up proper, place'll be packed. Still, makes up for the winter. Ain't that right, Alice?" he added to the barmaid who had come to take Vicky's order.

"It is. What can I get you?"

Vicky asked for two glasses of white wine, and glanced around at the crowd. She had noticed on their previous visit that among the locals there were few who appeared to be around her age — indeed, few who appeared to be under fifty.

"Is it very quiet here in the winter?" she asked.

Alice smiled crookedly. "You could say quiet — you could say dead. No jobs see, once the holiday crowd be gone. The hotel gets by on the golfing types, but the rest of us just keeps our fingers crossed and hopes for the best."

She set Vicky's drinks down on the bar.

"And even if there was enough jobs," she added, "there's nowhere for the young 'uns to live, not that they could afford. Some of 'em stops with their folks, but that don't do for all of 'em. Most of 'em just has to move away."

The old man nodded. "That's right. Lot of the houses down here has gone to holiday homes, see — landlords can charge a lot more, make a lot more money even if they stay closed up all the winter. Same in a lot of places like this. You're glad to have the tourists o' course, but then they edge the locals out. What can you do?"

"That's a shame."

It was exactly what Tom had been so annoyed about. It didn't excuse the way he had spoken to her, but she could understand how he felt.

It must be difficult for people who had grown up here, lived here all their lives, to see what must once have been a close community slowly dying, to be replaced by little more than a tourist attraction.

She nodded a polite goodbye and took her drinks, edging through the throng to hand one to Jayde — she didn't get a thank you, but then she hadn't expected one. She found herself a corner where she could comfortably people-watch, sipping her wine and listening to the conversations and laughter bubbling over the music playing on the old-fashioned jukebox.

If she could find a way to live here, some of these people would be her neighbours, maybe even her friends. She'd like that. She'd more or less lost contact with the friends she'd had before she'd started dating Jeremy — their social life tended to revolve solely around his circle, and she'd never really felt able to get close to any of the women. Not meet-up-for-a-casual-coffee close, not 'let's go shopping' close.

The darts match ended in a home win, much back-slapping and a fresh round of drinks. Jayde seemed to have forgotten that Vicky was even there — she was in her element, flirting wildly with both darts teams and their supporters.

"Your sister seems to be very popular tonight."

Vicky glanced round, startled by Tom's voice close behind her. "Oh . . . Yes, she is." She laughed a little unsteadily. "Nothing unusual in that."

"I don't suppose there is. She's a very pretty girl."

"Yes." Somehow she managed to keep her smile in place. She was *not* jealous.

"Is she staying long?"

"I . . . don't know. A few days."

"Well, I hope she doesn't stay too long." There was a lilt of amusement in his voice. "Our lads are liable to lose their heads completely." He leaned past her to put his empty beer-glass down on the bar, brushing so close to her that she was sure she could sense some kind of magnetic forcefield between them. "Goodnight then."

"Uh . . . goodnight."

She didn't intend to watch him go, but her gaze followed him as he eased his way across the room, pausing now and then to chat with his neighbours, slapping shoulders, kissing cheeks, laughing at shared jokes.

Dammit, what was happening to her? One good-looking farmer and suddenly her heart was all a-flutter like some Regency virgin kidnapped by a dangerous duke. Her head was in a spin — the solid, steady, sensible life she had been living no longer seemed to fit.

Was she really thinking of leaving her job, leaving her home, leaving her fiancé and the wedding that was already being planned, to move two hundred miles away, to a place she barely knew, where the chances of employment were limited, all on a whim?

Yes she was. Though it was nothing to do with Tom Cullen. Of course not.

It was that letter from the solicitor about Aunt Molly's will that had shaken her out of the lazy drift she had settled into, made her stop and think about what she really wanted in life.

After all, if Aunt Molly could dance at the Moulin Rouge in those exotic costumes, maybe it wasn't so foolish to have dreams after all.

Jayde had been so caught up in the admiration she was getting that it was several moments before she looked around to find Tom. Frowning, she pushed her way back to where Vicky was standing.

"Where is he?" she demanded, as if Vicky was hiding him in her pocket.

"Tom?"

"Of course Tom."

"I think he left."

"Left?" Jayde's mouth thinned with annoyance. "Why didn't you tell me?"

Vicky returned her a bland smile. "Sorry."

Jayde shook her head. "Oh, well — I suppose we might as well go home then." She threw back her wine — Vicky had counted at least three bought for her by her new admirers. "If we hurry we can be home in time for *Billionaire Bachelors*."

Without waiting for Vicky she set off for the door, weaving a little. Vicky followed, relieved to get away while her sister was only slightly tipsy.

But Jayde hadn't entirely forgotten about Tom. "Why would he just walk off like that?" she complained, pausing abruptly in the doorway as the fresh air hit the wine in her bloodstream. "We were getting on really well the other night."

"I expect he was jealous that you were getting on so well with all those other guys," Vicky suggested, tongue in cheek.

"I know." Jayde giggled. "I told you he fancies me."

And she teetered off up the hill at such a sharp pace, Vicky strongly suspected she was hoping to catch up with Tom. Small chance of that — Vicky had seen the way he could stride out.

* * *

"So this is it?" Jeremy cast a disparaging glance around the room. "Not much, is it?"

"This is just the kitchen," Vicky protested defensively.

"I can see that. It's going to need a lot of work to make it saleable."

"Of course." It was a struggle to keep her smile in place. "Would you like to see the rest of it before we have lunch?"

"I suppose so."

She led the way down the passage. "This is the sitting room."

"Hmm." Jeremy wasn't much impressed. "A bit on the small side."

"It's cosy."

"Yes, well . . . it might look a bit better without the bulky furniture. You may be able to get something for that sideboard."

"How much do you think it's worth?" Jayde asked eagerly.

"I really couldn't say. I'd suggest you ask a legitimate antique dealer to take a look at it — you don't want to get ripped off by some fly-by-night con merchant."

"I rather like it," Vicky insisted. A rich, dark mahogany with roses carved on the door panels, it would polish up well.

"Don't be silly. It couldn't be more out of place in the flat." He was even more dismissive of the bathroom. "You're right to get something done about this — the whole thing needs to be ripped out and replaced. It's a shame the toilet can't be separated into another room — buyers aren't keen on having them in the bathroom these days."

She was going to argue for re-enamelling the bath but decided not to waste her breath.

The main bedroom he declared, "Not too bad — and it's quite a decent view." But then he spotted Molly's painting on the wall. "What on earth . . . ? I've never seen anything so hideous."

That fired Vicky up in defence. "I thought I might try to find out who painted it. See if it's worth anything."

"Of course it isn't." His voice was laced with scorn. "It's a piece of junk — amateurish junk, at that. The best place for it is the skip."

"I suppose so." Though she was reluctant to throw away something that Aunt Molly had obviously valued.

"We did find some good stuff in the attic," Jayde put in. "Come and see."

Vicky couldn't imagine that Jeremy would be interested in the contents of those old trunks, but her sister was already dragging him up the stairs.

"I'll put the lunch on then . . ."

At least it would give her a few minutes alone to think. Although she wasn't sure that she wanted to think. Thinking might lead her to a conclusion she wasn't quite ready to face just yet.

Because when Jeremy had walked into the cottage she hadn't felt a thing — or rather, instead of the electric tingle she felt around Tom Cullen she had felt a thud like a cold lead weight.

Which was a bit scary.

She had lain awake for hours last night, her mind churning with the dilemma that she had posed for herself in the pub. Her heart was nudging her to find a way to stay here, but her head was reminding her to be sensible. After all, it would be a huge decision to overturn her whole life in one go.

But if she felt so uninspired by the future mapped out in front of her now, when she was supposed to be looking forward eagerly to her wedding, how would she feel five years, ten years down the line?

To distract herself from that uncomfortable train of thought, she bustled around the kitchen, preparing lunch. She made a Mediterranean chickpea salad — she used canned chickpeas and bottled vinaigrette, but Jeremy wouldn't know the difference if she tucked the evidence well out of sight in the bin.

She cut up a couple of bread rolls and left them to warm in the oven while she mixed the garlic butter. The other two seemed to be taking a long time upstairs — a glance at the clock on the wall told her they'd been gone for more than twenty minutes. Jeremy must have been more interested in the costumes than she had expected.

She was thinking about going to call them when she finally heard their footsteps coming down the stairs.

Jayde breezed into the room, her eyes bright. "Mmm — something smells good. I love garlic bread."

It looked as if she'd been trying on some of the costumes — her hair was ruffled and her T-shirt was caught up in the back of her jeans.

"Come and sit down." Vicky set the bowl of salad on the table and took the rolls from the oven. "Help yourselves."

She sat down and picked up her fork. "So what did you think of that stuff?"

"Very . . . interesting." Jeremy reached across and took a roll.

"I wonder where she got them from?" Jayde mused, carefully sorting out the ingredients in her salad to choose which ones were okay with whatever diet she was on today.

Jeremy shrugged in casual dismissal. "She probably picked them up in a sale of old theatrical costumes."

"You don't think it's possible that they were hers?" Vicky suggested tentatively. "That she was actually a dancer?"

"It's possible," he conceded loftily. "There were lots of those kinds of exotic cabarets in the forties and fifties."

"Like the Moulin Rouge?"

"Oh, yes — there would no doubt have been copycats. Here in London as well as Paris. But don't get carried away thinking your aunt danced at the Moulin Rouge — that's most unlikely."

"Yes — I suppose so . . ." Why did he always have to pour cold water on her dreams?

Lunch was enlivened by Jayde's chatter about one of her favourite celebrities who had been in the news. To Vicky's relief, Jeremy restrained his usual impatience with her, even responding with a show of interest.

When they had finished, Jayde rose from the table and began gathering up the plates. "I'll do the washing-up."

Vicky glanced up, startled at her sister's unexpected offer. What about her precious nails?

Jayde's smile was dazzlingly bright. "You need to get down to the party."

Jeremy shot a questioning glance from one to the other. "Party? What party?"

"Oh . . ." Jayde bit her lip, her impression of feeling guilty almost convincing. "I assumed you'd told him. Sorry."

"What party?" Jeremy repeated sharply.

Vicky sighed. "I promised to help out my friend Debbie. She and her mum run a café down by the seafront. She's got a kids' birthday party this afternoon, but her mum's been poorly and is under doctor's orders to stay in bed. Debbie couldn't get anyone else in to help, and she can't manage on her own."

"But why does that fall on you?"

"I promised . . ."

"But I'm here now."

"I know." She tried an apologetic smile. "But I promised before I knew you were coming."

He exploded. "Oh, this is ridiculous! Ring her and tell her you can't come."

"I can't do that." She confronted his angry glare. "I can't let her down. Anyway, it's only for a couple of hours. Why don't you both come down too?"

"To a kids' party?"

"It's only taking up part of the café — the rest will be open." She was struggling to suppress the irritation that was building inside her. She had *told* him not to come down. "And Debbie makes fabulous cakes."

"I don't eat cake."

"We'll come down later," Jayde suggested. "I haven't tried any of the cakes yet — they look delicious. And she has lots of other things if you prefer. Men always like savouries better than sweet stuff." Thus spoke the oracle on men's tastes.

"Ah. Yes, okay." Jeremy's cheeks looked a little flushed, his eyes darting around as if to avoid looking directly at anything.

"And I can show Jerry round the house properly," Jayde added, inspired. "So he can check all the things that need to be done."

"Okay." Vicky smiled thinly.

Jerry? He hated being called Jerry. And when had her sister become so familiar with him?

An unpleasant suspicion was niggling in the back of her mind. But Jayde and Jeremy? No — her sister was absolutely not his type. And he wasn't hers. They had nothing in common — they didn't even like each other very much. She was just being stupid.

81

CHAPTER SEVEN

"Ah, they're so cute."

"Aren't they?"

The birthday party was in one corner of the café, cordoned off with an archway of pink and blue balloons tied to a frame of garden canes. Eight small children — several fairies, a couple of juvenile cowboys and a pirate, and two clones of Elsa from *Frozen* — were seated around a table cluttered with the remains of mini pizzas and fruit jellies and multicoloured ice cream, and glasses of home-made lemonade.

"They do seem to be enjoying themselves."

"Of course they are." Vicky smiled at her friend. "You've done a great job. And Amy looks so pretty in that little dress."

"She does, doesn't she?" Debbie beamed with pride. "Mum made it."

"How is your mum?"

"Not too bad today. The doctor says she can come down to the café next week, but only to sit at the till." She laughed. "I may have to tie her to the chair!" She turned as the door opened, and a sudden blush spread up over her cheeks. Bill. She glanced quickly at Vicky. "Oh . . . er . . . will you . . . ?"

Vicky laughed, shaking her head. "No — you serve him."

A look of desperation flickered in her friend's eyes, but she hesitated only for a moment then hurried behind the counter. "Hello, Bill." A shy smile. "Your usual?"

"Yes, please." If anything he looked even more awkward. "Two pasties."

Little Amy had spotted him and ran over to hug him. The awkwardness vanished and he picked up the child and swung her high in the air. "How's my best girl?"

She giggled excitedly. "We're having a party. It's Robyn's birthday. She's my bestest friend."

"Ah. Is that why you've got that pretty party dress on?"

"It is pretty." As he set her down on her feet again she spread her skirt and did a little dance on her pointed toes. "Nanna made it for me."

"That was nice of your nanna, wasn't it? Now run along and sit at the table — I think the birthday cake will be along in a minute."

The child ran back to her friends, wriggling into her place. "That's Uncle Bill," she informed them proudly. "He milks cows."

Debbie, usually so deftly efficient, was fumbling to put two pasties into a paper bag. She finally managed it and held them out to him with another shy smile.

"Thank you." He took out his wallet and tapped his credit card on the reader, but he didn't leave at once. "Um . . . Will . . . will you be coming to the cricket tomorrow?"

"Of course." Another blush. "You know I always do the catering."

"Oh yes — of course." He grinned, glanced away, glanced back. "I'll see you there then. Goodbye."

"Yes. Goodbye."

Vicky had been clearing one of the tables. She paused as she stepped past Debbie to put the things in the dishwasher. "He likes you."

"Um . . ."

"And you like him."

If Debbie had blushed any deeper she would have rivalled the tomatoes on the pizza.

"So why don't you get it together?"

"It's not that simple." Debbie had picked up a tea towel and was twisting it in her hands. "There's Amy."

"But she adores him," Vicky insisted. "And he seems very fond of her."

"I know. That's the problem. If I . . . if we . . . I don't want her to get too attached to him in case . . . What if it turns out like Alan again?"

"Why would it?" Vicky arched an eyebrow. "Is he like Alan?"

"No! Nothing like him — not at all. But . . ." Debbie shrugged, trying to smile. "I don't think I'm a very good judge of men."

"Rubbish. He seems like a really nice bloke. Sometimes you just have to take a chance."

"I suppose . . ." She shook her head, fussing with hanging the tea cloth back on its hook. "Um . . . It's time for the birthday cake."

Vicky let the subject drop. But she hadn't forgotten about it.

The birthday cake was met with squeals of excitement. Debbie had made a plain sponge, but covered it with pink fondant icing and designed a castle gate complete with drawbridge, and arrow-slit windows all round. Set around the top were five turrets made of icing sugar, each with a candle, and in the middle was a tiny princess and a white knight.

"Oh, that's fabulous!" Vicky exclaimed. "How did you make the little figures?"

"They're just the bride and groom figures you get on a wedding cake. I added a few bits, and coloured them different with food colouring." She smiled crookedly. "Actually they're from my own wedding cake. I thought it was about time they made themselves useful."

Vicky laughed. "Too right!"

The candles were blown out and the cake cut with due ceremony. By the time the last few crumbs had been demolished, some of the children were getting fidgety, leaving the table and starting to run around the café.

"Oh dear." Debbie watched them anxiously. "I hope none of them are going to be sick."

"Don't worry — their mums will be here soon to pick them up."

As she spoke the door opened. But it wasn't a parent — it was Jeremy and Jayde. And at the precise moment they walked in, a miniature Wyatt Earp ran towards them — and threw up a virulent amalgam of pink cake, jelly and ice cream all over Jeremy's highly polished shoes.

"What the . . . ?" He leaped back, roaring in anger. "Get away from me, you disgusting child!"

Wyatt Earp promptly burst into tears.

Vicky hunkered down to put her arms around the child. "It's okay, sweetie." She glared up at Jeremy. "Really, Jeremy, there was no need to get angry with him — he's just a child."

"I'm not angry." The thin line of his mouth belied his words. "But these are new shoes. Anyway, we just came down to see if you were coming home yet."

"Not yet. There's still some clearing up to do."

Debbie had run to grab a roll of paper towels from behind the counter to clear up the mess. "Here — let me wipe your shoes."

Jeremy snatched the roll from her. "Don't bother. You'd do better to clean the floor up before someone slips on it."

"Oh . . . yes."

Vicky could see that Debbie's eyes were filling with tears as she hurried to fetch the mop and bucket. The little cowboy was still wailing, and several of the other children were ready to join in.

The door opened again. Tom. He took in the scene in one swift glance, and swooped to swing the weeping cowboy up onto his hip. "What have you been up to, you unspeakable brat?"

The insult brought an instant beaming smile to the child's cake-smeared face. "I was sick," he announced with pride. "As sick as anything."

"I'm not surprised. I bet you've been stuffing your face all afternoon, and then whirling around like a screaming banshee. I'm sorry," he added, his apology taking in both Debbie and Jeremy. "Are there any damages?"

Jeremy glared at him. "My shoes. Just look at the state of them."

"They'll clean." Vicky's voice was sharper than she had intended. Not just because of Jeremy's arrogant manner but . . .

Tom — and his son.

Of course — she should have known he'd be married. A man like that — there was no way some woman wouldn't have made sure of him. Well, so what? She'd acknowledge that he was superficially attractive, but that was all. She'd put him out of her mind easily enough — after all, she was only staying for another few days.

Anyway, he shouldn't be smiling at her like that, his eyes warm with humour as if they were sharing a private joke. He had a wife, and a child. That told her a lot about the sort of person he was — not the sort that any sensible woman would want to get involved with.

And besides, she was engaged. She slanted a guilty glance at Jeremy, but he was still busy wiping the vomit from his shoes and didn't seem to have noticed.

"Come on then, brat." Tom had put the child down, but kept a firm hold on his hand. "Let's get you home and get you cleaned up before your mum sees the state of you. Thank Auntie Debbie for the party, and say sorry to the gentleman for being sick on his shoes."

The child obeyed, though the thanks were rather more enthusiastic than the apology. "Can we watch *Pirates*?" he demanded as they left.

"If you behave yourself."

As the door closed behind father and son, Vicky let go the breath she hadn't realised she was holding. At least seeing them together should put an end to her silly fantasies. Even if she wasn't engaged herself, married men were strictly off limits.

More parents had arrived to collect their little ones, and there was a general melee of goodbyes and thank yous. Each child left with a party bag and one of the balloons from the arch.

Debbie surveyed the remaining debris with a wry smile. "Well, that wasn't too bad. Only one of them was sick. Thank you so much for helping."

Vicky laughed, snaffling a leftover scrap of icing from the birthday cake. "No problem — it was fun. Their little faces — especially when you brought out the cake."

"I hope . . . I mean, I hope your sister's friend is okay, after what happened." Debbie spoke quietly, glancing back over her shoulder to where Jeremy had seated himself at one of the tables. "It's not very nice to be sicked over."

"Ah . . ." Vicky managed a crooked smile. "He's not Jayde's friend — he's my fiancé."

"Oh . . ."

And he had behaved appallingly. She felt as if she should apologise to Debbie for his attitude, but why should she? It was on him. But he never apologised. He was always right — somehow it was everyone else who was wrong.

Jayde had finished cleaning up Jeremy's shoes. "There you are — good as new."

"Thank you." He slanted a chilly glance at Vicky — a glance clearly meant to inform her that it should have been her cleaning his shoes. "So, are you ready to come home?"

"I'm just going to help Debbie finish clearing up — I'll be about half an hour. Would you like to stay and have a coffee?"

"All right." It was a grudging concession, but probably as much as she was going to get.

* * *

Vicky eased herself carefully in the bed. Jeremy was beside her, his back to her, and she didn't want to risk waking him.

She had been uncomfortable about sharing the bed with him, but she hadn't been able to think of an excuse not to — especially as it would have meant one of them sleeping downstairs on the sofa.

Fortunately, after a rather stilted evening — dinner in the restaurant of the Carleton Hotel, followed by a few drinks in the pub and a slow walk home up the hill — he had bestowed a casual goodnight kiss and had been asleep by the time she had returned from the bathroom.

A glance at her bedside clock told her that it was almost two o'clock. In London there would still be the roar of traffic on the busy main road, but here the only sound was the occasional gust of wind rattling the window.

She slipped silently out of bed and crept over to the window, and parted a narrow crack between the curtains. In the pale glimmer of moonlight the garden was a fairy kingdom of silver and shadows.

The soft night breeze drifting up from the sea rustled in the leaves and the long grass, swirling around this old cottage — and on to the rambling stone farmhouse a few hundred yards up the lane.

Where Tom would be sleeping.

Lying in bed, that lithe male body totally relaxed, those long dark lashes shadowing his cheeks. What did he wear in bed? Pyjama pants? Boxer shorts? Or . . . nothing at all . . .

But of course he wouldn't be alone, she reminded herself sharply. There would be a wife in bed beside him. And his son sleeping in another room nearby.

So, no more silly fantasies. Tom Cullen was strictly off limits.

Drawing in a long, slow breath to steady the rapid beat of her heart, she tiptoed back to bed. Jeremy was still fast asleep, snoring quietly. Slipping under the duvet she closed her eyes and tried to will herself to sleep.

* * *

She must have drifted off eventually, waking as Jeremy began to stir beside her. She slipped quietly out of bed and picked up her clothes, and escaped to the bathroom before she had to face him.

She needed these few moments to gather her thoughts. This situation couldn't drag on any longer — she had to face the truth. It wasn't just arrogance — Jeremy was a bully.

When had he started to get like that? He hadn't always been like it. When she had first met him he had been charming, considerate. Confident, yes, but not arrogant — and certainly not a bully.

He had always known what he wanted — and she had been happy enough to go along with him, because there hadn't really been anything she felt strongly enough about to argue with him.

And somehow, imperceptibly, that had slipped into a situation where he dominated the relationship, assumed she would agree with whatever he wanted, and got petulant if she disagreed.

And she had been letting him get away with it. But no more. It was time to stand up for herself, refuse to be manipulated. Tell him that their relationship, their engagement, was over. Start a new life.

It was a scary thought — it would alter the whole course of her life.

The image in the mirror above the sink gazed back at her. "Come on," it scolded. "You're a grown woman. You're twenty-six-years-old — you're intelligent, you're not bad looking even if you're a bit on the skinny side and your hair isn't quite blonde. You can do this."

"That's easy for you to say." Oh Lord, as if it wasn't bad enough arguing with her satnav — now she was arguing with her own reflection. Was that worse?

A tap on the door brought an end to the debate. "Vicky? How much longer are you going to be in there?"

"Just coming." She flushed the loo, washed her hands, and opened the door. "Sorry. It's all yours."

Jeremy merely grunted and stepped past her. He was never at his best first thing in the morning.

* * *

They met again at the breakfast table. Jeremy was wearing a clean white shirt — he always wore a clean shirt every day, perfectly ironed. He ironed them himself, being very particular that it was done correctly.

"Good morning." He bent to drop a brief kiss on her cheek, and took the seat opposite her. "Did you sleep well?"

"Yes, thank you." How formal, how polite! Beneath the table she twisted the diamond ring on her finger. Should she take it off now, hand it to him, end their engagement — quick and clean?

"What's for breakfast?"

"Bacon and eggs?" she offered.

"Yes, that will do."

Focussing on the frying pan gave her a few moments to think about what she wanted to say. *It's not you, it's me.* A cliché, which didn't even have the virtue of being true.

I don't feel this is working. We're drifting apart. But that would give him something to argue against, an opportunity to browbeat her into backing down. *I don't want to marry you. I don't love you — I don't even like you very much* . . .

"Morning everyone!" Jayde bounced into the room, her cheerful greeting a startling contrast to her usual early morning manner. "Mmm — breakfast. That smells good."

"You want bacon and eggs?" Vicky queried, startled.

"Yes, please."

Apparently the diet she had been so fussy about yesterday had been abandoned. Jayde was prone to do that, then moan that she never managed to lose weight. Not that she needed to — she had a great figure, slim but with the sort of curves that Vicky had always envied.

At least her arrival meant there was no chance of settling the situation with Jeremy. Maybe she was a coward, but she was forced to admit that it was something of a relief. Later . . .

Or maybe when she got back to London. After all, it was a big decision she was making. It would help if she had some concrete plans in place for her future. A job, at least. She was pretty sure she wouldn't get a glowing reference from Jeremy's mother.

The bacon was sizzling in the pan. She shifted it onto the warmed plates, and cracked the eggs. In a moment she brought the two plates over to the table and sat down to finish her toast.

Jayde frowned down at her plate as if slightly surprised that she had asked for so many calories. Picking up her knife and fork she began to carefully trim the rind and fat from the bacon. "Are you coming home today?" she asked, cutting off a tiny piece of bacon and forking it into her mouth.

Vicky slanted a brief glance at Jeremy. "Not today. There are still a few more things I need to sort out here. I have another week of annual leave."

Was it her imagination, or was there something in the look that passed between him and her sister? No . . . she was just being paranoid — maybe because of her own guilty conscience.

Although they did seem to be getting on better than usual this weekend. And what had they been doing yesterday afternoon, when they had been alone together for more than an hour . . . ?

She watched them covertly as she ate her toast. Every look, every smile . . . was she reading more into it than was really there?

Jeremy finished his breakfast and placed his knife and fork neatly side by side on his plate. "Well, since there's nothing more for me to do here, I'll be leaving. Forward the quote to me when you get it. And arrange for at least two more. I've identified several other builders who seem suitable and emailed their details to you."

"Thank you." Somehow Vicky kept her smile in place.

"I'll fetch my bag."

"Right . . ." Vicky began to clear the table and load the washing-up into the sink.

"I don't suppose you need a hand with that, do you?" Jayde asked.

"No, thanks — I can manage."

"Okay." She swirled out of the kitchen.

At least she was in a good mood, Vicky reflected as she wiped the plates and propped them in the wire drainer. Maybe the next couple of days wouldn't be too bad after all.

She heard Jeremy's footsteps on the stairs and turned from the sink to say goodbye. He came into the kitchen and slid his arm around her shoulders and kissed her — a proper kiss this time, but quite brief.

"I'll see you in a few days then."

"Yes. Well, probably Saturday. I'd like to get everything sorted out, so I won't need to come down again for a while."

"Good. Don't forget about the quote, and the other builders."

"I won't." It was easier to agree with him than to argue.

He opened the door, then glanced back over his shoulder as Jayde came dancing down the stairs, bouncing her suitcase behind her. "Ah — you're ready."

"Bye, Vicky!" Jayde trilled. "See you at the weekend."

"But . . . what . . . ?"

"Jerry's offered me a lift back to London. Isn't that sweet of him? You know how I hate the train." And with that she was off, trundling her suitcase down the path.

Vicky could only stare, lost for words, as Jeremy piled Jayde's suitcase in the boot with his own, and the pair of them settled into the front of the grey BMW, not even bothering with a wave of farewell as they drove off down the lane.

So . . . what did all that mean — if it meant anything at all? Was it entirely innocent or was there something going on — absurd as it seemed?

Whatever, she had made up her mind. Climbing the stairs to Molly's bedroom she stood for a moment gazing out over the garden, the fields, the sea. Then with a decisive movement she twisted off her diamond ring and left it in the trinket tray on the dressing table.

CHAPTER EIGHT

Cricket. It wasn't her favourite sport, but Vicky felt she deserved a break from sorting through Molly's things. And rattling around in the cottage by herself, there was a risk that she might begin to have second thoughts about Jeremy.

The cricket club was down a rough path just past the church — the number of cars parked along the hedge and in the car park told her that the match was a popular event.

A wooden gate stood wide open — apparently there was no charge to get in. The pitch was a wide green oval, ringed by trees in their early summer leaf, providing welcome shade for the spectators ranged around the boundary line on deck-chairs and picnic blankets.

The game had already started. The two teams seemed to be made up of whoever they could scratch together — grand-sons and granddads, some who looked as if they might risk a heart attack if they tried running between the stumps, and several women. Some of the players wore traditional cricket whites, the others an assortment of shorts and T-shirts and baseball caps.

She recognised the figure on the far side of the pitch at once. Tom, on the fielding team. He had glanced briefly in her direction, but she wasn't sure if he had noticed her. She wasn't going to watch him — of course not. She was just here to watch the play.

The bowler ran in and threw his pitch, and the umpire called, "No ball." There was a bit of mild grumbling, then the wicketkeeper tossed the ball back to the bowler.

He walked back to his start point and ran in again. The batsman got his bat to it, but it wasn't much of a hit — it bounced and rolled, and one of the fielders picked it up. The batsmen hadn't even bothered to try running.

The pavilion was a wooden hut with a veranda along the front, and wooden benches where the rest of the batting side were awaiting their turn at the wicket. A long trestle table had been set up in front of it, with plates of sandwiches, finger rolls and cupcakes, rows of cardboard cups, and a stainless-steel tea urn.

Debbie was pouring tea. As she spotted Vicky she waved. "Hi! Come to cheer our boys on?"

"I didn't think you were supposed to cheer at cricket matches — isn't it just a smattering of polite applause?"

Debbie laughed, shaking her head. "Would you like a cup of tea?"

"Thank you."

A cheer went up as the batsman scored a single. "Ah, that means George Evans is up. He's their best player."

That was soon apparent as he began racking up runs on the makeshift scoreboard — a double and two boundaries in one over.

"Come on, lads — get him out," Debbie urged, bouncing excitedly.

Vicky smiled to herself. Sweet, shy Debbie? Not when it came to the village cricket team, apparently.

A couple of customers had arrived, keeping Debbie busy for a few moments serving tea and sandwiches. When it was quiet again she came back to stand with Vicky. "Didn't your sister and your boyfriend want to come and watch the cricket?"

Vicky shrugged in careless dismissal. "Oh, they've gone home."

"Oh . . ."

If Debbie had noticed that she wasn't wearing her ring, she made no comment.

"How's your mum?" Vicky asked to divert the conversation.

"Feeling a bit better." Debbie lifted a cake tin from under the table and unloaded the contents to fill another plate with her fresh, home-baked scones. "She's getting very restless — she always likes to be doing, she was never one to sit watching telly and doing her knitting."

Vicky laughed. "So who's minding the café today — or are you closed?"

"We close on Sundays during the low season. Once it starts to pick up, around the middle of June, we open every day. But it's nice to get a day off."

"So instead you've set up shop down here. A busman's holiday!"

"Oh, I enjoy it." That was clear from the glow in her eyes. "Anyway, I can watch the cricket."

"Is Bill playing?" Vicky asked, all bland innocence.

"Yes." A vivid blush. "He's the wicketkeeper."

Vicky smiled. "You really do like him, don't you?"

Debbie couldn't even look at her. "Yes," she admitted in a small voice.

"Well?"

A long hesitation as Debbie fiddled with rearranging the scones on the plate. "I'm . . . thinking about it."

"Good."

Someone else had come to ask for two cups of tea and some cupcakes. Vicky moved away — she wasn't going to push the subject anymore today. And how ironic, that she was trying to matchmake for her friend when her own love life had gone down the tubes. No fiancé, and attracted to a man who was married.

Ah, well.

She took her cup of tea, strolled over to an empty deck-chair and sat down. She had never really understood the joys of cricket, even when Jeremy had tried to explain it to her. 'Short leg' . . . 'silly mid-off' — it all seemed so arcane.

But there was something very relaxing in watching a village match. The warm sunshine on the green grass, the soft rustle of the breeze in the trees, the thwack of leather on willow. The occasional shouts of protest or approval, the smattering of applause for a good hit or a good stop.

She let her gaze wander lazily around the spectators. The age range was as diverse as the players on the field — it seemed the match was a family day out for the locals. Bright summer dresses and rolled-up shirt-sleeves were the predominant fashion.

Which one was Tom's wife? The petite blonde in a yellow sundress? The attractive redhead chatting to a middle-aged woman over to the left?

A group of children were playing with a bat and ball under the trees, mimicking the adults' cricket. She wasn't sure, without his Wyatt Earp outfit, but she thought the little dark-haired lad who was bowling was Tom's son.

Apparently she had been wrong with both guesses about Tom's wife. As the children's game broke up, the junior Wyatt Earp ran to the young woman who was helping the scorekeeper, hugging her leg and begging for something from her bag. She ruffled his hair and produced a packet of crisps. He took it and ran off again to share with his friends.

Vicky studied the woman from behind her sunglasses. Tall, with dark hair in a neat French plait — Vicky envied her the ability to do that; she'd never been able to manage it. Not really beautiful, but there was something very attractive about her smile.

And she was heavily pregnant.

Oh.

Girl Code:

Rule #1: You never mess with another woman's man.

Rule #2: You NEVER mess with another woman's husband.

Rule #3: You never ever EVER mess with another woman's husband when she's pregnant.

So that was it. Tom Cullen couldn't be more off limits if he'd had a barbed-wire fence, a minefield and a few radio-active warning signs around him.

Resolutely she focussed her attention on the match again. The away team's top batsman was still at the crease, clocking up the runs. And then he took a wild swipe, and the ball soared towards the outfield.

There was a collective holding of breath all round the pitch as Tom ran, his eye on the ball as it arced across the sky. He reached out, dived sideways, rolled . . . and came back to his feet with the ball held high in his hand.

Vicky leaped up, joining in the cheering. So much for a smattering of polite applause! A little embarrassed and hoping Tom hadn't noticed her slight overreaction, she sat down again. The elderly man in the next deckchair was chuckling.

"Good catch. That's our Tom! He could have played for the county if he'd stuck with it."

Vicky smiled. "I don't know much about cricket, but that did look like a good catch."

"One of the best players we've got, is Tom."

"You've played yourself?"

"Oh, ah." He nodded slowly. "More'n sixty years, from when I were just a lad, up till me knees wouldn't let me run no more."

She glanced across at him. She'd guess he was almost as old as Aunt Molly. His face was all creases, his pale eyes over-hung by bushy white eyebrows, which seemed to have won a competition with the sparse white hair over his freckled skull.

"O' course I had a couple of years out for me National Service." He chuckled. "Just copped right for that, I did. Off to Korea, to fight for the king. Though why I could never work out — thousands of miles away it is and none too happy about us being there. But I says to meself, Arthur Crocombe, it's not for you to question what the king wants. So I did me bit, and managed not to get meself shot."

Vicky listened with interest as he reminisced about times long past. He was rambling a bit, as elderly people often would, his memories disjointed and skipping from one thread to another. But she was fascinated — any period of history fascinated her, even as recent as the Korean War.

He seemed to enjoy chatting to her. There didn't seem to be anyone with him. He was probably lonely — as Aunt Molly had probably been. She still felt guilty that she had let her aunt down — maybe she could make up for that a little by sitting with Arthur.

If the old man had seemed absorbed in memories of his younger days, he was still alert to what was happening on the pitch. "Ah — that's forty overs." He rubbed his hands with glee. "Time for lunch."

"Would you like me to fetch you something?"

"Oh, no, my luvver — I want to see what they've got. But you can help me up out of this damned deckchair. Stupid things — who designed them? You get your thumbs caught when you try to put them up, then when you want to get out of them you can't."

Vicky laughed as she helped him carefully to his feet and offered her arm as they walked up to the pavilion.

The trestle table had been laid out with more selections for lunch. Plates of traditional sandwiches, sausage rolls, bacon baps, pizzas and paninis. Several other people had come to help serve — including Tom's wife.

She greeted Arthur with a warm smile. "Hello, Arthur. What can I get you?"

"Those sausage rolls — are they proper home-made?" he demanded.

"Of course."

"Then I'll have a couple."

"You want ketchup on them?"

He chuckled. "What do you think? And give 'em plenty — don't stint it." He turned to Vicky. "What about you, my dear?"

"Oh, but . . ."

"You're my date," he insisted. "The gentleman always pays for dinner."

As Vicky was about to protest again, Tom's wife shook her head discreetly. "Let him," she mouthed, smiling.

Vicky couldn't help smiling back. "Okay — thank you. I'll have a panini, please."

"We've got chicken, pulled beef, or mozzarella with tomato."

"I'll have the mozzarella."

"And two teas," Arthur added.

"Coming right up."

As she bustled away, Vicky felt a hand on the small of her back, and a voice murmured close to her ear, "So you're a cricket fan then?"

She glanced up sharply. Tom was smiling down at her — and he was standing much too close. Fortunately, his wife was at the far end of the table, slathering Arthur's sausage rolls with generous dollops of ketchup.

She flashed him an icy glare and turned her shoulder on him, and stepped away from his hand. She sensed his flicker of surprise — apparently he was accustomed to women welcoming his attention.

"Your sister didn't want to come down to watch the game?"

She took a pause to ensure that her voice would be ice-cool. "She's gone home."

"Ah . . ." A brief hesitation. "Hi there, Arthur. How are you keeping?"

Arthur's pale eyes lit with mischief. "All the better for having this pretty young thing to take care of me."

Tom laughed. "Enjoying the game?"

"I will if you win. That was a lucky catch."

"Lucky?" Tom feigned indignation.

"Lucky. Ah, thank you, my dear," he added as Tom's wife brought their lunch order.

"Enjoy." Her smile suddenly thinned into discomfort, and she eased her hands down her back.

Debbie was there immediately. "Now then, Mrs Cullen," she scolded, bringing a wooden chair. "You know you shouldn't be on your feet for so long. Come along, plop yourself down on this."

"Stop fussing," Tom's wife protested, laughing merrily. "I'm not an invalid — I'm just pregnant."

"Do as you're told." Tom's voice was warm with affection. "Make the most of it — you'll be dying for a sit-down once the baby comes."

"Okay, okay — I'll be a good girl." She eased her bulky frame onto the chair. "There — you can all stop nagging me now."

Vicky had stepped back, watching. It seemed that Tom was fond of his wife, even while trying to set up something on the side.

And she seemed to be a really nice person. *Damn.*

"Here you are, Vicky — you can use this for a tray." Debbie had brought the lid of a cardboard box and set their paper plates and cups on it.

"Thanks." She managed a smile, glad to get away while she still had a little sanity left.

Arthur tottered along beside her as she carried their lunch over to their deckchairs and set it on the ground beside them while she helped him to sit down. He grinned up at her, mischief dancing in his pale eyes.

"Ah — it's been a long time since I've had lunch with a pretty girl."

Vicky laughed. "I bet there were plenty of them in your day."

"Oh, ah — that there were. But not a one of them could hold a candle to my Betty."

"Your wife?"

"Yes, God rest her. Near on sixty-five years we were wed." He lapsed into a moment of melancholy silence.

"How did you meet her?" Vicky prompted, handing him his sausage rolls and a paper napkin.

He smiled in fond reminiscence. "We were childhood sweethearts. She used to help me with my sums in school — I always had trouble with 'em. And we used to go bird-watching up on the moors — we'd walk for miles. Not like your youngsters today, with their noses always glued to their phones."

"You must have been very happy."

"Oh, happy . . . yes, we were — very happy. Mind, we quarrelled often enough — she could certainly say her piece, could Betty. But we always made up — we never went to sleep in bad blood."

"That's a very wise policy." She took a sip of her tea. "Did you have any children?"

"Just the one boy — our Simon. We'd have liked more, but it never happened. He lives in Canada now. Works in television — produces one of those quiz shows. It's very popular." There was a note of pride in his voice. "I don't see him that often. Well, he's very busy with his work, and then there's the kids and the grandkids. But he rings me every weekend."

"That's nice." It seemed that she wasn't the only one who was neglectful of their older relatives. And she had less of an excuse than Arthur's son.

It was pleasant to while away the afternoon sitting in the sunshine as the fat bumblebees hummed gently in the long grass under the trees and the runs clicked up on the scoreboard.

Tom was third in to bat. He had a good eye, swiping the ball away with ease, running between the stumps with a long, athletic stride. He stayed in for nine overs until one fierce strike too many got him caught out, to groans from the home team and wild cheers from the opposition.

He waved genially to the players who had dispatched him, and strolled back to the pavilion. Vicky refused to let herself watch him go.

Arthur had dozed off and was snoring gently. The match ended in a draw. She couldn't work out how that had happened — another of the incomprehensible rules of the game that Jeremy could probably have explained to her at length.

The two teams had gathered beside the pavilion to toast each other with cool beers as the spectators picked up their deckchairs and brought them over to be stored until the next match.

A couple of people were helping Debbie stack the remains of the buffet in boxes and carry them back to her van; the trestle table had been dismantled and put away in the pavilion.

Tom was helping his wife take down the hanging number plates from the scoreboard, their son eagerly helping them by placing them in their storage box. Vicky turned away from them as Arthur roused himself.

"Well, that was an excellent match," he declared. "Best I've seen in a long time."

Vicky smiled to herself — she didn't bother pointing out that he had missed most of the second innings. "Time to go home." She offered him her arm and together they walked back up the path to Church Road.

A short distance past the convenience store they came to a short lane, trees on one side, the other lined with a row of narrow terraced houses. Arthur stopped by the gate of the second one. "Well, here we are." He fumbled in his pocket for his door key.

Vicky glanced along the row. The other houses all had gravel front gardens and UPVC front doors — what in her former life she would have called 'easy maintenance'. And they all looked empty. Second homes.

Arthur's stood out like a bad tooth.

"Is there anything you need?" she asked, opening the gate for him.

"No, no, my dear. I'm absolutely fine. You go on home — your husband will be waiting for his tea."

"I don't . . ." But no, there was no need to correct him — he'd probably forget anyway. Instead she gave him a little wave. "Goodbye then."

"Goodbye."

She hesitated, watching as he opened the door and stepped safely inside, then she turned back up the hill.

* * *

It was nice to have the cottage to herself again. Vicky brewed herself a cup of coffee and took it into the sitting room, settling down on the sofa to phone her mother.

"Hi, Mum — how's everything?"

"Oh, it would be fine if this rain would just stop. Honestly, it's supposed to be coming on for summer, but it's been pouring down all week."

"Really? It's glorious down here."

"Oh, yes — Jayde said it had been nice."

Vicky drew in a breath between her teeth. "Did she?"

"Jeremy just dropped her off. I thought you'd be coming home with them."

Oh? Eight hours for a journey that should take around four — five at the most? They must have taken quite a detour. Or maybe stopped for a long lunch?

"Uh, no, Mum." Vicky kept her voice as casual as she could. "I won't be home till the weekend. There's a few things I need to sort out about the cottage."

"Oh. But what about work?"

"I've another week's leave."

"Oh, right. By the way, you remember Mrs Simmonds at number twenty-three? Her Alison is getting married again. That'll be her third time! Can you believe it? Mind you, apparently this one's got a good steady job, so at least she's being a bit sensible this time."

Vicky laughed, relieved that her mother had diverted the conversation herself. "Sensible isn't the only criteria for a happy marriage, Mum."

"Of course not — but it doesn't hurt."

They chatted for a while — Vicky was relieved that her mum didn't mention Jeremy. She could just imagine her response when she told her she was breaking off her engagement — the word 'sensible' would definitely be in there somewhere.

At last, her mum had exhausted all the local gossip. "Well, I'd better be going — I've got the tea on."

Vicky smiled to herself, imagining the quiet house in north London, with its bright white net curtains and comfortable three-piece suite, the kitchen where her mother enjoyed her baking, the smart wooden front door.

"Bye then, Mum — I'll speak to you again later in the week."

"Goodbye, dear. Look after yourself."

"And you."

Vicky closed the call and put the phone down. She hadn't mentioned Molly's mysterious poet to her mother. Thinking about it, it seemed unlikely that Molly had ever told her mother about him — they hadn't had that sort of relationship.

She hadn't told Jayde, either — and certainly not Jeremy. She had kept the poem in the book, tucked in her suitcase among her own things.

The late afternoon sun was slanting in through the French windows, soft golden rays warming the room. A light breeze was ruffling the leaves of the apple tree, and somewhere a robin was singing.

The roses she had put in the fireplace were fully open now, their fragrance sweet and heady. Strange how a scent could take you back in time, stir up memories so vividly that closing her eyes she could almost be a child again, tired and happy after a long day at the beach.

A child again, sprawling out on the sofa with her head on her mother's lap, her feet on her dad's. Aunt Molly in the recliner, her dad chuckling at some comedy on the television.

But those days of innocent contentment were long gone. And the problem with having the cottage to herself was that there was nothing to distract her thoughts. There was nothing on the television that she wanted to watch, and she didn't feel like reading.

Tom . . . She didn't want to think about him. About that smile, that rich, deep voice, the smattering of dark, curling hair across his wide chest. But he was stuck in her head and she didn't know how to get him out.

In his cricket whites, grass stains on one hip, reaching for that catch, lithe as a panther. That low, husky laugh, those dark eyes . . .

If she was honest, a small part of her had been hoping to find that he was separated from his wife, even divorced. But that hope had been thoroughly extinguished by the sight of them together after the match, with their little boy.

With an impatient sigh she shook her head, rose to her feet, and went into the kitchen to sit down at the table with her laptop. Maybe it was time to take advantage of this quiet time to get on with the book she had been planning to write.

At least it would give her something else to think about.

* * *

It really wasn't working. Reading over the chapters she'd managed to write so far, she had to admit that it was falling flat. The characters weren't coming to life, the backstory about battles and political intrigue was dragging it down.

Resting her chin in her cupped hand she stared at the screen, her mind blank. Elizabeth and Edward — their secret wedding, at her family home, with only her mother and two other ladies present. It should be a really romantic scene — easy to write. You'd have thought.

But even a short break to cook herself some supper didn't help. By ten o'clock she was ready to give up. Saving her work — though it hardly seemed worth it — she closed down the laptop, washed up her supper things and climbed the stairs to the bedroom.

But she wasn't ready to sleep yet. Sitting on the edge of the bed, she surveyed the room. She had finished sorting Molly's things — there were two large bin bags to go to the dump, and a couple of suitcases she had found in the attic packed with the better items to go to the charity shop.

The only thing left was a couple of hatboxes on the top shelf of the wardrobe. She lifted the first box down and opened the lid.

Inside, carefully layered in tissue paper, was a hat. A cream straw hat with a wide bell-shaped brim and a scarlet ribbon around the crown. Very chic, very Audrey Hepburn.

"Oh, wow!"

She hurried over to the mirror to try it on. It was gorgeous. She turned her head from side to side to view it from different angles. She could just imagine Aunt Molly wearing it — maybe on afternoon walks in Paris between performances at the Moulin Rouge.

But unless Debbie and Bill got married it was unlikely that she'd get much opportunity to wear it herself, she acknowledged wryly. With a sigh she took it off and put it back in its box.

The second box was heavier and when she moved it, she heard things shifting inside. She carried it over to the bed, lifted the lid, and gasped in delight — inside was a treasure trove of photographs and magazine clippings.

Any thought of sleep was forgotten. The photographs were a jumble of sizes, some spotted or creased with age. Some were black-and-white snaps mostly taken around Paris — the Eiffel Tower and the Arc de Triomphe in the background left no doubt of that. Groups of young women, all of them beautiful, chic, laughing at the camera.

And among them, unmistakeably, a young Aunt Molly.

Oh, wow — she had been stunning! Tall and slender, with a dancer's grace. Dark glossy hair tumbled in waves over her shoulders or twisted into a neat chignon at the nape of her neck. Her eyes were dark and lustrous, her soft lips painted scarlet, her cheekbones carved from creamy ivory.

Some of the photos were clearly professional shots — on the backs were the stamps of the studio. *Studio Lenoire*. The dates were from 1948 to 1955, many of the same young women, but in sumptuous costumes of beads and satin and feathers — just like the ones they had found in the trunks upstairs.

The setting was just as sumptuous — a brightly lit stage draped with richly coloured satin curtains. And above the proscenium arch, spelled out in scarlet lights, the words *Moulin Rouge*.

Her heart leaped with excitement. So Aunt Molly really *had* danced at the Moulin Rouge! How incredible was that?

And the clippings . . . fashion plates, Molly, modelling lingerie like the pieces they had found in the drawers, and fabulous dresses — gold brocade, black velvet, elegant columns and corselet bodices and sweeping skirts.

Most of the images were labelled *Elyna Chastain Couture, Paris*. There were a few others, names she recognised — Schiaparelli, Balenciaga. She shook her head, bemused. What else was she going to find out?

At the bottom of the box was a dark blue velvet bag, embroidered with gold thread. She loosened the draw-cord and tipped the contents out onto the bed.

Jewellery.

Gold and silver, diamonds and emeralds and garnets and pearls, earrings and bracelets and rings. A watch in a marcasite surround; a choker necklace of rich red garnets with matching earrings and bracelet; a brooch in the shape of a dragonfly, its wings set with diamonds.

And a gorgeous ring — two intertwined hearts set with pavé diamonds, and, in the centre of each heart, a clear, vivid emerald, which sparked fire as they caught the light from the lamp on the bedside table.

She slipped it onto her finger — it fitted perfectly.

She stared at the pile as it lay shimmering on the bedspread. She had no idea of the value, but with luck she could sell them and put the money towards the cost of the renovations to the cottage. Maybe even with a little bit left over.

"Oh, Aunt Molly — where did you get all these? Were they gifts from your poet?"

There was something left at the bottom of the bag — an old copper coin, a penny . . . or . . . no, it seemed to be a medal — there was a bar at the top where a ribbon would be threaded.

On one side was a cross with an extra cross-bar — she recognised it as the Cross of Lorraine. Around the edge was a set of Roman numerals. On the other was a raised inscription in Latin: *PATRIA NON IMMEMOR*. She held it in the palm of her hand, frowning.

The numerals looked like a date — 18 June. She couldn't work out the year — she'd have to look up what the letters meant. And the inscription — something about the unforgotten country, perhaps?

But for now . . . where to put this stuff, to keep it safe? It made her edgy to have such valuables lying around. Tomorrow she'd drive into town and see about selling it. But tonight . . . scooping the jewellery back into the bag, she tucked it under her pillow, and hurried off to the bathroom to get ready for bed.

CHAPTER NINE

She had been a little too optimistic about the weather. Vicky woke to the sound of rain pelting against the window. After a glorious week, normal British summer had returned.

Memory came back to her quickly of the small fortune tucked under her pillow. She pulled out the bag and opened it again, just to check that she hadn't been imagining it.

No — there they were, a fistful of bright jewels, still sparkling in the cool morning light. "Thank you, Aunt Molly." She tipped the treasures back into the bag. "I had no idea that you had stuff like this, but . . . thank you."

She tumbled out of bed and had a shower at top speed, dressed quickly and scoffed down a bowl of cereal. Then she went out to load the car with the two suitcases of clothes for the charity shop, and a couple of coats — she might as well kill two birds with one stone.

The jewellery. She laid it out on the bed and stood gazing at it for a moment. It was a bit bulky, but it didn't feel safe to put it in her bag.

There was a silk scarf in one of the drawers, and she wrapped the garnet set in that and stuffed it into the pocket of her jeans. The rest, in the velvet pouch, went into the other pocket.

It was still raining as she drove down the lane and turned right onto Church Road. She had to drive carefully — the potholes were now puddles, and she wasn't sure how deep they were. She didn't want to risk damaging the car again.

Tom's cows were in the top field, quietly cropping the grass — apparently that thing about cows lying down when it rained was just a myth.

But she wasn't letting herself think about Tom. Well, she'd indulge herself for just a few moments at a time — it was a struggle to cut him out completely from her mind, especially when he lived next door and she could see his cows every time she looked out of her window.

Rounding a bend in the road she saw someone waiting at the bus stop, huddled into a parka as rain dripped from the hood, a hefty-looking backpack weighing down their drooping shoulders.

As she drew level she recognised her — Bethany, Brenda's teenaged daughter from the little convenience store. She stopped and lowered the passenger-side window.

"Hi — would you like a lift?"

The girl huffed and turned away. "No, thank you."

Vicky hesitated. But she was reluctant to leave the girl standing there in the rain. And she wasn't so far from her own adolescence that she couldn't remember those days when everything and everyone seemed to be against you.

"I think you've missed the bus," she said.

The only reply was a grunt.

"There won't be another one for ages."

"It doesn't matter."

Vicky suppressed her amusement — she was quite sure she had been equally as rude in her day. "Look, I'm going into town. I can drop you off anywhere — it won't be out of my way. You're going to get soaked standing there."

The girl hesitated, then grudgingly opened the passenger door.

"Stick your pack on the back seat," Vicky suggested, keeping her voice bland.

Silence. Bethany climbed into the car and hugged the backpack on her lap as if it was going to try to get away.

"Seat belt?" Vicky prompted.

Another grunt — but at least she fastened the seat belt.

The traffic on the main A road was quite busy — a dozen cars passed before Vicky could slip into a gap. "Phew!" She laughed. "I thought we were going to be stuck there till Christmas. It's like they're afraid they'd choke on their chewing gum if they gave way for you."

That produced a brief snigger.

Vicky tried a friendly smile. "It's Bethany, isn't it?"

That earned her one of those patented sardonic adolescent girl glances.

"Bez."

"Oh . . . right. Bez."

Bethany — Bez — turned her head away to look out of the window. This was going to be an entertaining drive!

For a while she concentrated on finding a place to slip into the outside lane to overtake a caravan.

"So, you're off school today?" she asked.

Bez hunched into her shoulders. "I'm not going back to school."

"Oh?"

"Mum wants me to finish my A levels and go to university."

"And you don't want to?"

"No." Her pretty face creased into a dark scowl. "I'm not going to let her rule my life."

"No — quite. Although . . . not doing something just because it's what she wants you to do is . . . still kind of letting her rule your life. Just . . . backwards. Kind of." She wasn't sure if that made sense.

The girl rolled her eyes. "I suppose you're going to tell me to go to university."

"Certainly not — not if it isn't what you want to do. That would be a complete waste of time." There was another caravan to overtake. "What do you want to do?"

Bez glared at her, all adolescent defiance. "I'm going to London."

Vicky stared at her in alarm. "What, now?"

"Yes. I'm seventeen — almost eighteen. I can leave home if I want."

"Ah." Yikes — what could she say to that? "Uh . . . does your mum know?"

"I left her a note."

"Oh. And . . . um . . . what will you do in London?"

"Get a job."

Of course — get a job. As if it was the easiest thing in the world. "Right . . . what sort of job?"

"I dunno." The girl shrugged, unconcerned. "Whatever."

Damn — what should she do now? She really ought to turn around and take her straight back home — but she suspected that the girl would just run off again at the first opportunity. She might even kick off in the car, possibly causing an accident on this busy road.

The traffic ran smoothly for a few minutes and Vicky took the opportunity to covertly study her passenger. Seventeen . . . She sighed to herself. At seventeen you knew everything — or thought you did.

She wasn't quite sure of the legal position, but she didn't think Bez could be forced to return home if she didn't want to. Even if she didn't have her mother's permission.

She'd never been in a more tricky predicament. She had to stall for time while she tried to come up with something.

"Well, there's certainly lots of jobs going if you're not too fussed what you do." She kept her tone light, casual. "There's plenty of hotels in London — they're always looking for people to clean the rooms, wash up in the kitchens, that sort of thing."

Another defiant glare. "I'm not going to clean someone else's scuzzy room!"

Vicky nodded sagely. "No — I can see that wouldn't be too much fun. And they don't pay much, I believe. You might be able to get a job in a shop. Not the posh ones in the West End, of course — they'd probably say you're too young."

"I'm not too young!"

"Oh, *I* didn't say you're too young, but they probably would. But there are plenty of places in the suburbs — supermarkets and that." She smiled encouragingly. "And you have experience, so that would help."

"I don't want to end up working in another shop. Not ever again as long as I live."

"No? Well, that's one thing to tick off your list then. What do you want to do? What do you like?"

Another silence — but this one seemed to have a different quality. Not sulky, more . . . contemplative. Vicky slanted her a swift glance. The girl was chewing her lip, apparently deep in thought.

"Reading," she volunteered at last.

Oh. That wasn't the response she had been expecting. "That's good," she responded carefully. "I'm not sure what sort of job you could get where you could do that. Unless it was in a bookshop, of course." She caught the eye-roll almost before it happened. "No . . . well . . ."

"Did you go to university?" For the first time there was genuine interest in Bez's voice.

"Yes."

"Did you enjoy it?"

"It was brilliant." There was no need to lie about it — the memories still danced in her mind. "Parties every weekend . . ."

"*Every* weekend?"

"More or less. Friday and Saturday nights. There was a film club, and a drama society that put on plays and revues every term — some of them were really good. I was a member of the hiking society — though I don't suppose that would interest you."

"I like hiking."

"Oh. Well . . . there you go. There was a debating society — in fact there was a society for just about anything you could think of."

113

Bez had visibly relaxed — the tension had eased from her shoulders, and she was no longer hugging her backpack so tightly.

She hadn't set out to give advice — who was she to give advice to anyone, considering the doldrums she'd let her own life sink into? But nevertheless it did seem as if she'd given the girl some food for thought. She wouldn't push it anymore.

It had given her food for thought, too. What had happened to the lively, fun-loving girl *she* used to be? She'd got buried in 'sensible'. Aunt Molly hadn't been sensible — at an even younger age she'd danced at the Moulin Rouge in little more than a few strings of pearls.

"I'm looking for a charity shop to donate some of my Aunt Molly's clothes to," she remarked.

At last, a friendly response. "Which one?"

"It doesn't matter. Do you know where they are?"

"Of course. There are three, right on the High Street. One's for animals, one's for cancer research and one's for heart diseases."

"Well, I've got two suitcases and a couple of decent coats. Maybe I'll share them out between all three."

"She was nice, your Aunt Molly." Bez was almost smiling. "Not grumpy like some old people. She told me once that she was in the war."

"Oh?"

"I was doing a project for history and she told me she'd lived in Paris during the war, when the Germans were there. She was younger than me." Now there was real animation in her voice. "She said sometimes it was horrible — there was never enough to eat, and you couldn't go where you liked, and if you forgot to take your identity papers everywhere you could get into real trouble. But sometimes it was dead exciting. She told me she used to run messages and that, for the Resistance."

Vicky glanced at her in surprise. "She did?"

"Well, that was what she said, anyway. Mum said she was probably making it up." Her tone indicated what she thought of any opinion her mother might hold. "Do you think she was?"

"I don't know," Vicky conceded. "I could ask my mum."

"What subject did you do at university?" Bez had put her backpack in the footwell between her feet.

"Medieval history."

"Why did you pick that?"

"I was fascinated by it. Well, any era of history, really, but that one most of all. There was so much going on — kings and queens fighting each other over the throne, deadly plagues, the odd revolution . . ."

Bez laughed. "It sounds like fun."

"I'm not sure I'd have wanted to live then, though," Vicky confessed. "There was so much disease — most people only lived into their thirties."

"A lot of women died in childbirth, didn't they?"

"They did — it was the main cause of death among women. And the men got killed off in the endless battles."

"Things haven't changed much there." Bez's voice lilted with cynical amusement. "They still like nothing better than a good punch-up. Football, whatever . . . any excuse will do. Stupid."

They slid into an easy conversation — Bez seemed to have entirely forgotten her earlier sulks. Until they reached the roundabout and the turn-off for the town.

"Could you drop me at the train station?" she asked — though Vicky detected a distinct lack of enthusiasm for the adventure now.

"Okay."

What to do? She couldn't just let the girl go off to London like this — but how could she stop her? As she followed the signs for the train station her mind churned with a dozen ideas, all of which she rejected as likely to make matters worse.

She was no closer to a solution as she turned into the car park in front of the station. "Do you want to leave an address to let your mum know where you're staying?" she suggested as Bez picked up her backpack and opened the passenger door.

A long hesitation. "I . . . don't know where I'll be staying yet. I'll probably find a hotel or something."

"Do you have enough money for that?"

"Yes — I looked up the room prices on the internet. And I've been saving up my babysitting money for months."

"Okay. But do let your mum know as soon as possible. She may be a pain in the bum — mine can be at times, even now. But I'm sure she loves you."

"Right. Yes. Um . . . thanks for the lift."

"No problem."

Bez clambered out of the car. It had almost stopped raining, but it was still a dismal day for running away from home. Vicky's heart went out to her. Even with nothing seriously wrong — a comfortable home, a caring if naggy mother — a lively teenager could feel suffocated in a small village so far away from the beguiling city lights.

Before she closed the door, Vicky leaned across and delayed her. "I'll tell you what — let me know where you're staying too." She reached for her bag and pulled out one of her business cards. "I'll be coming back to London in a few days, and I'll look you up. And this is my mum's phone number." She scrawled it on the back of the card. "If you have any problems, give her a ring. *Any* problems. Don't worry — she's really kind."

She'd ring her as soon as she got home to give her the heads-up. She knew her mum would be more than willing to help out if she was needed.

Bez glanced at the card. "Oh . . . you live in London?"

"Yes."

"And you're an estate agent?"

"That's right."

"Is that a good job?"

"Well . . . I suppose so." She kept her tone flat, with no spark of enthusiasm — which was easy, as she felt none. "Of

116

course, you usually need to have a university degree, and then train with an agency for another year."

"Oh . . ." Far from looking as if she was about to embark on an exciting adventure, the kid looked as if she was going to the dentist. "Well . . . um . . . goodbye."

"Goodbye. Stay safe."

Vicky watched as she crossed the car park and disappeared into the booking hall. In spite of this crazy plan to go to London, she did seem to have her head screwed on. She could only hope that things would work out for her. Maybe after a few days in London she would find out that it wasn't all it was cracked up to be, and come home.

In the meantime she was going to have to let Brenda know what had happened, and her part in it. Which was going to put her in even worse grace than selling the cottage. With a small sigh she put the car in gear and drove out of the car park.

The town was quite small, but the High Street was bustling, lined with shops, with a small car park just round the corner. She picked out the charity shops as she drove past — it wouldn't be too far to walk, even making three separate journeys. She'd get that job out of the way first.

Patting her pockets to make sure the jewellery was safe, she hefted the first suitcase out of the boot of the car and set off.

It had finally stopped raining but the pavement was wet, and heavy drops were dripping from the trees. The charity shop was warm and welcoming, a jumble of clothes racks and bric-a-brac, a couple of shelves of CDs and DVDs and several tables full of toys. The plump lady behind the counter greeted Vicky with a broad smile when she offered the suitcase.

"Ah, thank you, my luvver. I'll put them out the back for now, till we can get them sorted. Do you want the suitcase back?"

Vicky smiled back. "No, thanks — you can keep that."

Half an hour later the car boot was empty. Vicky glanced at her watch. She still had plenty of time on her parking ticket. How was Bez getting on? Unfortunately she didn't have Brenda's phone number so she couldn't call her and let her know what was happening. She'd have to go into the shop as soon as she got back to Sturcombe — and risk getting her head blown off.

Anyway, for now it was time to deal with the jewellery. Vicky strolled back to the shops, a small fizz of excitement bubbling inside her. This could make a lot of difference to the next few months.

There were two jewellers on the High Street. One was a national chain, selling all modern stuff. The other was more interesting — a small, personal-looking shop with a window full of mixed modern and vintage pieces. Above the window it bore the legend *Digby's Jewellers*. That was the obvious one to choose.

The bell above the door jingled as she opened it. Inside, the shop was narrow and dimly lit, the walls lined with glass cases displaying more jewellery, clocks, silver cups and some items of crystal glassware.

An elderly man with grey hair and a pair of rimless glasses perched on his nose came through a bead curtain from the back room and greeted her with a smile. "Hello, my dear. What can I do for you?"

"I have some jewellery to sell. I inherited it from my aunt." She pulled the bag from her pocket. "I've brought a copy of her will to show you that I really own it."

"Ah, yes — excellent, excellent. Well, let me see what you have." He produced a red velvet cloth from under the counter, spread it out smoothly and invited her to set out the pieces.

She tugged open the draw-cord and tipped out the contents onto the cloth. "I had no idea Aunt Molly had these things. I only found them yesterday, in a box of old photographs."

"Molly?" He peered up at her sharply. "Would that be Molly Marston, from down Sturcombe?"

Vicky's eyes widened in surprise. "That's right. You knew her?"

"I did, yes." He nodded, smiling sadly. "I heard that she'd passed." He picked up the watch and examined it closely. "She would come in now and then to sell me a piece. Gifts from her lovers, she said — I used to tease her that she must have had many of them. Some of them she said were very famous, but she wouldn't even whisper their names."

"Did you know that she was a dancer at the Moulin Rouge in Paris?" Vicky asked, thrilled to find someone who might know a little about her aunt. "I found some photographs, and some of her costumes."

"Oh, yes — the Moulin Rouge. That was where she met some of them, of course. There were many men who would go to watch the cabaret, then take flowers and chocolates round to the stage door and try to date the girls. And often they would bring gifts of jewellery to their favourites."

"Did she ever tell you . . . was there ever anyone special?"

"Well, yes — I believe there was. A long time ago. I never knew his name."

"A poet — a painter?"

He shook his head. "I don't know about that. But she certainly lived quite an adventurous life."

He placed the watch carefully on the cloth and picked up the pearl earrings. "I'm sad that she's gone, but she'll have gone with no regrets."

"No regrets." She smiled. "That's a good thought."

"It certainly is." He picked up the ring with the entwined hearts. "Ah, now this is a pretty thing."

"That's my favourite." She sighed in wistful regret. "I'd have kept it, but I need the money. She left me her cottage too, but it needs quite a lot of work, and there'll be a big inheritance tax bill to pay."

His kindly eyes twinkled at her. "Of course."

He continued to examine each piece, placing them down side by side. The final piece he picked up was the dragonfly brooch — he seemed to have deliberately left that till last.

"Ah . . ." He switched on a light at the side of the counter and removed his glasses, and lifted the loupe-glass that hung on a cord around his neck.

She watched anxiously as he held the brooch under the light, turning it in his hand, peering at it closely through the loupe-glass. After a few moments he let the loupe-glass drop and laid the brooch down separately to the other things.

"Now, these I can buy from you." He laid his hand over the pile on the right. "But this . . ." He picked up the brooch again and held it out to her on the palm of his hand. "No."

"Oh." The fizz inside her went as flat as day-old beer. "The diamonds are fake? I thought they must be."

He shook his head. "On the contrary, they are very fine stones indeed. Together I would estimate that there are about fourteen carats. If I were to put a price on it, I'd say perhaps twenty-five thousand pounds."

"Oh . . . !" *Fizz!*

"I don't have the market for a piece like this here, and I won't cheat you by buying it to sell on. If you want my advice, you should sell it in London."

"Oh . . ." Fortunately there was a chair beside the counter, and she sank onto it, her head spinning. Twenty-five thousand pounds . . . ! Even after paying the inheritance tax on it, that was going to go a long way towards paying for the renovations on the cottage.

"I can give you the name of a friend of mine whom you can rely on to deal with you honestly."

"Th . . . thank you."

"Now this is very interesting." The jeweller had picked up the medal, which had spilled out of the bag with the jewellery. "The inscription — do you know what it means?"

"No." She shook her head. "I meant to look it up, but I didn't have time this morning."

"*Patria non immemor.* I've not seen it before, but I think . . . Would you mind if I take a photograph and send it to another friend of mine? He's very interested in medals — he's quite the expert."

"No — of course." She sat forward eagerly. "Go ahead."

He took his phone from his pocket and photographed each side of the medal, and then tapped a message into the keyboard. "In the meantime, why don't you put this back in your bag to keep it safe, and I'll work out a price for you for these other pieces." He handed her the brooch. "Would you like a cup of tea while we wait for Leonard to get back to us?"

"Oh . . . yes, please."

They drank tea together and negotiated a very good price for the trinkets as they waited for the medal expert to call back. The response came sooner than Vicky had expected. Mr Digby read the message, and smiled.

"I thought so. Your Aunt Molly's real name was Meline, wasn't it?"

"That's right."

"Meline Marston. My friend says this is a French Resistance medal. The meaning of the inscription is 'the nation does not forget'. It was awarded to those who participated in the Resistance during the war."

Vicky stared at him. "But . . . Molly would only have been about fourteen or fifteen when the war ended."

"That's right. But there were quite a few young people who took part, carrying messages, that kind of thing. It seems that Molly's adventuring days started early."

"Wow!" Vicky laughed a little unsteadily. "And I only knew her as a slightly eccentric old spinster."

The old man chuckled. "Oh, she was certainly that. Leonard would like to look into this a little further. May I give him your email address so that he can get back to you?"

"Of course." For the second time that morning she pulled out a business card and handed it over to him. "Thank you."

"Do let me know what he finds out. It's a very interesting story."

"It is."

CHAPTER TEN

Vicky was in a dream, not really looking where she was going as she walked back to the car park. She had to skip out of the way of a cyclist, and stop for a moment to remember where she had parked the car.

"Hi."

She glanced round, startled.

Bez was standing by the car, smiling a little sheepishly. "I changed my mind. Can I have a lift home?"

"Of course." She was careful to show no surprise. "There's room in the boot for your backpack now."

It was probably best to take the situation completely for granted. Don't ask why she'd changed her mind, don't say she was being sensible . . . No, for heaven's sake, don't say *sensible*!

She popped the boot open and Bez dropped her backpack in it. As they settled in the seats, the girl fastened her seat belt without being prompted, and slanted Vicky a quirky little smile.

"Can you drop me back at school?"

"Of course."

"Only . . . could I leave my pack with you and pick it up later?" She glanced away, awkward. "I don't want people asking questions."

"That's okay," Vicky assured her. "Pick it up when you like." She put the car in gear and drove out of the car park. "Shall we have some music?"

"Okay."

They drove out of town as the rich voice of the Queen of Soul filled the car.

"Who's that?" asked Bez with genuine interest.

"Aretha Franklin."

"Never heard of her. She's good though."

Vicky felt the warmth of pure relief surging through her — she had been dreading having to tell Bez's mother what had happened. Whatever the reason for Bez changing her mind, she could only be thankful that she had.

The sun had come out, shimmering on the wet road and sparkling like diamonds on the leaves of the trees. From time to time she could catch a distant glimpse of the sea. A small smile tugged irresistibly at the corners of her mouth.

Bez glanced at her, seeming to pick up on her thoughts. "Are you going to stay here?"

"I'm not sure." The smile widened. "I'll be staying for a while, at least."

She could afford to now. The money Mr Digby had deposited in her bank for the purchase of Molly's jewellery would keep her going for a couple of months. And if the brooch was worth as much as he had suggested, she would be able to pay for the renovations without having to take out a loan, in spite of having to add it to the inheritance tax bill.

"You were right, by the way," she said.

"Oh?"

"About Molly being involved with the Resistance in Paris during the war. Even though she was only fourteen. I found a medal, a Resistance medal, and I went into that little jewellers on the High Street."

"Digby's?"

"That's right. He has a friend who knows about medals and he identified it and looked up Molly's name. Would you like to see it?"

They had reached the roundabout. As they had to wait for a couple of cars ahead of them, she fumbled in her pocket and pulled the medal out of the bag.

Bez took it, turning it over in her hand. "*Patria non immemor. Patria* . . . Does that mean country? *Non* would probably mean not, or does not. *Immemor*? I'd guess that means something about memory, remembering."

"Well done — close. It's 'the nation does not forget'."

"I like languages. I'm doing French at A level — and Spanish. I think I might do a degree in modern languages."

"That would be good." Vicky nodded encouragement. "There's plenty of career scope with that."

"I don't know which university I'd like to go to," she mused. "What do you think?"

"I don't really know — it depends on which course you're doing. There's a website that gives you all the rankings, and what the students say about them. Have a look. Search for Student Reviews."

Bez pulled out her phone and typed in the search request. The rest of the drive was occupied with debating the pros and cons of each university, and whether she wanted to stay near home, at Plymouth or Exeter, or go to London, or even venture further afield.

* * *

"The school's just down here. Turn left, then first right."

Vicky followed the directions, turning into a quiet street with smart houses on one side, and a long green hedge on the other. Above the hedge she could see a two-storey red-brick building. To one side was a large car park, to the other a row of tennis courts.

"This is it?"

"Uh-huh. Stop just down there by the gate. Thanks very much for the lift and . . . everything."

"You won't get into trouble for being away this morning?"

"No — I had double library, so no one will have noticed. Oh . . ."

Brenda was bustling across the car park towards them, her face like thunder. "Where on earth have you been?" she demanded. "I've been worried sick. I found your clothes and your backpack gone, and that stupid note, and when I rang the school they said you hadn't been in."

"No." It wasn't with defiance but a new-found confidence that Bez greeted her mother. "I was going to London."

"*What?*"

"I changed my mind," she announced simply. "I decided to try to get into university after all."

"Well, I . . ." Brenda stared at her daughter in astonishment. "What brought that on? And what are you doing in that car?"

"I bumped into Vicky in town and she gave me a lift back."

Vicky thanked her silently for skipping the earlier part of the episode.

"She went to university and she told me all about it. It sounds like fun."

Brenda hadn't yet recovered. "Well, yes, but . . ."

"I'm going to do modern languages. Vicky says it would give me lots of career options, and most of the courses include a year abroad." She hefted her backpack out of the boot of the car. "I need to get to class. Could you take this home for me?"

"Okay . . ."

Brenda stood shaking her head in bewilderment as her daughter hugged her and strolled off with a jaunty step across the car park.

Vicky rolled down the car window. "Um . . . could I give you a lift?" she offered. "That pack looks heavy."

Brenda hesitated before conceding a wary, "Thank you." She took Bez's place in the passenger seat, tucking the pack into the footwell. "And thank you for bringing her home. I don't know what she was thinking, going off like that."

Vicky let a small sigh escape her lips. "Um . . . I think I should tell you the truth. I saw her standing at the bus stop in the rain and offered her a lift into town before I realised what she was planning to do."

"Oh?"

"So I drove her to the train station."

"Oh."

"I didn't know what else to do. I suppose I should have turned round and brought her straight home . . ."

"She'd only have run off again." Brenda's voice echoed with strained patience. "She's been threatening to do it for a long time."

"That's what I thought. But I think she really has changed her mind. She asked me loads of questions about university, and she seems quite excited about the idea." She slanted her passenger a swift glance. "For heaven's sake don't tell her it's sensible."

"Of course it's sensible. I've been trying to drum that into her for months."

Vicky shook her head. "Look, I don't want to tell you what to do with your own daughter, but maybe trying to drum stuff into her is having the opposite effect." Her mouth curved into a smile of wry amusement. "Did it ever work with you at that age?"

Brenda conceded a brief laugh. "Well . . . no."

Vicky laughed too. "Teenagers — they're always contrary. She said she didn't want to let you run her life — I pointed out that doing the opposite of what you wanted was the same thing as letting you run her life."

Brenda frowned. "That sounds a bit contrary."

"I suppose it does. But it seemed to do the trick."

They turned down Church Road, the atmosphere between them much more relaxed.

"What are you planning to do with Molly's cottage?" Brenda asked. "Are you still going to sell it as a second home?"

"I don't know. I'd really like to live there, but I'm going to have to find a way to pay the inheritance tax."

"Could you get a mortgage?"

"Possibly — I'd been thinking about that. The problem is that if I stay, I won't have a job, and mortgage companies tend not to be too keen on lending under those circumstances. Still . . ." She pulled up outside Brenda's shop. "I have a little while before I have to make up my mind."

"Well . . . thank you for the lift." Brenda's smile was now warm and friendly. "And for talking some sense into my Bethany. It's more than I could ever do."

"I'm not sure that it was anything I said. I just hinted at some of the difficulties she might have finding a job and somewhere to stay. She began to realise that the streets of London might not be paved with gold after all. She's a good kid, and very bright. She'll do all right. Just go easy on her."

"I'll try."

Vicky sighed with relief as she turned the car round and drove back up the hill to the cottage. Instead of a potential disaster, that had turned out pretty well after all. Bez seemed really enthusiastic about going to university, and hopefully her mother wouldn't nag her quite so much.

And she had a piece of very valuable jewellery in her pocket. Tomorrow she'd go up to London, to the jewellers that Mr Digby had recommended — she was too excited to wait any longer.

She turned through the gate, parked on the drive and climbed out, and reached into the back for her bag . . .

"Hi."

Her heart thumped and she turned sharply, banging her head on the car roof. Tom. "Oh . . ." She managed to fix a smile in place. Standing there with his thumbs hooked in the pockets of his well-worn jeans, he could have stepped straight out of one of her hot dreams. "Hello. You . . . made me jump."

"I'm sorry. I'm looking for Rufus. He often comes into Molly's garden. He's been gone since before breakfast — it isn't like him to miss his food."

"Oh . . ." *And breathe* . . . "Sorry, I've been out — I haven't seen him."

"It'll serve him right if he misses his supper too, the little rat."

Numbly her mind sought for something casual to say. "Does he run away often?" Did her voice sound a little too bright?

"Quite often, but he never goes far."

She took a moment to steady herself. The sensible part of her brain was warning her to freeze him out; temptation was whispering to her to stay. *He's married.* She was struggling to remember that, to conjure the image of him at the cricket match with his wife and his little boy.

But when he smiled like that . . .

"Um . . . how old is he?"

"Almost eighteen months. Still a pup, really. I'm hoping he'll grow out of the habit."

"You can't shut him in?"

He laughed. "Are you kidding? Houdini had nothing on him. Anyway, it isn't really practical on a farm. At least he knows not to bother the cows. And he's a great little ratter."

Oh, dammit, that laugh. Low and slightly husky, it sent a shimmer of heat over her skin. And the glint in those dark eyes, the slight lift at the corner of that beguiling mouth.

That mouth . . . it would be warm and firm on hers, sure and confident, easing her lips apart as those strong arms drew her against his hard body . . .

Careful, she warned herself sharply. She suspected that Tom Cullen was far too perceptive to miss the effect he had on her. Which could make things difficult if they were going to be neighbours.

But if they were going to be neighbours, even if only for a short time, she ought to try to establish some kind of friendly relationship. She just had to ensure that she kept that simmering sexual attraction under control. She could do that.

"Have you looked in the back garden?" she asked.

"I was just going to, if that's okay."

"Of course." She led the way down the side of the cottage. "It's a bit of a jungle back here." She tried for a note of light humour. "There are probably elephants hidden in the grass."

He quirked one dark eyebrow in amusement. "I didn't know Molly kept a herd of elephants."

"Well, she was pretty eccentric." She laughed. "I wouldn't put it past her."

He stood with his hands fisted on his hips, surveying the area. "You're going to need a lawnmower on this."

"There's one in the garage — a petrol thing. It looks pretty ancient though, so I don't know if it still goes."

"Let's have a look at it."

The garage door creaked in protest as they dragged it open. "Needs a drop of WD40 on those hinges," Tom suggested.

Vicky flicked on the light — a single naked bulb swinging from the roof, casting weird shadows among the random junk. "It's a bit of a tip. I think there could be a whole new species of spider evolving in here."

There was an old spin-dryer — the top-loading sort dating from the 1960s. A broken deckchair, paint tins, garden tools. In the middle, under a dusty tarpaulin, was Molly's motorbike and sidecar.

"Oh, I remember this old thing." Tom flipped up the tarpaulin. "She gave me a ride in the sidecar once — I've never been more scared in my life. She thought speed limits were nothing more than a casual suggestion."

Vicky laughed. "No wonder my mum would never let me go for a ride in it. Here's the lawnmower." She edged past the motorbike. "I don't know if there's any petrol in it."

"There's a jerrycan here." He picked it up and shook it. "Yes, it's full."

"Right."

The lawnmower was heavy. Tom came to help her manoeuvre it out of the garage and over to the edge of the lawn. "We'd better check if there's any oil in it."

"Ah — yes." She wouldn't have thought of that.

He messed about, checking the engine oil and filling the tank with petrol, and finally managed to get it started. It rattled alarmingly, but then to Vicky's relief it settled into a steady throb.

"There you go. Try it."

She took the handle and pulled up the starter lever . . . and found herself sprawling on the ground as the mower leaped forward.

"Oh . . . !" Laughing, she eased herself to her knees, awkwardly aware that any dignity she might have hoped for had been shattered. "What a klutz."

"Are you okay?" Tom took her elbow to help her to her feet.

"Yes, thanks . . ." He hadn't moved his hand. A small glow of heat was spreading up her arm, and when she lifted her gaze to those deep, dark eyes she felt as if she was caught in some kind of spell.

Had he stepped closer to her, or was it just that he was the only thing she could see? There seemed to be some kind of static charge in the air, like the moments before a thunderstorm. She couldn't move, had forgotten to breathe.

His hand slid slowly up from her elbow to her shoulder . . .

A burst of ecstatic barking shattered the moment. A small brown-and-white terrier scrambled out of the bushes at the side of the garden and hurled himself at his master as if he hadn't seen him for months.

Vicky stepped back sharply, alarm bells ringing in her head. If Rufus hadn't saved her . . . *Girl Code: Off Limits*.

And what the hell did he think he was doing? He was married, with a kid — and another on the way. He had no right — *no right* — to play flirty games with other women. In a small village like this he was probably the number one babe-magnet, and clearly it had resulted in an outsized ego — not to mention a sense of entitlement.

Well, this was one babe who had no intention of being magnetised. She had too much respect — for herself, for his wife, for any woman — to fall for a man who collected women like teenagers collected TikTok followers.

"Ah — he's decided to come back." She forced a smile, cool and friendly. "That's good. Well, I'd better get on with mowing this lawn. See you around."

She sensed his brief hesitation. But as she started up the mower again and set off down the garden he called to the dog, and by the time she risked a glance back over her shoulder he was gone.

* * *

How had she forgotten, in just ten days, how awful the London traffic was? It wasn't helped by the roadworks on Hammersmith Bridge. Vicky sighed as she pulled up behind yet another traffic queue.

There were two options — driving all the way across town to Hatton Garden and hoping to find a convenient parking space, or leaving the car in the car park beneath her apartment block and catching the Tube. Of the two, the latter was probably the best one to go with.

Molly's diamond brooch was safe in her pocket, in its velvet pouch and covered by her sweater. It was a quick ride on the Circle line, thirty minutes, almost door to door. If anyone was going to mug her they'd take her bag and be satisfied.

It was a relief to turn off the main road onto the quieter side street. A few hundred yards along was the entrance to the cavernous car park beneath the apartment block. Jeremy's car was in his allocated space next to hers.

That wasn't unusual — most days he walked to the office. Unless he needed to go out to a viewing — then he felt it gave a more professional impression to arrive in his BMW rather than on foot.

The other advantage of parking here was that she could nip up to the apartment. After the four-hour drive from Devon she was ready for a cup of coffee and a chance to freshen up before she set off for Hatton Garden.

After she finished the business at the jewellers she'd come back and pack up all her stuff and load it into the car. By the time Jeremy got home from work she'd be ready to sit down and have a calm conversation with him, give him back his ring. And leave.

The lift took her to the fifth floor. Strange to think that after almost twelve months she wouldn't be living here anymore. She wouldn't miss it.

The corridor was stark but spotlessly clean and brightly lit. There were six doors, three on each side — theirs was the middle one on the right. She slid the key into the lock and opened the door.

And froze.

Something was off. The curtains were still drawn, and there were two empty wine glasses on the floor beside the sofa. A lingering hint of perfume in the air — a familiar perfume, but not hers.

A giggle from the bedroom. Then Jeremy's voice: "You little minx."

And as if she needed any further confirmation, there was a red leather jacket on the coat rack on the wall. Jayde's red leather jacket.

Very quietly she stepped back into the corridor and closed the door, and stood staring at it.

There were two options. She could open the door again, storm in, catch them red-handed — create an almighty scene with them all screaming at each other and probably ending up with everything being twisted and making her the one who was in the wrong.

Or she could leave now, come back after they'd gone, collect her things and be on the road back to Devon before Jeremy came home. Leaving her engagement ring and a brief note telling him that she had decided not to marry him, leaving him to try to figure out her reasons.

She smiled grimly. Of the two, the latter was probably the best one to go with. Cold, dignified. Making it clear that she was the one doing the rejecting, not the one being rejected and cheated on.

With her own stepsister! That would certainly be an explosive relationship. They'd either be good for each other, compensating for each other's flaws, or they'd end up killing each other.

She smiled again. Of the two options . . .

CHAPTER ELEVEN

The motorway traffic westbound out of London was quite heavy until she got past Bristol, then she was able to put her foot down. Soaring along the elevated section of the M5 above the Gordano Valley with her headlights spearing through the gathering dusk, Vicky felt as if she was flying.

Thirty-two thousand pounds! Incredible. She had almost hugged Monsieur Laurent, the jeweller. He had identified the dragonfly brooch as a Cartier piece, and had been delighted with it, cooing over it as if it had been a fluffy kitten.

And that wasn't the only cause for satisfaction. Any doubts that maybe she had leaped to the wrong conclusion about Jeremy and Jayde had been blown away within twenty minutes of leaving the apartment.

She had popped in for coffee and a bite of lunch in the café on the ground floor of the block. Watching out of the window, she had seen them come out — holding hands. And at the bus stop they had kissed. And not just a brotherly kiss on the cheek, either.

Apparently Jayde didn't adhere to the Girl Code. But even for her, it was a new low — pinching her sister's fiancé. Well, ex-fiancé, but neither of them had known that.

Anyway, good riddance to the pair of them — they deserved each other. So much for 'sensible'. Maybe it was time to follow her dreams instead. And now, thanks to Aunt Molly, she could afford to do that — at least for a while.

It had taken her little more than an hour to pack up her clothes and the few other things she wanted to keep — her books, a couple of photo albums, some CDs and DVDs, and a few other bits and bobs she had brought back from holidays when she was younger.

She had left her engagement ring with a carefully worded note for Jeremy on the kitchen table, and a letter of resignation without notice from the Thorington estate agency. Let them try to sue her — that could be fun!

Then she had walked away from the apartment with no regrets.

It was dark by the time she got home. Pulling onto the gravel drive she glanced up at the cottage, welcoming in the moonlight, and smiled. Home — how quickly Molly's cottage, and Sturcombe, already felt like home!

After the long drive to London and back in a day she was tired. A light snack and an early night beckoned. A couple of cheese toasties and a cup of coffee — one of the first things she was going to treat herself to, as well as a new television and a WiFi connection, was a good coffee-maker.

Ten minutes later she was curled up on the sofa, watching one of her favourite comedy panel shows. Jeremy hadn't liked it, she recalled — in fact he hadn't liked many comedies. Or movies, unless they were 'art house' movies with subtitles.

But she didn't have to take account of Jeremy's tastes anymore. She could watch whatever she liked.

She had taken her phone out of her bag and set it down on the coffee table beside her, but she hadn't turned it on — she could guess what would be awaiting her. She'd finish her coffee first.

Or maybe she wouldn't bother to answer it at all tonight. They could all wait until tomorrow.

* * *

Vicky didn't wake until the sun was already climbing up the sky. She lay for a while, reliving that moment in the very exclusive Hatton Garden jewellers.

In that moment everything had changed. She wasn't sure that she had fully absorbed all the implications yet. The first thought that came into her mind was that she was going to be able to keep the cottage.

At least, she was still going to have to take out a mortgage to pay off the inheritance tax, which meant she was going to need a job. But it was no longer the mountain it had once seemed.

And she could afford to have the kitchen she had liked, which she had rejected as being too expensive. She'd better ring Dan the builder and let him know about the change.

Energised, she rolled out of bed and skipped into the bathroom.

Twenty minutes later she was in the kitchen, singing along to the radio as she fixed herself scrambled eggs on toast for her breakfast. Her happy warbling was interrupted by a knock on the door. Her heart thumped so hard it was almost painful.

Tom.

Why would he be knocking on her door? After that brief episode in the garden the other day did he think she'd invite him in for a repeat? But who else could it be? Debbie? Bez? Unlikely . . .

Damn him! Was he going to give her the old 'my wife doesn't understand me' routine? Did he think she was stupid enough to fall for that one? Anger surging inside her, she threw the door open, not bothering with a smile.

It wasn't Tom. It was Bill.

"Oh . . ."

"I'm sorry." He blinked, bobbing his head. "I didn't mean to bother you, but I saw your car was there today, so . . ." He took a step back. "I'm sorry. If it isn't convenient . . ."

"No — no. It's fine." She made her smile extra-warm to compensate for her initial reaction. "Come in."

"No, I won't if you don't mind — my boots are terrible muddy. I just came to say . . . thank you."

"Thank you?"

"About my niece — Bethany. Bez, as she likes to call herself. She told me about how you talked to her, how it did the trick. Brenda — my sister — isn't always wise, nagging on at her. You can't do that with teenagers, can you?" He chuckled. "They think they know everything. So anyway . . . thank you."

"It was nothing," Vicky assured him readily. "She's a nice kid — I enjoyed chatting to her. I hope she'll settle down a bit now."

"I think she will. She was real excited about the idea of going to university. She showed me that website on her phone — she's still deciding which ones she'd like to apply to. Of course she's got to pass her A levels first. But if she does . . . she'd be the first in the family to go to university." He beamed. "We'd be that proud of her."

"I'm sure you will. Bill . . ." Impulsively she caught his arm as he turned to go. "Look, while I'm interfering, I might as well add something else." She took a deep breath and plunged on. "Why don't you ask Debbie out?"

His cheeks flamed scarlet as he opened and closed his mouth like a stranded fish. "I . . . I did once. She said no."

"Once?" She laughed, shaking her head. "How long ago was that?"

"A year ago, mebee."

"Just after she'd split up with her husband?"

He dropped his head, looking sheepish. "Um . . ."

"Probably not the best time to choose, was it?"

He hesitated, returning her a crooked smile. "No . . ."

"Maybe it's time to try again," she suggested gently.

"You . . . you think so?"

Vicky smiled. "I know she likes you. She's just been wary of getting involved because of Amy."

His eyes widened in surprise. "But I love that kid — she knows that."

"She does know. But she's afraid that if she gets involved with you and it goes wrong, it will break Amy's heart."

"I would never break her heart." Suddenly his voice was assertive. "Or Debbie's. I'd rather cut out my tongue. I want to marry her."

Vicky suppressed the impulse to punch the air. "Then go for it," she urged. "If you don't take the risk, you'll never know if you could have found the best thing in your life."

He stared at her for a long moment, then nodded slowly. "Yes. Yes, I . . . I'll try." His smile was very sweet, and suddenly she saw why Debbie was attracted to him, in spite of his bashfulness. "Thank you."

"Good luck."

She watched him as he walked away, down the drive and into the lane. Oh dear — had she done the right thing? It had been bad enough meddling with Bez, but at least that had had a positive outcome.

Perhaps that was a good omen. She could only hope so.

She brought her breakfast to the table and sat down, eyeing her phone with reluctance. As soon as she switched it on, it started pinging to tell her that there was a stack of voicemail messages for her. Four from Jeremy, two from his mother, one from Jayde, three from her mother — and one from Leonard, the medal expert.

She wasn't going to answer the ones from Jeremy or his mother. And she certainly wasn't going to answer the one from Jayde. She opened the one from the medal expert.

"Hello, my dear. It's Leonard Kovacs here. I've discovered some very interesting information about your relative Meline. Do call me back as soon as you can."

Intrigued, she dialled his number. He answered after only two rings.

"Herr Kovacs? It's Victoria Marston. I got your message."

"Ah hello, my dear — I'm very happy to hear from you. You really will be fascinated by this. I found some more details about your Aunt Meline's adventures in Paris during the war. Apparently she was quite the little heroine."

"Really?" She put the phone on speaker while she poured herself a coffee.

"Yes, indeed. She worked with a local Resistance group — not just relaying messages between members, but also conveying weapons and explosives in her schoolbag, concealed beneath her books."

"Wooo!"

"The group leader who recommended her for the medal spoke very highly of her. He said she was a key to the group's success. And that's not all. She also acted as a courier, helping airmen who'd been shot down, and escaped prisoners of war, guiding them between safe houses and putting them in contact with the escape lines to Spain."

"Wow — that's amazing," Vicky breathed. "She really was quite a character."

"She certainly was. And thank you so much for introducing me to her — I've been absolutely fascinated to find out about her."

"Yes. Thank you for telling me about her."

"My pleasure."

They said goodbye and ended the call. Vicky sat staring at her phone for a long moment. Auntie Molly, that eccentric old lady with soft white hair and the lingering fragrance of roses . . . Incredible.

She wasn't going to answer the calls from Jeremy or Jayde, or Charlotte Thorington. But she might as well speak to her mum — get it over with.

"Vicky! What on earth's going on?"

Vicky felt a small stab of guilt. Maybe she should have stayed over at her mother's last night, instead of dashing back here to Sturcombe.

But that would have meant facing the third degree. Not that she was going to escape it entirely. But at least on the telephone, with two hundred miles between them, it was a little easier to smile about it.

"I've had Jeremy calling me, asking where you've got to." Her mother's voice was shrill with agitation. "He's been so worried, and so have I. Where are you?"

"I'm at the cottage, Mum." She spoke calmly, reassuringly. "Where else would I be?"

"But . . . Jeremy said you came up to the flat yesterday, and took all your things."

"That's right. I've decided to move down here."

"What — for good?"

"Very much for good."

"But . . . just like that? Vicky, do be sensible . . ."

Vicky rolled her eyes. "I am being sensible, Mum. What could be more sensible than living where you're happy?"

"But what about Jeremy? What does he think about it?"

"It's none of his business anymore." Time to make the announcement. "I've ended our engagement."

"But . . . I don't understand." She sounded totally bewildered. "Why?"

"I've decided not to marry him — that's all there is to it."

"But what about your job?"

"I resigned."

"Oh, Vicky — have you gone crazy? What are you going to live on?" Now there was real distress in her mother's voice. "You don't know anyone down there. Oh dear . . . I don't know what to say."

Vicky smiled to herself. Her mother never had any trouble finding something to say.

"It's all okay, Mum. It's lovely here, and Aunt Molly has left me enough money to manage for a while." She'd tell her the details another time. "Once I've got the place done up you'll have to come down and visit me."

"Well . . ."

"Did you know that Aunt Molly lived in France during the war?"

"What? I . . ." Her mother sounded confused by the abrupt change of subject. "Yes, I believe she lived near Paris. Why?"

"I was just wondering about her. Why did the family stay there when the war broke out? Why didn't they come back to England?"

"Well, her mother had to stay to look after her grandmother. It's hard to remember the details after all this time. If I recall, the old lady was an invalid, bedridden — she couldn't be got away. Her father had already joined up, of course. And her brother — your grandfather — was at boarding school in England."

"But Molly wasn't evacuated?"

"Apparently not. I don't remember why. It was probably thought too dangerous to send a little girl away on her own — more dangerous than staying with her mother. They didn't live in the centre of Paris — it was somewhere on the outskirts. Boissy, or something like that."

"Did she ever tell you about what it was like?" Vicky asked.

"Well . . . she said they were always short of food. Everything was rationed and they had to queue for hours to buy anything — but of course it was much the same here. And they couldn't get shoes. She had a pair made of raffia, with wooden soles, or she wore her grandmother's stuffed with straw. And coal — that was hard to get, too."

"Did she tell you anything about the Resistance?"

A pause. Vicky could visualise her mother's face, mouth puckered as she considered the question. "I don't think so. She told me how there were German soldiers everywhere, but most of the time she was able to stay out of their way. And of course she was just a schoolgirl, so I don't suppose they would have bothered her."

"No . . ." Vicky smiled to herself. Sometimes her mother was wonderfully naïve. "Anyway, Mum, I've got a lot to do today — I want to make a start on the garden. Speak to you soon."

"Yes, dear . . ."

Vicky ended the call before her mother could remember to ask any more questions.

Well, she'd done it. She'd burned her boats. Now she had a whole new life to make for herself. She rose to her feet and strolled through to the sitting room, and opened the French windows to step out into the garden.

It was hard to believe that she'd only lived here for a little over a week — it really felt like home already. Much more so than the smart apartment in London that she'd shared with Jeremy.

Could she really find a way to keep the cottage? If she was going to take on a mortgage to pay the inheritance tax bill, she'd need to find a job. Not as an estate agent — she'd had enough of that. But there was bound to be something.

* * *

Vicky stood watching as the trailer turned carefully out of the drive and down the lane, bearing Aunt Molly's old motorbike and sidecar. Not 'old' she reminded herself, but 'vintage'.

Barry from the garage had almost wet himself with excitement when she had rung to ask if he knew anyone who might be interested in buying it. A genuine Royal Enfield from 1959 — he had positively drooled over it when she had opened the garage door. At least it would be going to a good home!

And she had a little more money in her bank account to live on until she got a job, or to put towards paying the inheritance tax bill that would be due in six months. She couldn't restrain a few little dance steps as she walked back into the kitchen. Even finding more messages from Jeremy on her phone couldn't dampen her mood.

Time for a stroll down into the village and a cup of coffee at Debbie's. Swinging her bag onto her shoulder she locked the door and set off at a brisk pace down the hill.

It was another glorious sunny day — Monday's rain had given the ground a welcome soaking and then departed. Bumblebees and bright butterflies were dancing among the wild flowers in the hedgerows along the side of the road, and the soft chirruping of birds filled the trees.

Oh, yes — she really wanted to stay. That brief trip to London — the traffic and the pavements and everyone rushing about and never even looking up at the sky . . . Who wouldn't choose this?

And that was before she'd even reached the beach.

The café was bustling with happy holidaymakers, children wide-eyed with excitement at the prospect of the pretty iced cupcakes being brought to their tables, parents munching on pizza slices and paninis, thankful that someone else was doing the washing-up.

A family had just left a table by the window. Vicky put her bag on it and collected up the debris of their meal to carry over to the kitchen.

Debbie greeted her with a happy smile as she passed. "Hi. I'll just wipe your table down. Your usual?"

"Yes, please." She couldn't miss that there was something special about her friend — her eyes were sparkling like stars, her cheeks softly tinged with pink. "You're busy this afternoon."

"The season's starting to build up. It'll get a lot busier than this. Oh — you remember my mum?" she added, indicating the older woman seated beside the till. She had Debbie's soft brown hair and soft brown eyes, but her skin was pale and her cheeks a little thin from her recent illness.

"Of course." Vicky smiled warmly. "Hello, Mrs Rowley."

"Why, it's little Vicky! You call me Kate, my luvver." Her accent was as rich as Devon cream. She came round from behind the counter and took both of Vicky's hands in hers. "Debbie told me you was here. How are you? My, you've grown up into a beauty."

Vicky laughed, squeezing her hands. "Well, I've grown up anyway. How are you? Debbie said you'd been poorly."

"Nothing serious — I get a touch of bronchitis now and then, and this time it turned into a bout of pneumonia, so the doc ordered me to bed. Silly thing to make a fuss over."

"Not at all — pneumonia can be very unpleasant. You have to take care of yourself. I hope you're better now?"

"Much better, thank you. And so bored of sitting up in bed with my knitting. I'm much better off down here, where I can make myself useful."

"And if you don't stay on that chair like the doctor told you, you'll be back up there again," Debbie chided as she passed.

Kate chuckled with laughter, but sat down again. "So are you planning on staying then?" she asked Vicky.

"Yes — at least I hope so. Aunt Molly left me some jewellery, as well as the cottage. I sold most of it to Digby's, in town, but there was a brooch that he said was worth more."

"That was a bit of luck."

"Yes, it was. That was why I went up to London yesterday, to sell it. And it *was* worth more — a lot more." She drew in a deep breath, feeling the excitement bubbling up inside her again. "Enough to pay for the work on the cottage, and a bit left over."

"Oh! That's wonderful."

"I still have to pay the inheritance tax. I'll need to get a mortgage on the cottage to pay it off, or arrange to spread the payments — though that will mean paying interest too. Either way, I'll need to get a job."

"Hmm — there's not a lot round here." Kate shook her head, frowning in thought. "The young 'uns struggle to find anything — I feel sorry for 'em. So many of them end up having to move away."

Debbie set down Vicky's coffee on the counter. "What about the Carleton?" she suggested.

Her mother's face brightened. "Oh, yes — of course!"

Vicky glanced from one to the other. "There's a job going there?"

"That's right. It's only temporary, mind. Lisa, their assistant manager, will be going on maternity leave in a few weeks, so they're going to need someone to cover."

Vicky hesitated. "I don't know. I don't know anything about managing a hotel. They'll want someone qualified, with experience. And I doubt if Jeremy's mother will give me a reference," she added with a humourless laugh.

"They'll just want someone smart, with intelligence — you'd soon pick it up. Why don't you pop up and speak to Mike, the manager?" Debbie urged. "At least it's worth a try."

"Well . . . I suppose so." She shrugged with a wry smile. "He can only say no."

CHAPTER TWELVE

The Carleton had probably seen better days, but it was still clinging bravely to some of its former elegance. The reception hall was quite spacious. The wooden floor was slightly scuffed, but the chandeliers swinging from the ceiling were sparkling clean. To one side there was a carpeted lounge area with a small bar that served drinks and snacks.

Its best feature was undoubtedly its view of the bay, spread like a wide swathe of blue silk out to the distant horizon. The sky was the same vivid blue, with just a few cotton-wool puffs of white cloud like peaceful grazing sheep.

A young girl maybe a few years older than Bez was sitting at a computer behind the reception desk. She looked up with a trained smile as Vicky approached.

"Can I help you, ma'am?"

"Could I see Mr Slade, please?"

The receptionist picked up the phone. "Who shall I say?"

"My name's Victoria Marston. I don't have an appointment — but if it isn't convenient at the moment I could make one."

"Okay." The girl exchanged a brief conversation with the person on the other end of the phone, then turned back to Vicky. "He'll be out in a few minutes, if you'd like to take a seat."

"Thank you."

She chose not to sit down — instead she strolled across to gaze out at the sea. She never seemed to tire of it — that feeling that beyond the horizon it went on for ever, lapping the distant shores of Africa and Australia and Antarctica, home to whales and penguins and giant squid.

A couple of seagulls were soaring in the high blue sky, swooping down to the waves to snatch up an unwary fish. She watched them for a few moments, smiling to herself. They looked so joyful and free — no taxes, no mortgages to worry about.

A door behind the reception desk opened, and the manager came out. "Miss Marston? I'm sorry to keep you waiting. Will you come through?"

"Thank you."

He beckoned her past the reception desk and into a lobby at the back. Here the hand of time had taken its toll — the carpet was almost threadbare, the once-cream paint on the walls dulled to a yellowish tinge, with brown fingermarks around the door frames and light switches.

His office, with its spectacular view of a whitewashed wall and a row of overflowing bins, was just sad. Barely big enough for a desk, a couple of chairs, a metal filing cabinet and a set of bookshelves rammed with lever-arch files, it probably never got even a glimpse of the sun.

Mike Slade looked to be in his fifties, but he was still quite a good-looking man. His hair was neatly trimmed and touched with grey, as was his beard, and his eyes were grey and gentle behind his glasses.

He smiled uncertainly. "I'm sorry — did we have an appointment?"

"No." She felt a little sorry for him. "I just popped in on the chance you might have a moment to see me."

"Of course, of course." He took off his glasses, wiped them with his handkerchief and put them back on again.

"Well, sit down, my dear, sit down. Would you like a cup of tea?"

"Thank you." She guessed that the offer was as much to make him feel comfortable as her.

He leaned out of the door to call to the receptionist. "Kerry, could you fetch me two teas, please?"

"Okay, Mike."

"Now." He moved round behind his desk and sat down, smiling again. "What can I do for you?"

Vicky smiled back — she found herself liking him. He was a bit like her stepfather — kindly, but always slightly harassed, as if afraid he'd forgotten something important. "I heard you may need a temporary assistant manager soon, to cover for maternity leave."

His pale eyes lit up at once. "Oh, yes — oh, yes, indeed. Indeed we do. And you're looking for a job, Miss . . . ah . . ."

"Marston."

"Marston, Marston." A line creased between his brows. "Any relation to . . . ?"

"Molly Marston — she was my great-aunt. She left me her cottage."

"Oh, yes, indeed." He beamed in delight. "Old Molly — well I never. She was quite a character. She fought a long battle with the council over the regulation banning dogs on the beach. I remember her standing up in the council meeting and telling them they'd do better to ban families as they were the ones who left all the litter. She was right, of course, and she won in the end."

Vicky laughed. "That sounds just like Molly!"

The door opened and Kerry came in carrying a tray with two cups of tea and a plate of chocolate biscuits. "Here y'are then, Mike." She put it down on the desk. "Anything else while I'm up?"

"No, thank you, Kerry. But could you just ask Lisa to step in here, please?"

"Right you are."

Vicky glanced from one to the other, suppressing a smile. The total lack of formality between them gave the whole place an air of warmth, friendliness. In spite of the slightly run-down air, this seemed to be a nice place to work. Much nicer than working for Charlotte Thorington.

And then Lisa walked in.

Oh. Tom's wife. Vicky's heart thumped. Maybe she should have connected the heavily pregnant woman at the cricket with the assistant manager due to go on maternity leave, but she had never even thought of it. Though she had done nothing wrong, except in her dreams, a sharp stab of guilt twisted in her gut.

"Hi, Mike — you wanted something?"

"Ah, Lisa. This is Molly's niece. Miss Marston."

"Please, call me Vicky."

"Oh, yes." The young woman smiled warmly. "I saw you at the cricket, looking after Arthur Crocombe. That was very kind of you."

"I . . . um . . . I enjoyed chatting to him." Vicky was struggling to keep her breathing steady. "He has lots of fascinating stories."

"Miss Marston — Vicky — was enquiring about the cover for your maternity leave," the manager explained.

"Really?" Her eyes, a pretty grey, lit up. "Oh, that's great! We were getting worried that we wouldn't be able to find anyone, weren't we, Mike? Most people seem to want full-time — you know it's only part-time, right?"

"Yes. But . . ."

"And if that doesn't put them off, they don't want temporary. Or they don't want to be tucked away down here." Those grey eyes danced. "We're not exactly the Las Vegas of the South West Peninsula. More like somewhere between the middle of nowhere and the back of beyond!"

Mike chuckled. "I'm afraid so."

Vicky was squirming inside. Lisa seemed so open and friendly — she really liked her, while at the same time she wanted to hate her for being married to Tom.

148

"This little bundle is due at the end of June." Lisa stroked her hand over her bump, smiling that secret smile of all pregnant mothers. "So I'd really like to start my maternity leave in two weeks. Would that be okay with you?"

"Yes. But . . ." Vicky drew a breath. "The thing is . . . I don't have any relevant experience. I've never worked in a hotel. I'm . . . I *was* an estate agent."

Lisa laughed, shaking her head. "Well, that's probably good experience — it's mostly about dealing with the public and being organised with paperwork. It's not that complicated — you'll soon get the hang of it."

"And I doubt if I'll be able to supply you with a reference. I left my last job for . . ." She hesitated. "Personal reasons."

"Don't worry about that," Mike assured her. "You're old Molly's niece — that makes you almost family. Look, if you have time, why don't you let Lisa show you around, give you a general outline of the job? Then you can sit down and sort out the details — wages, National Insurance number, that sort of thing."

"Um . . . yes, that would be fine. Thank you."

Vicky felt as if her head was spinning. So much was happening so quickly. She owned a cottage. She had more money in the bank than she had ever had in her life. She had thrown over one job, and now she had another.

Lisa had eased herself carefully to her feet. "Mike, don't forget you need to speak to the council about when they're going to be starting the repairs on Pear Tree Road."

"Don't worry — I'll get onto it."

"And next weekend it's the Three Counties Amateur Ladies' Tournament."

"Ah, yes — I have that in my diary."

Lisa laughed softly as she led Vicky back to the reception hall. "As you can see, one of the most important parts of the job is keeping an eye on Mike. He's a sweetheart, but he sometimes needs a bit of a reminder about things. The guests love him." Her eyes danced. "Actually some of them love him rather too much!"

"Right . . ."

"So you've decided to stay?" They were strolling across the reception area to the dining room. "Tom said you were planning to sell the cottage."

"I was originally. But I really love it here — the countryside, the sea. If I can find a way to pay the inheritance tax I'd really like to keep the place." She smiled. "Aunt Molly left me some jewellery, and I was able to sell that to help pay for the work that needs doing. But I need a job. This is ideal as a stopgap, but I'll need something permanent."

"What do you want to do?" Lisa asked with genuine interest. "Will you go back to being an estate agent?"

Vicky shook her head. "I don't think so. I'd like to do something different. Work for a charity, maybe."

"That would be interesting. Well, as you can see, this is the dining room. We do breakfast, and guests can have a packed lunch if they want it. And we do dinner, for hotel guests and the general public."

"Oh, yes — I had dinner here on Saturday, with . . . a couple of friends."

"Was it good?"

"Very good."

Lisa nodded, pleased. "Thanks for the positive feedback! The kitchen is through here." She pushed open another door into a bright kitchen full of gleaming stainless-steel worktops and appliances. "Chef comes on at four."

"Right . . ."

They walked back across Reception to a short corridor with two wide sliding doors. "These are the wheelchair-accessible suites." She opened one of the doors. "There's no guests in this one at the moment. They're both equipped with a fixed-track hoist system, here and in the bathroom, adjustable beds, adapted equipment. And each has a separate room for the carer."

French windows led straight out onto the terrace with its view of the bay. The room was charmingly decorated in shades of peach and cream, with gleaming mahogany furniture and a delicate chandelier light-fitting.

Vicky smiled as she gazed around. "It's lovely."

"Isn't it? We wanted these rooms to be at least as good as all the others. They can be booked out to non-disabled people, but it's best to book them last in case they're needed. Okay, shall we go upstairs?"

The two of them fell into an easy conversation as they strolled around the hotel. "We've got forty-two rooms," Lisa explained. "Three on the first floor are suites, and there are two singles, besides the two downstairs. Thirty-one of them are occupied at the moment — that's around seventy per cent occupancy. It usually averages about eighty, eighty-five during high season."

"Is that good?"

"Well . . . Not bad. It could be better — but as I said, we're not Las Vegas. A lot of our guests are repeat visitors — some of the elderly couples have been coming for years. They're often here to celebrate a birthday or anniversary, so we always try to make a note of those and make something a bit special for them."

"That's nice. And I suppose you get a lot of people coming for the golf?"

"Yes, we do. We host several tournaments a year, too. Not the big ones, obviously, just amateurs and a couple of semi-pro. Well, that's the grand tour." They had come back to the lift and Lisa pressed the call button. "Let's go down to my office and fill in the paperwork."

Lisa's office was next to Mike's, the same size and with the same non-view, but it somehow seemed much more comfortable. Maybe because it was considerably tidier, and the bookshelves held several pretty trinkets — seashells, coloured pebbles and sea-washed glass. On the desk was a small vase of flowers — and a photo frame. Well, the back of a photo frame — Vicky didn't want to see the front.

"Have a seat," Lisa invited. "Coffee?"

"Yes, please."

She poured two mugs from a coffee machine on the credenza. "Milk or cream?"

"Just a little cream, please. No sugar."

She brought the mugs over and sat down behind her desk, and opened a new file on her computer.

"Have you got your National Insurance number?"

"Yes." She recited it from memory.

"That's good. If you don't mind me asking, you said there were personal reasons why you left your previous job?"

Vicky smiled wryly. "It's not a good idea to be engaged to your boss. If you decide to break off your engagement, the job goes, the flat goes — everything goes!"

"Oh dear — it does sound like it could be unwise." Lisa laughed. "That's something I've been very careful to avoid!"

Vicky kept her smile in place. She couldn't quite imagine Lisa working on the farm, milking the cows and mucking out the barn. But it was all too easy to imagine her snuggling up on the sofa with Tom in the evening . . .

A little desperately she pushed that thought from her mind. "It's funny, in a way — it wasn't just because I inherited the cottage. I began to realise that I wasn't living the life I wanted. And finding out about Molly, all the amazing things she did, made me realise that being sensible was just a waste. It gave me the courage to think about what I really want."

Lisa laughed. "Sensible?"

"That's my mother's thing." Another wry smile. "I suppose it's understandable — mothers worry."

"We do. But you're right — being sensible isn't always the best way to live your life. Anyway, tell me more about Molly." Lisa leaned forward with eager interest. "My mum told me that she used to go swimming in a purple swimsuit, every day, right through the winter, until she was well into her seventies."

Vicky rolled her eyes. "That doesn't surprise me at all!"

* * *

152

Vicky's mind was still swirling with thoughts of Tom and Lisa as she walked up the hill from the hotel. Tom and Lisa. If she was going to stay here, living next door to them, she was just going to have to get used to it.

She could do that — of course she could. It was just a matter of . . . self-discipline. And finding other things to distract herself. Like working on her book. She really needed to get on with that, while she had this opportunity.

There were a few bits of shopping she needed, so she stopped at Brenda's. The shopkeeper greeted her with a friendly smile. "Hi, Vicky. How are you?"

"Great, thanks. And you?"

"*Tray beeyun, mercy.*" Brenda laughed. "I've got French in the house morning, noon and night! Linda, this is old Molly's niece I was telling you about," she added to the plump woman waiting at the counter.

"Oh, ah — I heard someone had got her cottage. So you be her niece, then?"

"That's right — well, her great-niece. My grandfather was her older brother."

"She talked my Bethany into going for university," Brenda declared proudly.

Vicky laughed, shaking her head. "She talked herself into it. I just gave her a bit of a nudge. Sometimes a kid'll take more notice of a stranger than their own mum."

"Well, anyway, she's really keen. I used to have to nag her to do her homework, but now I don't have to say a word."

"It'd be a good thing, her going to university." Linda nodded sagely. "I wish one of mine would have a bit of ambition. They don't want to leave Sturcombe. Can't budge 'em."

"I don't blame them." Vicky smiled. "It's a lovely place."

"So are you going to stay after all then?"

"I hope so."

"That's good. Morning, Arthur," Linda added as the old man appeared in the doorway.

"Morning, ladies." He chuckled mischievously. "Having a good gossip, are we?"

"Of course."

He picked up a wire basket and pottered off around the shelves. Vicky watched him a little anxiously. He seemed steady enough on his feet, if slow, and he was clearly very independent.

She wandered around the shelves herself, selecting a loaf of bread, some cheese and two pints of milk. Arthur had stopped at the shelves of tinned soup, studying them closely. He stretched up, but the one he wanted was too far back for him to reach.

"Here — let me," Vicky offered. "Just one, or two?"

"I might as well have two while I'm here." He beamed up at her. "Thank you, my luvver."

"Do you need a hand to carry your bag?"

"No, no, I can manage, thank you."

He returned to the counter, chatting comfortably with Brenda as she rang up his purchases. He pulled a coin-purse from his pocket and fumbled for the right change, then nodded goodbye and set off towards his house.

Vicky added some biscuits to her own shopping and went back to the counter.

"Got everything you wanted?" Brenda asked.

"Yes, thanks."

"I heard your neighbour Bill from up the farm has been having cupcakes with his tea," Linda remarked archly.

Vicky didn't need an interpreter to guess the implication. She really shouldn't be surprised that there was gossip in a small village like this. There was no point arguing about it, but she didn't want to get involved, so she simply smiled thinly as she tapped her credit card on the reader and packed her purchases into her bag.

In the doorway she paused to put her sunglasses back on . . . and cried out in horror. "Oh my God! Brenda — phone for an ambulance, quick. Arthur's had a fall."

The old man was sprawled on the pavement, his shopping bag spilled over the kerb. She ran to kneel beside him.

"Arthur? Can you hear me? What happened?"

He groaned, trying to lift his head.

"No, don't try to move." She took his hand, shocked at how cold it was. "Don't worry, there's an ambulance coming."

Brenda had run out from the shop, followed by Linda. "What happened? Did he trip?"

"I don't know. Do you have something to cover him with? I know it's warm, but he could be in shock."

"I'll get something." She bustled back into the shop and was out again a moment later with a tweed coat. "Here."

"Should we try to get him inside?" Linda suggested.

"No — we shouldn't try to move him. We don't know if he might have injured himself. He could have broken a hip or something." Vague memories of earning her first-aid badge at Guides was coming back to her. She laid her fingertips against the pulse point in his neck. "He's breathing, anyway, though his pulse is a bit weak."

Linda had collected up his shopping from the ground. "The ambulance will be here in about twenty minutes. I'll put these things back in the shop."

Brenda nodded. "Good idea. Someone ought to go to the hospital with him."

"I can go," Vicky offered.

"Are you sure?"

"Of course — no problem."

"That's very kind of you." Brenda smiled and held out her hand. "Give me your shopping. I'll get Beth to bring it up for you later."

"Okay — thanks."

"What about his son?" Linda asked. "Someone should get in touch with him — let him know what's happened."

Brenda shook her head. "I've no idea what his phone number is."

"We might be able to find out." Vicky pulled out her phone. "Arthur told me he lives in Canada, and he's a television producer. And Crocombe isn't a very common name." She pulled up the search engine. "He might have a Facebook page, or even be on Wikipedia." It only took a few minutes' detective work to track him down. "Ah — I've got him. At least his work contact. I'll send him an email."

Linda shook her head, bemused, as Vicky tapped in a message. "They're a marvel, those things. My two have both got them — they're always trying to show me how to use them, but I can't be doing with them."

"Everyone's got them these days, even the little kids," Brenda remarked. "People can even pay for their shopping direct with them. I'm going to have to get a new terminal so people can use them."

Arthur seemed to be coming round a little more, his eyes flickering open and trying to speak. He seemed to recognise Vicky, smiling up at her as she spoke soothingly to him, holding his hand.

"I've emailed your son, Arthur — he'll be getting back in touch soon, and I'll tell him what's happened. And the ambulance will be here in a minute."

I hope.

It was more than half an hour before the ambulance arrived — Vicky had never been more relieved than when she saw the flash of the blue light as it came round the bend in the road.

It pulled into the kerb, and the paramedic climbed out. She put her bag down and knelt beside the old man. "Okay, what have we got? Had a nasty fall, have we?"

"About half an hour ago," Vicky explained. "He seemed fine a moment before, in the shop — just a bit slow. But when I came out he'd fallen."

"Did he lose consciousness?"

"I don't think so — at least only for a few moments. His pulse was a bit weak."

"That's to be expected." She was bending over him, shining her penlight into his eyes. "Arthur? Can you hear me? Can you tell me if you have any pain?"

"Arm." It was little more than a weak groan.

"Ah, yes." The paramedic nodded briskly. "The one underneath him probably took the brunt of the fall. Okay,

Arthur, we're going to pop you onto a stretcher and take you off to the hospital. Is that all right with you?"

He managed a nod.

"Can I go with him?" Vicky asked.

"Of course."

The other paramedic had brought the stretcher. With infinite care they eased him onto it and lifted it onto a folding trolley.

"All right, Arthur?" They carefully laid his injured arm over his body and wrapped a blanket around him, then fastened the stretcher's strap to keep him safely in place. "Off we go."

CHAPTER THIRTEEN

Vicky was surprised — and pleased — to find Arthur already sitting up in a high-backed chair beside his bed when she visited on Saturday afternoon. It was a four-bed ward — the other three patients were gentlemen of a similar age to him, and clearly there was a lot of banter between them.

He looked around with a wide smile as Vicky walked in. "Ho there! Here's my girlfriend."

One of the others chortled loudly. "You should be so lucky."

"Don't go wasting your time with that one, girly. He's ticking."

Arthur chuckled. "No good. She's devoted to me, aren't you, my luvver?"

"Of course."

"What have you got there?" he demanded as she placed a paper bag on the table beside him.

"Grapes."

"Lovely!" He reached greedily for the bag with his good hand — the other was strapped with bandage and held in a sling. "You lot, keep your thieving fingers off them." He glared at his comrades. "They're all mine."

"Hah! Share and share alike."

He gestured towards a spare chair. "Well, drag that one over here and sit down, my luvver, and tell me what you've been up to."

"Not much. How are you feeling today?"

"Oh, not so bad. A few bumps and bruises. And they've fitted me up with one of those peacemaker things."

"A pacemaker?"

"That's what I said. It's got a little thing with wires inside me that keeps me ticking properly. What do you think of that, eh?"

"It's wonderful. I hope it'll keep you ticking for a very long time. Now I've got a surprise for you." She took out her phone and clicked on a few buttons. "Just a moment . . ." She held the phone out to him.

"Oh!"

"Hello, Dad." A smiling face appeared on the screen. "Good to see you. I hear you've been a bit poorly."

"Oh . . ." For a moment Vicky thought the old man was going to cry. But he recovered quickly. "Poorly? Nah — it was nothing. And now I've got a peacemaker in me chest."

"And lots of young nurses making a fuss of you, I don't doubt."

"Of course." He laughed mischievously. "What's the point of being in hospital if you can't have lots of pretty young things around you?"

Vicky left them to chat, and slipped away to find the charge nurse in his cubbyhole beside the ward entrance. He glanced up from his desk as she tapped on the door.

"Excuse me. Arthur Crocombe — he's looking quite well. How is he?"

"Are you his granddaughter?"

"No — I'm just a neighbour. A friend. He doesn't have any relatives in this country — his son lives in Canada."

"Oh, yes." He turned to his computer and called up the information. "We've got that. He'd be his next of kin. I gather he won't be able to visit."

Vicky nodded. "Unfortunately not. He had a hip replacement a few weeks ago, so he can't fly long-haul for another couple of months. But they're chatting on FaceTime at the moment."

"Ah — that's good. Are you Victoria Marston?"

"Yes, I am. Simon said he'd contact you to confirm that it's okay for me to deal with everything on his behalf."

"That's right — he emailed us. I've got it here. Okay, the doctor said he could be discharged in a few more days. But if he doesn't have any other relatives here, is there anyone to look after him? He won't be fit to cope on his own for a while."

Vicky shook her head. "I don't know of anyone. There are neighbours, of course, but . . ."

"Yeah, okay." He ran a hand over his face, then nodded. "I'll see if the discharge social worker can set up rehab for him for a couple of weeks. Then when he goes home they might be able to arrange for a carer to go in a couple of times a day."

"That would be a big help. Thank you."

* * *

Saturday night. The night for fun. Discos and wild all-night parties in her university days. Cinema dates and evenings in on the sofa with a movie and a bottle of wine with a succession of boyfriends, some more serious than others. Later, theatre and ballet and elegant little dinner parties with Jeremy.

Tonight she had her laptop for company. Driving back from the hospital, she had had an idea — maybe she shouldn't be thinking of writing a straightforward biography of kings and queens. That had been done.

Maybe . . . it might be more interesting to make it a story, a fiction, based within the actual events. She could focus on one of the lesser characters — a lady-in-waiting to the queen. She could give her adventures, a romance — a dangerous love affair with one of the enemy, a commander in the army of Henry VI.

Once the ideas had started to spin in her head she was on a roll. Pausing only to grill a couple of cheese toasties for her tea, she sat down at the kitchen table and began to scribble in her notebook — scenes, character sketches, snatches of dialogue, filling page after page.

It was after eleven when she decided to call it a day. With a yawn she closed the notebook and set it aside. She was about to turn off the laptop, but hesitated. She'd set up the WiFi that morning, and had used it to check the route to the hospital and to dip into some of the research she needed for the book.

But a compelling curiosity had been niggling in her mind. She had done her best to ignore it, but she knew she wouldn't sleep unless she gave in. She called up the search engine and typed in *Cullen Organic Mill*.

A website came up — a good one. Very professionally done, with a nice colour scheme and clear text. No thick country bumpkin here. The home page had a couple of paragraphs about the health and environmental benefits of organic farming — simple language, nothing preachy.

As she had expected, there was a page detailing the various organic animal feeds the company sold. But there was also a page of dairy products — yoghurt, cheeses, flavoured milk — and another advertising organic fruit and vegetables.

It appeared that the Cullen Organic Mill was a much more substantial outfit than she had imagined. No wonder Tom could afford a top-of-the-range SUV. That would have scored him extra points with Jayde — she always factored in the car a man drove when deciding whether she fancied him or not.

With a small shake of her head she closed down the laptop and went up to bed.

* * *

"What the . . . ?" Vicky scrambled out of bed and ran to the window. The garden was full of cows — a black-and-white mob, bellowing as they jostled their way through a gap they had broken in the fence to feast richly on the long grass and the vegetable patch. "Oh! Of all the stupid . . . Go! Go away!"

But yelling at the obstinate creatures through the window wasn't going to help. Throwing on some clothes she raced down the stairs, out through the kitchen and up the lane to the farm.

With luck, Tom wouldn't be there — just Bill. But, no, of course not. Bill was at the far end of the milking shed, scooping up the old straw and manure with the small bucket-loader.

As she hesitated, wondering if she should wait until he had finished his task, Tom strolled out of the farmhouse, a mug of tea in each hand, his scruffy brown-and-white terrier bouncing at his heels.

"Good morning." He smiled — and her heart bumped.

"Well, it would be good," she retorted tartly. "Except there are a bunch of your cows in my garden."

A glint of teasing amusement lit his eyes. "They're called a herd, not a bunch."

"Never mind what they're called, they're in my garden and they're eating my vegetables."

He laughed. "They like vegetables."

She glared at him. "I'm sure they do. But I don't want them there, depositing all their smelly . . ."

"It's called shit."

"I don't need a dictionary," she snapped. "I need your cows out of my garden — preferably sometime this century."

He held up his hands in surrender. "Okay — I apologise. I assume they got in through the fence? I should have fixed it before. I'll come and sort it out now."

She ground out a terse, "Thank you," between clenched teeth. She hadn't intended to sound so hostile, but maybe hostility was safer — a defence against that treacherous sexual tension that had been building since their first encounter.

It was difficult to keep her breathing steady as she walked beside him down the lane to the cottage. She had to

162

keep reminding herself that he was out of bounds — and that those warm looks and flirty smiles were just a game. He was a narcissist who thought he was God's gift to women.

And he made her pulse race just by looking at her.

"So you've decided to stay?" he enquired genially.

"Yes." She hoped he wouldn't notice the slight tremor in her voice. "I thought it might be nice to stay for the summer, at least. After that . . . who knows?"

"You've got a job down at the hotel?"

"Yes." *Please don't mention your wife.*

To her relief they had reached her gate. As they walked down the side of the cottage, Tom burst out laughing at the sight of the cows contentedly cropping the juicy grass in the back garden.

"Oh dear. Gertie, was this your idea?"

One of the cows lifted her head on hearing her name, regarded him with one liquid brown eye, then turned back to contentedly chewing.

"Okay, girls, fun's over. Gertie, Sheila — back to your own field now."

He tugged up a handful of sweet, long grass and wafted it under the nose of the animal he had called Gertie. She lifted her head, tempted . . . And docilely allowed him to lead her back through the gap in the fence.

Vicky watched in amazement as the cows waiting to push into the garden backed up politely as the matriarch strolled through, her large rump swaying with each step, and those already inside followed her out to their own field.

He turned back to Vicky, a provocative grin on his face. "There. All done."

"Great. Thank you. Except . . . I'm reluctant to point it out, but . . . What's to stop them coming back in as soon as you've gone?"

"The fact that I'm going to mend the fence for you."

"Oh . . ." That rather took the wind out of her sails. "Thank you."

"No problem."

Oh, that smile. It lit his eyes, made her feel as if she was the only woman he had ever smiled at like that. Which was a very dangerous fantasy.

"Do you have any wood I could use?"

"Um . . . I think there's some in the garage. There's probably a few tools in there, too — though I wouldn't guarantee that they haven't crumbled into a pile of rust."

That glint of teasing amusement lit his eyes again. "Well, let's take a look, shall we?"

She was very aware of him as he followed her to the garage. Her heart was beating too fast, her mouth felt dry. And the faintly mocking smile lifting the corners of his mouth warned her that he knew precisely the effect he was having on her.

Struggling to ignore him, she pulled open the garage doors and pointed to the bits of timber piled at the back. "Will that do?"

"Should be okay. What about a saw, hammer, nails?"

"Here on the shelf." She picked up an old jam jar full of nails. "These look a bit rusty."

He took the jar from her and shook some of them out into his hand. "There's enough that'll do." He picked out the best of them. "I'll just do a temporary fix for now, and get someone to come in and do a proper job for you."

He hefted the timber easily onto one wide shoulder and strolled off down the garden.

She stood watching him — she couldn't tear herself away. There was something about him. It was in the way he moved, the easy competence in everything he did. Yes, even in the gentle way he managed his cows.

So much for not falling for him — she'd never stood a chance.

With an effort of will she turned away and walked back into the cottage . . . only to find herself drawn into the sitting room, where she could watch him through the French windows.

Those hard muscles moved smoothly beneath his skin as he worked — all she wanted was to feel them moving beneath her hands, feel his body against hers, breathe the unique male scent of his skin . . .

An explosion of curses from the end of the garden broke through her fantasy. Tom had dropped the saw and was sucking on his hand.

"Oh my God! What's happened?" Without even thinking about it she threw open the door and raced down the garden.

"Damn knot in the wood. The saw slipped."

"Show me." She took his hand. There was a long slice across the pad of his thumb, oozing blood. "It might need stitches."

"No, it's not that bad. It just needs a bandage or something."

"Right . . ." She realised that she'd been holding his hand for rather longer than was necessary. "There's . . . um . . . a first-aid box in the kitchen — there should be something in there."

He followed her up to the cottage and into the kitchen — the room suddenly felt a lot smaller with him in it. Vicky fussed with digging the first-aid box out from the cupboard, hoping he wouldn't notice the faint blush of pink in her cheeks.

"Here we are." Her voice sounded over-bright to her own ears as she carried the box to the table. "Let's see . . . yes, there's bandages, and some gauze. And some TCP — maybe I'd better bathe it first."

"Go ahead."

He perched on the edge of the table and held out his injured hand. A strong, well-made hand, with long fingers and a powerful wrist. Soaking a pad of gauze with TCP she dabbed it gently on the cut.

"Ow!"

Her eyes flew to his face. "Oh, I'm sorry. Did that hurt?"

"Not really." There was a lilt of amusement in his voice. "I just wanted a bit of sympathy. I was hoping you might kiss it better."

Yes, he knew exactly what effect he had on her. "I . . . think the TCP will do a better job."

She kept her head lowered over her task as she sliced open another pack of gauze and wrapped it carefully over the cut. "Just hold that in place for a minute."

She found a roll of micropore and taped the gauze in place, then wound a bandage over it, anchoring it with a few turns around his thumb.

"There. I think it'll be okay without stitches, if you're careful. Try not to get it wet for a couple of days. You don't think you should go and get a tetanus jab, just in case?"

He laughed. "You obviously haven't been around farmers much. We always keep our shots well up to date. Accidents happen a lot on farms."

"Oh . . ."

"Thank you." Oh, that smile. "You make a good nurse."

"I . . ."

He lifted his hand and touched her cheek. Did she lean in to him, or did he lean in to her? Gazing up into those mesmerising dark eyes, she felt as if she was melting inside.

Her breathing quickened as temptation flooded her mind. His head bent slowly over hers, his mouth brushed her lips, light as a butterfly's wing. Her eyelids fluttered closed as pleasure swirled through her veins, heating her blood. Her lips parted on a soft sigh, and she could only let herself surrender to the exquisite sensations he was stirring inside her.

She had never known a kiss could be like this. She felt as if her bones had turned to liquid honey as his hand slid down the length of her spine, curving her close against his hard body. The subtle male scent of his skin was drugging her mind. This was what she had dreamed of . . .

She froze. This wasn't supposed to be happening — it was all kinds of wrong. He was married — to a very nice woman, who she would have liked to have for a friend. He had a little boy, and another baby due in just a few weeks.

He sensed her sudden withdrawal, and let her go. She stepped back, ice-cold anger surging inside her, instantly dousing the fever in her veins. How dared he treat her like that — treat his wife like that?

But she wasn't going to let him see how badly he affected her. *Cool*... "I think you're done here," she said, not looking at him.

He frowned, puzzled. "Done?"

Her heart was thumping painfully, but she shrugged her shoulders in casual unconcern, focussing on packing away the contents of the first-aid box.

"I don't think . . ." he began, but she pulled herself out of reach.

"No, clearly you don't." She spoke so sharply that it wiped away the playful smile that had crept back onto his face. She turned to put the first-aid box back in the cupboard. "Have you finished with the fence?"

"Just one more piece to put in place, then I'll be out of your way."

"Good. I have some things to do later today. Just put the tools back in the garage when you've finished with them."

"Of course. And I'll send young Wayne over to deal with any shit deposited in your garden."

"Oh, I don't think there's much — they weren't there very long. Anyway, I'll shovel it onto the compost heap — it'll make good fertiliser."

"Fine." He turned abruptly and walked out of the door.

Vicky slumped down on one of the chairs. She felt hot and dizzy, a thousand unwanted emotions churning inside her. She should never have let that happen.

And it couldn't happen again.

Maybe it would be better if she sold the cottage and moved away after all — safer. Living right next door to him might not be good for her sanity. But she hated the thought of leaving Sturcombe — she had begun to really love the place, and already she was building a circle of friends.

Why should she let Tom Cullen ruin that?

CHAPTER FOURTEEN

Chaos.

Vicky had been delighted when Dan the builder had rung to say that a last-minute delay on another contract, due to an unforeseen problem with the drainage on the site, meant that he could fit in the work on the cottage straight away, if it was convenient.

Since then it had been full on. Scaffolders had arrived at seven thirty the next morning so the men could get started on replacing the cracked roof tiles and the guttering.

The second-hand furniture shop on Church Road had been very happy to take Molly's bed and the recliner, but the mattress and the sofa were now sitting in the front garden waiting to be collected by the council's recycling lorry.

Keeping them company was a large yellow skip now full of building debris, including the old toilet and sink from the bathroom. The bathroom had been tiled and the new items installed — Dan knew someone who could come and repair the enamel on the bath.

The cottage was full of noise and dust, loud music blasting from a radio, and half a dozen beefy young men working around each other as they rewired the electrics and replaced the radiators. They were a friendly bunch — she knew all of them by name now, and how much sugar they liked in their tea.

She had been glad to escape to the garden most of the time, where there was plenty of weeding to do. In the evenings she'd been able to sit down at the kitchen table with her laptop and do some work on her book.

She had created her two main characters. She could see them so easily. Lady Cecily, lady-in-waiting to Queen Elizabeth Woodville, was fair, delicate. An English rose, but with a steel core and a deep loyalty to the queen.

And he — Lord William Beaufort — was tall, with wide shoulders and a face carved in strong planes and angles. And dark, dark eyes that could glint in sardonic amusement, or glow with a warmth that could ignite the fires inside her.

Her sketch of the genealogy had made William a cousin of the Duke of Somerset. She had decided that he had been wounded and captured in the Battle of Losecoat, and was being held at Ludlow Castle.

She had already written the scene when the two had first met. The queen had sent her with a special ointment to dress his wounds — a slash on his forehead and a sword-thrust beneath his shoulder. She had enjoyed writing that — Cecily's first reaction to a glimpse of his hard-muscled chest.

Now she was going to write a scene where they would *almost* kiss. With a coffee close to hand she closed her eyes and let her imagination roll . . .

"You're leaving tomorrow."

"Lord Richard has negotiated an exchange of prisoners."

"I'm glad for you."

"Are you?"

"Of course. You'll be back with your own people, your friends."

"Yes. But . . ." He lifted his hand and touched her cheek, so gently. *"You're crying."*

"I'm not . . . I am. I'll miss you. We've been . . . friends . . ."

"Yes . . ."

Did she lean in to him, or did he lean in to her? Gazing up into those mesmerising dark eyes, she felt as if she was melting inside. Her lips parted as his head bent over hers . . .

A clatter of footsteps on the stairs drove them apart . . .

Vicky dragged in a long, ragged breath. She had been drawn right into it — and it hadn't been Lord William in the vivid scene, but Tom Cullen. Her heart was racing, the image of that hard-boned face had seemed so close to hers — so close that she could almost feel the heat of his breath against her cheek.

Oh, boy . . .

Quickly she saved the file and put the laptop aside. She urgently needed a coffee . . . No, not coffee — she was going to have enough trouble getting to sleep. Camomile tea might help — if she had any. Or maybe a strong hit of whiskey.

Molly had left a half-full bottle of rather good eighteen-year-old triple-distilled Irish malt in the walnut sideboard, with a set of fine crystal tumblers. She poured herself three fingers, laughing as she toasted herself.

"Oh, Lord William — you're absolutely gorgeous. You're going to be one heck of a problem for poor Cecily." And the same could be said for Tom Cullen.

Draining the whiskey, she went up to bed.

* * *

"How's it going?"

Vicky rolled her eyes at Debbie's question. "Don't ask! I've been exiled from the sitting room while they're sanding the floor — there's dust everywhere."

She spread a generous scoop of rich Devon cream onto her scone and smeared a little jam on the top.

"But I've got my workroom done — I spent a very enter-taining couple of hours yesterday assembling the cupboards and drawers to make the base for my desk. It'll be great to be able to spread out in there. I'm getting a new desktop computer — the laptop's fine for a while, but if I'm going to do some serious writing a desktop will be better."

"Bill said they've got the new windows in. He said they look really smart."

"They do. My new bed came this morning, so I'll be able to move back into the main bedroom and get a good night's sleep — that mattress in the spare room must be fifty years old and it's as hard as concrete. And they're installing the new kitchen next week. I'll be glad when it's all done."

"I bet." Debbie turned to say goodbye to a family who were just leaving. "Are you going to have a housewarming party?" she asked when she came back from clearing their table.

"I hadn't thought of it, but . . . yes. At least a small one. You and your mum. And Bill, of course."

Debbie's blush told her everything.

"You're still seeing him?"

Her friend's shy smile put two tiny dimples into her cheeks. "Yes. We've been to the pictures a couple of times. And we're going out to dinner tomorrow."

"That's good."

"I . . . um . . . wanted to thank you."

"What for?" Vicky bit into her scone, letting the cream ooze into her mouth.

"He . . . Bill . . . he told me what you said to him." Again that shy little smile. "I suppose we both needed a bit of a push."

Vicky laughed, shaking her head. "I'm getting to be a real interfering bugger."

"Oh, no! At least, in a good way. Without it we'd both still be dithering around, I expect. And young Beth would have gone off to London, and heaven alone knows what would have happened to her."

"I don't think she'd have stayed, when it came down to it," Vicky mused. "She may be only seventeen, but she's got her head screwed on."

"Even so, you saved her mum a lot of worry. And now she's planning to go to university. That's brilliant."

Debbie's mum came through from the kitchen with a fresh batch of cupcakes to put on the counter. "What time's Arthur coming home?"

"I'm picking him up at two o'clock. I spoke to the social worker again — they're arranging for a carer to come in to him, at least for a while, to help him get dressed in the morning and make him some breakfast, and then help him to bed."

"That's good. Brenda said you're getting up a rota to go in and give him lunch."

"That's right. Bez is helping too, and Linda."

Kate laughed. "Ah — so we'll get to hear all the details then. Anyway, count me in. I'll see to him tomorrow. I'll take some meals down to pop in his fridge, that'll just need heating up. And I'll make some pasties, and the apple pie he likes — he can have them cold or heat them up."

"Brilliant." Vicky finished her coffee and glanced at her watch. "Anyway, it's half past — I need to be going. He'll fret if I'm late. See you tomorrow."

* * *

"Well, here we are." Vicky drew the car into the kerb and switched off the engine. "Home sweet home."

"Oh, ah . . ." Arthur beamed with pleasure. "Thank you, my luvver."

She climbed out of the car and paused to study the house. The garden was overgrown with bindweed and wild garlic, and the front door was in need of a coat of paint. Maybe there'd be a lad in the village who'd be willing to do a few odd jobs for a bit of extra pocket-money — she'd ask around.

Arthur was struggling with his seat belt, so she hurried round the car to help him out.

"Oops-a-daisy." He stood up with some effort and looked around contentedly. "It's good to be home."

172

"You were spoiled rotten in that hospital," she teased him. "You won't have a dozen nurses fussing around you now."

He chuckled as he took her arm to walk up the path. "That was a compensation. But, really, all I wanted was to come home."

Vicky opened the door for him. Inside it wasn't as bad as she had feared it might be — just the sort of mild neglect to be expected from an elderly widower with failing eyesight. A faint musty smell in the hall, dust-bunnies beneath the telephone table, a ragged cobweb in the corner of the ceiling.

She took him into the sitting room and settled him in a comfortable armchair. "There — you sit down, and I'll make a cup of tea."

She nipped out to the car to fetch his suitcase, then put the kettle on and made two cups of tea, which she put on a tray with a plate of Bourbon biscuits, and carried them through to the sitting room.

It was a cosy room, if a bit cluttered and faded, the chintz upholstery and curtains and the extensive collection of china cats evidence that a woman had once reigned here.

Several framed photographs were lined up along the tiled mantelpiece. Vicky moved closer to study them. "May I look?"

"Of course, dearie, if you like."

She picked up one of them — a proud young Arthur in his wedding suit, his darling Betty at his side in her long white dress and veil, clutching a bouquet of roses and lily of the valley, gazing up at him in open adoration. "Well, weren't you a handsome chap!" she remarked.

He chuckled. "Oh, ah — I was that." He took the photo from her and gazed at it, a smile of wistful reminiscence curving his mouth. "And my Betty, she was a real beauty."

"She was." She picked up another photograph — a lad of about twelve, proud as punch in his Scout uniform. "And this is Simon?"

"That's right."

Another photograph. "And his wife and kids — your grandsons. They're nice-looking kids."

He nodded, beaming. "Take after their grandmother."

The couple in the picture looked to be in their forties, the two boys in front of them early teens. "This must have been taken a few years ago?"

"Oh . . . yes — maybe. I don't remember." He waved his hand in vague dismissal.

"And that's Niagara Falls in the background?"

"Mmm." He was busy dunking his biscuit in his tea. Vicky smiled to herself — he never liked to admit that his memory sometimes had gaps in it.

She wandered round the room looking at the pictures on the walls — mostly rather kitsch pictures of cats, clashing with the flowery wallpaper.

"Betty was fond of cats?" she asked, amused.

"Oh, ah — allus had cats when she was alive. I didn't mind 'em — could be a bit smelly, some of 'em, but they was mostly right enough."

"You don't have one now?"

He shook his head. "Last one took itself off somewhere after she was gone. Never saw it again. They have a way of finding themselves a cosy billet, do cats."

She just hoped that was true, and that the poor creature hadn't met a more unfortunate fate, but she didn't say anything.

There were more family photographs on the oak sideboard and on top of an upright piano. But it was a framed portrait that caught her eye — a charcoal sketch, recognisably by the same hand as the portrait of Molly. In the bottom left-hand corner was the same rabbit-ears signature.

"Oh!"

Arthur looked over, smiling. "Ah, yes — that's my Betty, God rest her."

She gazed at the sketch, feeling a small surge of excitement. The portrait was very similar to the one of Molly, while still being undoubtedly the woman in the wedding photograph. It took a clever hand to do that.

"Do you remember who drew it?"

"O' course I do!" Clearly indignant that she might think he had forgotten. "It was John. Foreign guy. That wasn't his proper name, o' course — it was some funny foreign name. But I always called him John — that was near enough."

"He was . . . a friend of my Aunt Molly's?"

"Oh, ah." His pale eyes twinkled with mischief. "A bit more 'n a friend, I reckon."

Vicky gazed at the portrait, with its rabbit-ears signature. John . . . Molly's lover, who had painted her portrait and written that poem.

"So he lived here in Sturcombe?"

"I told you — he lived with Molly. They met up in Spain or some place and came to live here. Must have been maybe ten or fifteen years they lived here. Then he upped and got ill and died."

"Oh . . ." So that was what had happened to Aunt Molly's poet. Vicky brushed a tear from the corner of her eye — it was so sad. "When was that?"

He grunted. "A while ago."

"Do you remember when he died?"

"O' course I do." He glared at her. "It was not long after that test match when that young Botham chap scored a century and took ten wickets. India, that was. Great performance — never been bettered, before nor since."

"Cricket?"

"Well, it wasn't table tennis."

Vicky laughed. "You're an old devil. Do you mind if I take a photograph of the picture?"

"No — you go ahead, dearie. It's a pretty good likeness, though it does look a bit wonky, like. And that funny thing he's done with her hair — my Betty never had hair like that. Still, I suppose he done his best."

"Yes . . . I suppose so."

* * *

"There was a portrait of his wife on the wall." Vicky pulled her phone from her pocket and opened the image to show

Debbie. "There's one like it of Molly at the cottage, though that's an oil painting, not a charcoal sketch like this one. But it's by the same artist. He signs his work with what looks like a pair of rabbit's ears."

Debbie peered closely at the image, her eyes widening. "We've got one like that! It's of Granny." She beckoned to her mother. "Mum — come and look at this."

Kate put down the cloth she had been using to wipe some empty tables and came over to peer at the image on Vicky's phone.

"Oh, yes — that's just like my mother's picture. A little bit weird, I always thought, with the hair like that. But Mum was fond of it."

"Did she tell you anything about the man who drew it?" Vicky asked.

Kate thought for a moment, shaking her head. "Not really. She said that he was Spanish, and very handsome. But that's all."

"Arthur said he was foreign — he called him John, but he said that wasn't his real name. He lived here with Molly. He wrote her the most beautiful poem — I found it in a book when I was clearing out the bookshelves."

"Well I never!" Kate laughed. "She really was a one, wasn't she?"

"She certainly seems to have been a free spirit," Debbie remarked. "Living with a man without being married would still have been a bit of a scandal in those days, especially down here. We're about fifty years behind the times."

"I wonder why they didn't get married?" Vicky mused.

"Maybe he was already married."

Kate nodded. "If he was Spanish he was probably Catholic. He might not have been able to get a divorce back then."

"I'd really love to find out a bit more about him. Arthur said he died just after Ian Botham got ten wickets in a test match."

Kate laughed. "Trust Arthur to date things by cricket!"

176

"We could look that up. It's a good place to start, anyway. Wait — I'll go and get my laptop — it'll be easier to search on that." Debbie hurried away upstairs, while her mother went to serve some customers who had just come in.

Debbie was back in a moment, and set up the laptop at Vicky's table. "There. I just need to go and empty the dishwasher while you start searching."

"Right." She started with a search for Ian Botham — it didn't take long to find a stack of news items about his spectacular achievement in the test match. "Here it is — February 1980. So, let's look for Spanish artists who died that year."

There were plenty of famous artists listed, but some were still alive and others had died in the wrong year. She scrolled down a little further — and hit pay dirt.

"Yesss!"

Kate hurried out from behind the counter. "You've found him?"

"I think so." There was a bubble of excitement in her voice. "His name was Juan-Jorge Conejero. I think *conejero* means rabbit warren in Spanish — that's probably why he signed his work with what looked like rabbit's ears." She clicked on the link to a webpage. "This is him."

Debbie and her mum leaned in to look at the image that had popped up on the screen. "Oh . . . He really was very good-looking, wasn't he?" Kate chuckled. "Lucky Molly!"

"There's a few of his paintings on here." She scrolled down. There were several portraits similar to the one of Molly, some abstracts and still lifes, and half a dozen landscapes — wild, surreal, as if on another planet. "He seems to have been quite famous — some of these are in the Pradera in Spain."

"I wonder if yours is worth anything?" Kate mused.

"It could be. I'm really not sure if I should sell it, though. Molly was obviously very fond of it. She had it hanging in her bedroom."

Debbie shook her head decisively. "But it might mean you could pay the tax and keep the cottage, wouldn't it?" she pointed out. "Molly would want that."

Vicky frowned. "I suppose . . ."

"Of course she would. Anyway, why not just see if it's worth anything first, then you can have a think about it."

Vicky nodded thoughtfully. "You're probably right."

"Do we still have the one of Granny, Mum?" Debbie asked. "It didn't get thrown away when she died?"

Kate thought for a moment. "Yes, we've still got it — it's in the back of my wardrobe."

"Would you sell it?"

"Yes — why not? There's not much point in keeping it tucked away. I don't suppose it'll be worth anything like as much as your portrait, but even a couple of hundred would come in handy towards a new freezer."

While Kate hurried upstairs to fetch the drawing of her mother, Vicky and Debbie put their heads together to look up a couple of auction houses that sold modern art.

"This one looks the most likely — Cottesmore. I've heard of them, anyway. They're in Kensington, and they seem to sell quite a lot of this kind of thing." She typed out an email and attached the images of Molly's portrait and Arthur's and Kate's sketches. "I don't suppose we'll hear anything for a while — it could be weeks."

She needed to be sensible, she reminded herself — not let herself get carried away with the idea that the painting could really be valuable.

Sensible. Ugh!

* * *

"This is the most tedious part of the job." Lisa pulled a wry face. "Doing the staff rota. No matter how carefully you do it, someone will come and complain that they always have Wednesday afternoons off, or they need to take Friday because it's the kids' sports day."

Vicky laughed.

"I usually do it," Lisa explained, "because poor Mike gets in a terrible tizz, trying not to let anyone down, bless him. This is the spreadsheet. I work on a three-week rolling repeat — that way everyone knows in advance what shift they're on and there's plenty of time if there does need to be changes. Really, most of the staff are very good and willing to be flexible — this is a happy place to work; a lot of our people have been here for years."

Vicky studied the spreadsheet while she sipped her coffee. "That looks clear enough. When I worked in the café while I was at uni we had a similar system, and I'd sometimes help draw up the rotas when the manager was busy."

"Great — I'm sure you'll soon get the hang of it. If you have any problems with it, you can always give me a call. Finished your coffee?"

"Yes, thanks."

"Good." Lisa put down her own coffee cup and rose to her feet. "Now I did give you a quick tour of the rooms before, but let's have a proper look now, and I'll show you how to check that the cleaning and maintenance are up to standard." She lifted a clipboard down from a hook beside her desk. "This is the checklist. I do a walk-through once a day — that's usually enough."

"Right."

"Now, as you walk through, check that there's nothing left where someone could trip over it, and that there are no rucks or tears in the carpets. Particularly the stair carpet."

Vicky nodded. "Health and safety."

"That's right." Lisa's eyes danced. "Number one priority. Not just to avoid getting sued, but guests with broken legs are *so* not a good advert for a hotel."

Vicky laughed. She was trying hard not to think about Tom. How could he be such a rat as to be looking to play the field when he was married to such a nice woman? And how could she be such an idiot as to still feel that treacherous tug of attraction when she knew he was such a cheating rat?

Well, hopefully she had made it clear that she wasn't interested in being his bit on the side. Over the past two weeks she had spotted his car driving past a couple of times, but she had managed to avoid bumping into him — even at Sunday's cricket match.

Should she tell Lisa what had happened? That question had been tugging at the fringes of her mind for the past few weeks. She had decided against it — unless he tried it on again. Partly out of cowardice. And maybe Lisa already knew what he was like, and chose to ignore it? Maybe she thought that preserving her marriage for the sake of the children was a price worth paying?

"Let's use the lift." Lisa pressed the call button. "We can start at the top and work our way down. How's Arthur, by the way?"

"Very happy to be home." Vicky smiled. "And his new carer is very good — he knows just how much fuss to give him while letting him be as independent as he's able to be."

Lisa nodded as she stepped into the lift. "My husband said it's worked out for the best in the end. He was lucky — if he'd fallen after he got indoors he might not have been able to get help, and he could have been there for hours, even days."

Vicky felt as if her smile was fixed in place with super-glue. *Her husband. Don't think about him.*

The lift doors opened and they stepped out onto the top floor. Like the ground floor it had a slightly faded grandeur, with a red-and-gold carpet, feather-patterned wallpaper and a fancy crystal chandelier hanging from the ceiling. A vase of lilacs stood on a table in the corner, their fragrance scenting the air.

There were five doors on each side of the corridor. Lisa opened one of them with her pass-key. "This one's empty, so we can go in. Every room has an en suite. It's important to check them." She led the way across the room to the bath-room. "Make sure there are fresh towels every day, and the complimentary baskets are full."

She showed Vicky the checklist.

"Always check every light bulb. It's something that Housekeeping is likely to miss, but it can be very irritating for the guests to go into their room and find the light doesn't work."

"Oh . . . of course, I wouldn't have thought of that."

"Hence the checklist. It's very easy to overlook those little details." Abruptly Lisa grunted and sat down heavily on the bed, rubbing her bump.

"Are you okay?" Vicky asked anxiously. "It's not . . . ?"

Lisa laughed and shook her head. "Not yet. These are just practice contractions — Braxton-Hicks. They're nothing. Ollie worries about me all the time, of course — you'd think a GP would take it all in his stride. They say doctors make the worst patients, and they're just as bad when it's their own families."

"Uh, Ollie . . . ?"

"My husband. You've probably seen him at the cricket — tall guy, brown hair, glasses. He usually does the scoreboard."

"Oh . . ." Vicky's breath seemed to stop in her throat, her head spinning as if the planet had suddenly tipped off its axis. Fortunately Lisa didn't seem to have noticed her reaction.

"He'd like to play, but he's often on the call-out rota on Sundays so if there's an emergency he has to dash off, which would be a bit disruptive to the team." She stroked her hand over her bump. "I suppose it's understandable that he'd worry. We'd been trying for a second for a while, but nothing seemed to be happening. We were starting to think about IVF, but then we went on holiday to Greece, and bingo!" Her eyes danced with merriment. "Must have been the sunshine — or maybe the ouzo!"

Vicky managed a laugh. She had a vague recollection of the tall man who had been keeping score at the cricket, at least until shortly after the lunchbreak. Then he had disappeared. So he was Lisa's husband . . .

With an effort of will she brought her mind back to the conversation before the other woman began to think she was a bit odd. "Do you know if it's a boy or a girl?" she asked lightly.

"It's a little girl." Lisa rose to her feet and led the way back into the corridor. "We haven't chosen a name yet. I suppose we should — there's only a couple of weeks to go."

"So . . . um . . . are you related to Tom Cullen, who owns the farm next to me?" Vicky asked as she followed her.

"Tom? Of course — he's Ollie's cousin. Ollie's a few years older, but they grew up like brothers — both being onlies. That was why I wanted a second one after Noah — there's nothing wrong with being an only, but I do think they can miss out. I'm one of three. Do you have any brothers and sisters?"

"No — I'm an only too. But I have a stepsister. She's a year older than me." She smiled thinly. "She's a bit of a mixed blessing."

Lisa nodded agreement. "Sisters can be — even when they're full sisters. Especially when they're close in age. My sister Cassie and I fought like cat and dog when we were kids, but we get on much better now. Though of course that could be because she's on the other side of the planet!"

"Oh?"

"She was always the adventurous one — she was never going to settle down in Sturcombe. She's been all over — America, Africa, Australia. She's in New Zealand now, bungee jumping and white-water rafting." Lisa laughed. "She's always sending me pictures of her doing something wild." She pulled her phone from her pocket and clicked a few buttons. "That's her."

"Oh, wow!" A very pretty girl. Dark hair flying, face full of excitement, arms flung wide as she soared against a dizzying backdrop of steep mountains.

"That was at a place called Nevis Bungy — apparently it's the highest bungee jump in New Zealand." She rolled her eyes. "Trust Cassie. Anyway, as you can see, there are ten rooms on this floor. They're all pretty much the same, so there's no need to look in them all. Any questions?"

CHAPTER FIFTEEN

Well, she'd certainly mucked up, big time. Vicky felt as if she was dragging her heart with her like a lead weight as she walked up the hill. Tom wasn't married. If it wasn't for her stupid pride she could have just asked Debbie or someone, and resolved it in seconds.

Instead she had been so hostile to him when he had kissed her — which had had exactly the result she had intended. It had pushed him away, made damn sure that she had killed off any interest he may have had in her.

And she had the feeling that he didn't give second chances.

But it was probably just as well, she told herself firmly. Even though she had got it wrong about him being married, she doubted that he was looking for anything more than a casual fling — a 'friends with benefits' arrangement. Which wasn't her thing.

And if she did let herself succumb to temptation, it would be beyond awkward afterwards, living so close to him.

Oh, dammit — she had known from the start that it would be stupid to let herself indulge in fantasies about him. But it was just too easy to let herself dwell on the way he had kissed her. The way his strong arms had held her, the way the subtle male scent of his skin had drugged her mind . . .

"Vicky!"

She glanced around as she heard someone call her name. Bez came bouncing out of the shop.

"We heard about Kate's picture. We've got one too — of my granny. Do you think it would be worth anything?"

Vicky blinked, startled. "I don't know — I haven't heard anything back from the auction house yet. But it might be."

"Can you wait a tick? I'll go and fetch it."

"Of course."

Vicky followed her into the shop, smiling to herself. How many more of those drawings were there in the village? If they were valuable, it could be quite a bonanza.

Brenda greeted her with a wide smile. "Oh, that old picture! She's been so excited about it — I just hope she won't be disappointed."

Bez hurried out from the back of the shop with the picture in its frame. "Here. Is it the same?" Her eyes were bright and eager. "It's got the rabbit ears — there."

Vicky studied the sketch. "Yes — I'm pretty sure it's by the same artist. They've all got that weird thing he did with the hair. Do you want to sell it?"

Bez glanced at her mother. Brenda shrugged. "We might as well — it's been away in a cupboard for years. To be honest, I don't like it that much. And besides, I could do with the money — it'll help pay your university fees. I thought once about taking it along to one of those telly programmes where they value things for you, but I didn't have the time."

"That's a good idea," Vicky agreed. "If I don't get a reply from any of the auction houses I might try that."

"I've been looking him up online." Bez was bubbling with enthusiasm. "I'm going to do some research on him — it'll be a chance to practise my Spanish. Then I'm going to interview any of the old people in the village who might remember him, like Arthur, and make a blog. If that's all right?"

"Of course."

"*Très bien*. Can I have a copy of the picture you took of the painting? That should be the main bit of it. And the other pictures, so I can put them up too? How amazing is it, to have had a famous artist living right here in Sturcombe?"

She danced away with the picture, disappearing through into the back room. Brenda laughed dryly. "I think someone must have stolen my daughter and replaced her with a different one. I'm getting French and Spanish, morning, noon and night — I'll be speaking it myself soon! And she's really excited about this university thing — especially the idea of spending a year abroad as part of her course. I'm not sure, but I suppose it'll be all right."

"Don't worry — she'll be fine. I'm so glad that she's really into it."

"Thank you. I know you keep insisting that you didn't do anything, but you really did help. And you were right — I've backed off the nagging, and that seems to have worked too."

"I'm glad. She's going to have to work hard to get good grades, but this idea of researching Juan-Jorge Conejero could give her an extra boost."

"It's really quite exciting, isn't it?" Brenda was almost girlish. "Even if it's not worth much, it's fun to know that a famous painter did a drawing of my mum."

"It is," Vicky agreed. That was a good way of looking at it. 'Sensible' her mother would say. But in this instance, she was probably right.

* * *

The workroom was perfect. Vicky sat in her office chair and admired the length of light-oak kitchen worktop that she had laid on top of a cupboard and drawer unit to give her plenty of room to spread out.

Her new desktop computer had been delivered and took pride of place. A pretty china pot she had found in one of the kitchen cupboards held pens and pencils, another was for paper clips, and a flourishing peace lily stood at the end of the desk.

To her left she had set up her printer, and to the right a three-tier paper tray. And on the wall in front of her she had fixed a cork board to pin up the pictures she had collected of the people and places that were going to feature in her book.

Smiling to herself she trailed her fingers lightly over the keyboard, then opened the file she had transferred from her laptop. She had sketched out the first four chapters, and had an outline for the rest.

Opening a new document, she began to type.

Lady Cecily had quarrelled with Lord William and now she was trying to convince herself that she didn't care a fig for him. But there were rumours that the Earl of Warwick was scheming to get the deposed King Henry released from the Tower of London, and restore him to the throne. It was vital to learn more of his plans . . .

The buzz of the phone cut across her train of thought. She cursed it mildly, ready to ignore it — until she saw the number. Her heart thumped as she scrambled to open the call.

"Hello?"

"Good afternoon, Miss Marston. It's Clive Loughton from Cottesmore's."

"Oh, yes — hello, Mr Loughton." She closed her eyes for a moment, drawing in a slow, steadying breath. "How are you?"

"Very well, thank you. Thank you for sending me those pictures. They do indeed appear to be by Conejero, but I'd need to see them to form a firm opinion. Could you bring them up to me, do you think?"

"Of course." She spoke quite calmly, but inside she felt like dancing around the room.

"Would Friday be convenient? Or is that too short notice?"

"Oh . . . no — yes. Friday would be fine."

"Excellent. Shall we say two o'clock?"

"Yes, of course." *And breathe.* "That would be fine."

"You'll be able to park outside — I'll arrange for Reception to give you a permit. I look forward to meeting you."

"Yes . . . thank you . . ."

"Until Friday then. Goodbye."

"Goodbye . . ."

She closed the call and put the phone down beside the computer. She hadn't really let herself believe that anything would come of that approach to the auction house. But now . . .

She wasn't going to let herself get her hopes up too high. *Sensible* — she could almost hear her mother's voice. Although as Brenda had said, it really was quite exciting.

And at least it was something to take her mind off her neighbour.

* * *

"I think I'm still in shock." Vicky laughed unsteadily. "He said to set the reserve at two million pounds! When he told me, I thought I was dreaming."

"I'm not surprised." Debbie looked equally stunned. "Come on, have a cup of coffee and tell us all about it. Was it very grand, the auction place?"

"*Very* grand." Vicky waited at the counter while Debbie poured her coffee. "All pale-grey walls and thick carpets, and swish chandeliers. The auction room itself is pretty impressive — it reminded me a bit of the lecture halls at uni, except the seats looked a lot more comfortable."

Debbie brought her coffee, and one for herself, and leaned on the counter, her eyes bright with excitement. It was early yet, and the café wasn't very busy.

"The auctioneer, Clive Loughton, was very nice. He was very interested to hear about Aunt Molly. Apparently she and Juan were part of an artists' colony in a small town several miles up the coast from Barcelona. He painted several portraits of her, and so did some of the others. Some of them were nudes!"

"Wow!" Debbie's eyes danced. "She really did live an incredible life."

"She certainly did. I'd like to write her biography one day."

"What did he say about your portrait?"

"He was pretty confident that it's genuine, but he's going to get in a second expert to definitely authenticate it — and the sketches. If that goes okay, he'll put them all in the next available auction of contemporary art."

"Two million pounds!" Debbie breathed, awed. "What will you do with the money?"

"I don't know. I don't know if it will make that much — it's an auction, so it's anybody's guess. It depends on how much interest there still is in him — he's been dead for over forty years. People could have forgotten about him."

"But artists often make more money after they're dead," Debbie pointed out. "Like pop stars. You could go on a world cruise."

Vicky laughed, shaking her head. "Oh no — I don't think I'm the world cruise type."

"You'll think of something. It's so exciting . . . Oh, hi, Tom — your usual?"

"Yes, please."

Vicky felt a shiver of heat run over her skin at the sound of that familiar voice — it was like standing too close to a high-voltage electrode. She took a sip of her coffee to avoid looking up at him.

"Vicky's just been telling me about her trip to London."

"Oh?" The polite interest was shaved down to the thinnest veneer over ice-cold steel.

"She took an old painting that Molly left to be valued." Debbie babbled on innocently. "And they said it could be worth two million pounds!"

Vicky caught the sardonic glance he slanted down at her. "Congratulations."

"Did he say whether the charcoal sketches would fetch anything?" Debbie asked.

"He thought maybe a few thousand each."

"Alice at the pub has one too, and she'd like to sell it." Debbie had bagged up two pasties and handed them over to Tom. "Though I suppose if there are a lot of them, you wouldn't get so much for each one."

"Not necessarily." Tom tapped his card on the reader. "Being sold as a group might make them worth more."

Debbie's eyes were bright. "Do you think so?"

"It's possible. Thanks for these, Debs — cheerio. Goodbye, Vicky."

"Mmm." That was as much as she could manage to say. You could have cut the hostility with one of Debbie's cake slices.

"Bye, Tom." As the door closed behind him, Debbie leaned over the counter to speak softly to Vicky. "Have you had a row with him?"

"What?" She tried to laugh. "Of course not."

"Because he looks at you that way — you know, the way men do when they're interested. And you like him, don't you?"

"Oh, he's good-looking, I grant you that." She tried for a note of casual dismissal, but she knew the wobble in her voice gave her away. "But he's really not my type. Though I don't suppose that'll bother him — I expect he's got half the women between here and Bristol after him."

"Well, yes . . . at least, he used to. But since last year . . ."

"What?" She didn't want to ask, but she couldn't help herself.

Debbie hesitated — she looked as if she was wishing she hadn't mentioned anything. "He was engaged — to an actress. Nyree Donovan. She was really gorgeous — red hair, and a fabulous figure. She's been on the telly a couple of times."

"An actress?" Vicky felt as if her smile was cemented in place. "How did he meet her?"

"She was down here filming a part in that detective series — you know, the one with that guy who was in *EastEnders*."

Vicky thought back, but she couldn't remember whether she'd ever seen it. She could probably look it up on the internet — if she was feeling really masochistic. "What happened?" she asked.

Her friend's gentle face darkened. "Just a month before the wedding she got offered a part in some American soap

189

series — *Mandate*, I think it was called, about politicians and all their shenanigans."

"And she went for it?" Well, that would explain why he had been so contemptuous when he had thought she was just a city girl who couldn't wait to cash in on her inheritance and hightail it back to London as soon as possible.

"She was off the next day — just like that! Tom must have been pretty cut up about it," Debbie mused. "Though he's never said anything. But he's hardly dated anyone since."

"Oh . . ."

At that moment there was a rush of customers, so Vicky finished her coffee and waved Debbie a cheerful goodbye, making her escape before she gave herself away.

So — a stunning actress who had broken his heart. Whom he still carried a torch for, if he had rarely dated since then. Which in a way made him almost as inaccessible as if he had been married.

She walked slowly up the hill — she didn't want to risk catching up with Tom. At Brenda's shop, she popped in to pick up some milk and a newspaper. Brenda was as excited as Debbie over the news about the sketches.

"It'll certainly help pay Beth's university fees. Thank you so much for what you've done."

Vicky smiled. "We don't know yet how much it might sell for, if at all," she warned. "Best keep your fingers crossed."

"I will — both hands!" She chuckled as she held them up. "What about Arthur — is he going to sell his?"

Vicky shook her head. "I spoke to his son about it, and he said to let him keep it. He's arranged to send money to pay for the carer. He's coming over to visit as soon as his doctor gives him the all-clear to fly."

"That's good." She waved aside Vicky's card as she went to pay. "On the house."

Vicky laughed. "You won't stay in business long that way!"

"It's today's special offer." Brenda smiled awkwardly. "To be honest, I've been feeling a bit guilty about Arthur.

He's lived just round the corner from us all my life, and I hadn't thought he might need a bit more help."

"Don't beat yourself up over it — he's very independent. You should have heard how he grumbled about having a carer. It was only when his son insisted that he gave in." Vicky tucked her shopping into her bag. "Well, goodbye then."

"Goodbye — see you soon."

* * *

"Donna said she'd swap the Friday with me."

Vicky smiled to herself. Lisa had warned her that arranging the staff shifts could be the most complicated part of her new job. "That's okay, Kerry — I'll switch the rota around."

"Thanks. Oh, by the way, the Donaldsons in room twenty-four asked for a seven o'clock wake-up tomorrow — they're going to drive down to the Eden Project, and want to make a full day of it."

"Okay — I expect they'll want an early breakfast too . . ."

"Hi." A light tap on the door, and Lisa appeared, a tiny pink bundle in a baby-sling on her chest. "Can I come in?"

"Of course!" Vicky laughed. "It's still your office. And you've brought the baby."

Lisa's face was warm with maternal pride. "Do you want to hold her?"

"Can I?"

"Even Ollie says it's quite safe. Kyra — meet your Auntie Vicky." She lifted the baby out of the sling and laid her carefully in Vicky's arms.

"Oh, she's gorgeous." Vicky gazed down at the delicate pink face topped by a curl of dark hair, then dipped her head and sniffed. "Mmm — that baby smell."

"I know. I could just eat her!"

"How old is she now — five days?"

"Six. She arrived a week early, the little minx — and she's just as impatient for everything now she's here."

191

"How's Noah been with her?"

"He's great." Lisa smiled fondly. "Every little noise she makes he goes running to check she's okay."

"That's lovely. He'll make a brilliant big brother. Cup of coffee?"

"Yes, please. Stay there — I'll get it."

Vicky laughed. "You know where everything is. I hope you don't mind me using your coffee-maker?"

"Of course not." She poured two mugs, adding cream, and brought them over to the desk. "So how's everything going?" she asked as she sat down.

"Not too bad." Vicky shifted the sleeping baby so that she could pick up her mug. "I don't think I'm making too much of a mess."

"I'm sure you're not. How does it compare to being an estate agent?"

"It's quite similar, in a way — trying to make sure the guests get the perfect holiday, and trying to help people find their perfect property. But the walk home's a lot nicer."

Lisa's eyes danced. "I'm sure it is. I've visited London a few times, but I don't think I'd want to live there. It's too big — I find it a bit overwhelming, with all the buildings and the traffic."

Vicky nodded agreement. "It can be overwhelming. Though there are a lot of green spaces — more than you'd think. But nothing can beat having a beach on your doorstep."

"Absolutely!"

They sat chatting for a while as little Kyra slept contentedly, her tiny fingers curled around Vicky's thumb.

"Feeling broody?" Lisa teased.

"What? No!" Vicky laughed, though it sounded a little forced to her own ears. A baby? With Jeremy, it had been out of the question — a baby wouldn't have suited his lifestyle. But with Tom . . . *oh, don't be stupid.* "I mean . . . one day, of course . . . maybe . . . but not yet. Not for a while yet." Again that edgy laugh. "Anyway, it's usual to have a partner or something first."

"Or something?"

"Well, someone who can fix the car and do the gardening would come in handy."

"It would. Mine could remove an appendix, but can't fix a dripping tap."

"Ah, well — at least he'd come in useful if you had appendicitis."

"And he's a whizz at changing nappies."

"Clincher!"

* * *

"Goodnight, Vicky. See you tomorrow."

"Goodnight, Pete." Vicky smiled at the night manager as she crossed the reception hall. "See you tomorrow."

A soft breeze was rustling the leaves overhead as she strolled up the hill. She liked every time of day here — the early mornings with the lambent glow of the rising sun, the heat of noon with the sky and the sea a jewel-bright sapphire.

But this time of the evening was special. The sun was drifting down towards the horizon, the sky in the east was darkening to a soft cobalt blue. The bees and butterflies had retired for the night, but an owl was hooting softly from the trees.

As she turned into the lane, she was surprised to see Tom emerging from the small patch of woodland beside the cottage. He was carrying a torch and a shovel, and his brow was creased in a worried frown.

She hesitated. There had been so many times over the past couple of weeks when she had wanted to walk up to the farm, quite casually, just to say 'hi' and see if it might lead anywhere, but she hadn't had the courage.

But she was going to have to speak to him now.

"Is there something wrong?"

He glanced up, seeming startled to see her. "Have you seen Rufus?"

"No. I've just come from work."

193

"He's been missing for two days." His voice was tense with anxiety. "He's never been gone for this long before."

"Oh . . ." His genuine concern for the little dog broke through her reserve. "Wait — I'll just drop my bag and change out of my work clothes, then I'll come and help you look."

His smile was brief, distracted. "Thank you."

As she hurried up the lane to the cottage she peered from side to side, hoping to spot a small bundle of brown-and-white fur. But there was no sign of him, no scrabble of small paws.

She let herself into the kitchen and raced up the stairs, stripping off her business suit and grabbing a pair of jeans and a cotton sweater, throwing them on at top speed. Without stopping to brush her hair she ran back down the stairs.

Tom had walked a little further down the lane to the junction with Church Road.

"Where have you looked already?" she asked as she caught up to him.

"Up the lane and along the top road." He pointed up past the farmhouse. "All the way down to the caravan park. And along here up as far as the main road. I . . . suppose I should look along there, but I'm afraid that . . . with all the traffic . . . speeding . . ."

He didn't need to finish the sentence. "Has he ever gone up there before?"

"No. But if he caught a scent, or was chasing a rabbit or a squirrel . . ."

"Okay. Let's go and look."

"Thanks."

The strain around his eyes made her long to reach out to him, but she held back. It had all got so complicated, and now wasn't the moment to sort it out. They needed to find Rufus.

They walked up to the busy main road and along it for a good distance in each direction, one on each side, checking the hedges for any gaps that a small dog could wriggle through, calling his name.

It was a mixture of relief and disappointment when they found nothing.

"How about the cricket ground?" Vicky asked. "Have you looked there?"

"Not yet."

"Okay — let's try it. And the golf course."

"Thanks — I really appreciate your help."

"No problem."

"Here." He smiled crookedly as he handed her half a dozen dog biscuits. "A little bribery usually works with him."

"Right." Her heart creased in sympathy for him, as well as her own concern for the lively little terrier. "We'll find him."

She could only hope that she was right as they hurried down the hill to the cricket ground. He loved that dog — it must be awful to have him missing for so long, not knowing what had happened to him, imagining all sorts of dreadful outcomes.

The sun was sinking below the horizon, leaving its memory in streaks of gold and magenta across the darkening sky. They scoured the narrow lane leading to the cricket ground, and all round the ground itself, calling to Rufus, peering under every hedge and thicket, listening for any bark or squeak.

Nothing.

The golf course was just as disappointing. Set on the long green swathe on the rising ground behind the hotel, the view was stunning. All along the Esplanade, the swags of coloured lights shone like a jewelled necklace. Beyond the houses around the bay, the hills were fading into shadow as the indigo cloak of night spread over the sky.

But Vicky barely spared it a glance. There were so many places a small dog could have got himself stuck — trees and bushes all around the perimeter and in clumps between the fairways.

They didn't speak much as they worked their way around the edge of the course. Vicky could feel the sharp sting of tears in her eyes — the grim possibility that Rufus may never be found was beginning to sink in.

It was harder to search in the dark. Tom's torch had a powerful beam, penetrating the tangled undergrowth of brambles and goosegrass and bindweed, but it cast confusing shadows that made it difficult to be sure what was there.

Vicky was almost ready to admit defeat when she bent to pull aside a long thorny runner of bramble . . . and caught her breath.

"Tom — here." A small tuft of fur was caught on the prickles.

He hurried over and shone the torch on the ground. It was slightly damp beneath the thatch of weeds, and imprinted in the mud was a small but very distinct pawprint.

"It could be just a cat, or a badger . . ."

Tom shook his head, pulling more of the undergrowth aside and shining the torch down. Among the tangle of roots, there was a hole. A hole just big enough to lure a small dog.

"Here, hold the torch." He thrust it into her hand and bent to drag the weeds aside, calling to the dog. "Rufus? Hey, boy."

As they listened intently there was the faintest sound . . . It could have been a bird. Then it came again . . .

"Rufus!"

Vicky aimed the beam carefully at the hole as Tom knelt and reached into it, stretching his arm down as far as he could.

"Is he there?"

"Yes. I can just touch him, but he's stuck." He drew back. "Pass me the shovel."

She tried not to let her gaze be distracted by the powerful movement of the hard muscles beneath his T-shirt as he stabbed the shovel into the earth around the hole, widening it. As he reached his arm into it again, she heard a distinct squeak.

He grunted, and pulled slowly back — and to Vicky's delight a small bundle of muddy fur appeared. With a whimper the little dog scrambled into Tom's arms, huddling against his chest and managing to lift a weary head to lick his chin.

At last Vicky could breathe. "Oh, thank God."

Tom was kneeling on the ground, hugging the dog, and she could see his shoulders shaking as he buried his face in the muddy fur. He was crying.

She waited in silence until at last he rose to his feet.

"Stupid mutt." His voice was a little huskier than usual. "I hope you've learned your lesson."

Vicky laughed. "I don't suppose he'll be doing that again in a hurry." She stroked a finger round the little dog's ear. He turned his head to gaze at her with eyes that lacked their usual sparkle, then snuggled against Tom's chest again. "Poor little mite — he must be starving."

"Yes. But he'd better not have his usual dinner — it'd be too much for his stomach, after eating nothing for so long. It could make him ill."

"I could do him some scrambled egg?" she offered.

He smiled, and reached out to take her hand. "That would be perfect."

CHAPTER SIXTEEN

They took the shortcut through the cricket ground. The sky was dark now, filling up with stars. Walking beside Tom as he carried his little dog, Vicky knew that her heart was lost. To both of them.

"He's a cute little thing," she remarked for something to say. "How long have you had him?"

"Since he was around two weeks old. He and the rest of his litter were dumped in a sack in one of the bins at the recycling centre in town. He was the only one who survived."

"Oh, that's awful!" A sharp tear stung the corner of her eye. "Why do people do that? They could have just handed them in to a vet or the RSPCA or something."

"Quite." There was a grim note in his voice. She suspected that if he had ever found out who'd done it, they would have lived to regret it.

"It must have been a lot of work, rearing such a tiny thing."

"It was." He rubbed his cheek against the dog's head. "Bottle-feeding for the first couple of weeks, getting him to pee and poo. Good job I'm used to that sort of thing, looking after a couple of hundred cows."

And it would have cemented them closer than most owners and their dogs, she reflected. "He was lucky to have found you."

He smiled down at her, all the tension eased from his face. "I was the lucky one." He nuzzled the top of the little dog's head again. "He's my best buddy."

They reached the lane and turned in through her gate, their footsteps crunching on the gravel path. Vicky felt a little flutter in the region of her heart. She had invited him into her house . . .

Of course it was just because of Rufus — to warm him up, give him something to eat. But even so, could this be a chance for a reset . . . ?

She opened the door and flicked on the light. "Come on in."

He stepped inside and glanced around. "Ah, your new kitchen. I like it."

"Dan did a really good job." She hoped he wouldn't notice the slight tremor in her voice. "Thank you for recommending him."

"And the rest of the place?"

"Just as good. He sanded and sealed the floorboards, and they look fabulous. And my new sofa came this morning — it's one of those really big old-fashioned-style ones, with huge squashy cushions. It looks perfect in the sitting room, in front of the fire."

She knew that she was babbling, but she couldn't help it. Her heart was beating so loudly she thought he must be able to hear it.

"You can wash the mud off him in the sink while I do his scrambled egg." She lifted the washing-up bowl out of the big Belfast sink and put it to one side. "I'll get some towels for you to dry him with."

"Thanks."

She hurried upstairs to fetch the towels from the linen cupboard, glad of the excuse to escape for a moment to try to compose herself. The sight of him in her kitchen, so big, so . . . *male*, really wasn't good for her sanity.

She returned to find that he had put Rufus in the sink and was gently splashing him with warm water. A little to her surprise the little dog didn't seem to mind at all. She laughed as Tom took the towels from her.

"You're almost as muddy as he is."

He glanced down at his T-shirt, laughing too, then in a move she hadn't anticipated he tugged it off over his head.

So much for composure. The sight of his powerful body — the smooth sun-bronzed skin, the swell and dip of hard muscle, the smattering of dark curling hair across his wide chest . . .

Quickly she turned away. "I'll . . . get that scrambled egg going — he can have it as soon as he's had his bath."

Her hands were shaking so much she was afraid she'd drop the eggs. But she managed to whip up the mix and pop it in the microwave without any disasters.

"Coffee?"

"That would be good."

He lifted Rufus out of the sink and wrapped him up in one of the towels to scrub him dry. "He's exhausted — he usually fights like mad when I try to give him a bath. Unfortunately he likes to roll in stinky things, so it's a frequent necessity."

Vicky filled a dish with water and set it down on the floor. "Here — he'll probably want this."

"Thanks."

Tom put the pup down beside the bowl and he lapped it up thirstily. The microwave pinged and she took out the scrambled egg, and tipped it onto a plate. It disappeared as swiftly as the water, and then with a huge sigh he just lay down, his head on his paws, and immediately fell asleep.

"Here." She folded a spare towel and laid it on the floor of the inglenook, close to the warmth of the range cooker. "He'll be more comfortable on this."

Rufus didn't even open his eyes as Tom lifted him onto the towel. He just curled round in a tight ball, snuffling, and slept on.

"He'll be okay." He covered the little dog with another warm towel. "Dogs have incredible powers of recovery." A dark shadow crossed his face. "Though I don't know how much longer he would have survived if we hadn't found him."

"But we did find him." Without conscious intent, Vicky laid her hand on his shoulder.

"Yes . . ."

He put his hand over hers as if to keep it there, his eyes dark as they gazed down into hers — so dark she felt as if she could drown in them. His forehead tipped against hers, resting there for a long moment as their breathing fell into the same slow rhythm.

She closed her eyes, letting herself absorb the emotions that were swirling through her brain, all the reasons why she shouldn't be allowing this to happen.

It was far too soon. If she had a fling with him her heart would be far too vulnerable, and if she stayed she would have to go on living next door to him.

And that actress. Yes, she'd been a masochist — looked her up online, read all about her and watched several episodes of the detective series Debbie had mentioned.

But none of that weighed against the surge of temptation sweeping aside all rational thought. Nothing mattered but this moment — she couldn't remember that she had ever felt this way. Out of control.

And then he was kissing her, his lips warm and enticing, coaxing hers apart, his languorous tongue plundering deep into her mouth. And she was kissing him back, her tongue sparring with his, her hands tangling into the crisp curls at the nape of his neck.

Her heart was racing so fast she felt dizzy. Pinned against the kitchen table by his hard body, she was made devastatingly aware of the rising tension of male arousal in him.

And she felt the same urgency. She slid her hands up over his chest, tracing through that smattering of rough, dark, curling hair, moaning softly as she felt the warmth of his skin and the ripple of hard muscle.

With little finesse he tugged her sweater off over her head. His work-roughened hands stroked up her back and round over her midriff, rising to encompass the ripe curve of her breasts, constrained in the tight lace cups of her bra, and she gasped as his thumbs teased over the taut buds of her nipples.

He laughed, low and husky. "Are you going to show me the rest of the cottage?"

"Uh . . . ?"

A glint of pure sensuous promise lit his eyes. "Let's start with the bedroom."

Vicky drew in the breath that had been trapped in her throat. Her legs felt so wobbly she wasn't sure that she would be able to climb the stairs. But Tom solved that problem for her by scooping her up in his arms as if she weighed nothing at all.

She laughed a little unsteadily. "Tough guy, huh?"

"You'd better believe it. Wrangling a ten-stone calf who wants to go one way when you want it to go the other is better than hours in the gym."

She smiled up at him, tipping her head against his shoulder. "I'm not complaining."

He nudged open the bedroom door. Vicky was glad that all those roses had gone — this didn't feel like a moment for pretty roses. The walls and carpet were a soft, rich plum that matched the satin bedcover, creating a sensuous atmosphere, enhanced by the scent of the fresh potpourri in the crackled-glass bowl on the dressing table.

As Tom laid her on the bed she wrapped her arms around him and drew him down to her. He reached over to switch on the bedside light, bathing the room in a warm golden glow. Propping himself up on his elbow he smiled down at her.

"Looks like we're postponing the tour of the cottage."

"Looks like it."

"Maybe later . . ." He let his gaze wander down over her body. "Mmm — delicious."

A bubble of laughter rose to her lips. "You make me sound like one of Debbie's cupcakes."

He shook his head, laughing softly. "No comparison."

With slow deliberation he traced one fingertip along the lacy edge of her bra. Anticipation was sizzling through her veins. As she gazed up into his dark eyes it seemed as if all her wild fantasies had sprung to life.

With a deft movement he unfastened the clasp of her bra and tossed the lacy scrap aside, and began to trace lazy circles over her bare skin. His touch was slow and sure, lingering over every contour, and she moaned softly, aching for more.

He laughed, warm and husky, and lowered his head, his mouth claiming hers, hard and urgent. She slid her hands over his shoulders, savouring the smooth movement of those powerful muscles.

Then his hot kisses moved on, tracing a scalding path over her trembling eyelids, across her temple and around the delicate shell of her ear, then on down the slender column of her throat.

Her breathing was ragged as she moved against him, his name a sigh on her lips as she begged incoherently for more. But he was making her wait, driving her out of her mind.

His hands and mouth roved over every contour of her body, stirring her blood. He was tracing a teasing path over the aching curve of her breasts, his tongue swirling languorously around each taut pink nipple, his lips and teeth teasing them and sparking fire along her taut-strung nerve fibres.

At some point they had both shed the rest of their clothes — she hadn't even noticed until his hand smoothed down over her bare thighs, then slipped between to seek the most intimate caresses.

Heat was flooding her veins, pooling like molten gold in the pit of her stomach. Then as the pad of his thumb stroked over the tiny seed-pearl hidden deep in the velvet folds, a shaft of pure pleasure shot through her and she gasped convulsively, her fists clenching as she dragged in a breath.

Some part of her mind had registered that he had torn open a small foil packet. She took it from him and eased the gossamer sheath over his hard length. But now everything was swirling heat and darkness as she twined her legs around him, arching her spine and drawing him deep inside her.

He took her mouth with a raw hunger, fierce and possessive, and she slid her hands down his back, responding without constraint, moving beneath him in a dance as old as time.

Tension was coiling inside her like the warning sizzle before a lightning strike. Delirious, she clung to him as they soared together, higher and dizzily higher, in a vortex of flame, until at last it exploded around them, tipping them over the edge, and they tumbled together to collapse on the bed, breathless and sweating, in a tangle of arms and legs.

* * *

Time spun slowly back into its normal course. Vicky lay curled up in the crook of Tom's arm, her eyes closed — if she could have her wish, she would stay there for ever.

Her fingers were trailing lightly through the smattering of dark hair across his chest.

"Do you always carry condoms in your back pocket?" Dammit, why had she asked that? She didn't really want to know the answer.

He laughed softly and propped himself up on one elbow. "Not always. I was just kind of hoping you might change your mind about me. And if there was a chance . . ." He twirled one finger into a curl of her not-quite-blonde hair. "I'm not sure if that's hopelessly optimistic or insufferably arrogant."

"Hmm." She pursed her lips, pretending to give the matter due consideration. "A tad arrogant, maybe — but not insufferably so." She hesitated briefly. "Actually the reason I was so off with you that day was because I thought you were married."

His eyebrows rose in surprise. "Married?"

"To Lisa."

"Ollie's Lisa?"

"Yes." She managed a crooked smile. "I saw you with Noah — at the kid's party, and . . . I thought he was your son."

He looked faintly puzzled. "I was babysitting. Lisa was on a late shift and Ollie had got caught up with something at the surgery, so he rang me to pick him up."

"Oh. Then at the cricket, I heard Debbie call her Mrs Cullen."

"And like following your satnav instead of using your head you went off down the wrong track." There was a lilt of mocking amusement in his voice.

"Well, you did too, didn't you?" she retorted. "You assumed that I was just the grasping kind who was only interested in selling Molly's cottage for as much as I could get, then scooting off back to London."

He laughed, and kissed the tip of her nose. "Okay, we're quits."

His hand stroked down over her body again, stirring the still-smouldering embers. A warm sigh escaped her lips, and she curved against him, breathing in the subtle male scent of his skin.

"Will Rufus be all right on his own downstairs?" she murmured.

"He'll be fine. After his adventure, he'll sleep right through till morning."

Which implied that Tom would be staying till morning, too. She had no argument with that.

* * *

The café was busy, as usual. Debbie was flitting about serving customers — there seemed to be a brighter light than usual in her eyes. She danced up to Vicky's table.

"You're looking like the cat that got the cream," Vicky teased.

"Am I? Well, yes, I am. Bill asked me to marry him last night." She did a little shimmy. "And I said yes!"

"Oh, that's wonderful! Congratulations."

"Thanks. I haven't told Amy yet. We're taking her to the zoo on Sunday, and we're going to tell her then."

"She'll be thrilled," Vicky assured her.

"I hope so. It's just been the two of us, and Mum, for a while . . ."

"She adores Bill."

"Yes, she does." She held up her hand, her fingers crossed. "I just hope Alan doesn't make trouble."

"Your ex?" Vicky shot her a startled look. "Why would he?"

Debbie bit her lip. "He can sometimes be a bit . . . awkward."

Vicky shook her head. "You know what, I'll bet he takes one look at Bill and decides to back off."

"Oh, but Bill would never get into a fight," Debbie protested quickly. "He isn't the type."

"I know that and you know that, but I bet Alan wouldn't want to risk it."

Debbie laughed. "You're right. I've let him bully me long enough — I'm not going to let him do it anymore."

"That's the spirit!"

"Anyway, do you want some of Mum's coffee cake?"

"Yes, please."

Debbie went back to the counter, and Vicky fell into gazing out of the window, as she usually did. But her mind wasn't on the view today. She was replaying every moment of last night, so vividly that she could almost feel the brush of Tom's mouth over hers, the warmth of his body, the smooth movement of those hard muscles beneath his skin.

She'd woken this morning as he had slipped out of bed and pulled on his clothes.

"I was trying not to wake you." He'd kissed the tip of her nose. "Go back to sleep."

Of course — milking. She'd snuggled down under the covers and slept again.

She'd have liked to ask Debbie more about him — his other girlfriends before that Nyree, how many there had been, what they had been like. But she'd feel stupid, probing like that — like some love-struck teenager Bez's age.

So, what now? Had last night been just a one-night stand, a brief fling? Or might there be a chance of something more?

* * *

The question still lingered in her mind into the evening, distracting her from the chapter she was trying to write. Memories of the night, wrapped up in those strong arms, their naked bodies hot against each other . . .

Curled up on her new sofa in the sitting room with her notebook, the French windows wide open to let in a soft evening breeze, she closed her eyes, trying to make herself focus on her heroine's attempts to . . .

A flurry of excited barking startled her back to the twenty-first century. A small bundle of brown-and-white fur hurtled in through the French windows and scrabbled at her knees.

"Well, hello, you." She scooped him up onto her lap, laughing as he bounced up to lick her chin. "Have you run away again?"

"No — he just wanted to come over and say thanks for the scrambled eggs."

Vicky felt her heart thump as Tom came into the room. "Oh, he was more than welcome. He's looking very well, in spite of his adventure."

"Dogs usually recover very quickly. I just hope he's learned his lesson." Tom strolled over to the sofa and leaned over the back of it to kiss her ear. "What's this?" he asked, glancing at the notebook.

"Oh . . . um . . . it's just . . ." She laughed a little unsteadily. "I'm trying to write a book."

"Oh? What about?"

"It's . . . a novel. Set in the time of the Wars of the Roses. I did my degree at university on that period. It's . . . kind of a bit of a romance, a bit of a thriller."

"Sounds good." He came round to sit beside her. "Can I read it?"

"I . . . um . . . it's not finished yet." She bent to tickle Rufus's ear to hide the blush in her cheeks. She had felt as if her writing was a guilty secret. But he hadn't mocked it, as Jeremy had — he seemed genuinely interested.

He dropped an arm around her shoulders and drew her close. "Bill's on calf-watching duties tonight, so I'm free and clear. If you can take a break, fancy coming out for a drink?"

"That sounds like fun."

"Although . . ." His eyes glinted with unmistakeable intent. "The pub will still be there in an hour or so."

A mischievous smile spread across her face. "I like your thinking."

He brushed his lips across hers, and, taking her hand, he drew her to her feet.

Rufus bounced along beside them to the stairs. Tom laughed, shaking his head. "We don't need company," he scolded gently, pointing back to the kitchen. "Stay."

With a sigh of disdain the pup turned his back on them and strolled into the kitchen as if that had always been his plan, and settled himself on the towel that was still beside the range cooker, his head on his paws.

* * *

Vicky and Tom strolled along the beach, their feet crunching on the damp sand. And he was holding her hand. The moon was almost full, tracing a path of shimmering silver across the dark water of the bay. Rufus had been let off his lead and was chasing in and out of the waves, barking like a loon.

She had felt a little awkward walking into the pub with Tom. Maybe she should have thought of that before, and come up with some excuse, but her brain had seemed to seize up. She had been conscious of the interested gazes that had followed her, but everyone had been very friendly.

"My mum and dad are coming home on Monday."

"Oh, that'll be nice." She smiled up at him, a hint of teasing in her eyes. "Have you missed them?"

"The farm's missed them. I certainly didn't begrudge them the trip — I've been on at them for years to go out for a visit, before they got too old for it to be comfortable, flying all that way. But it'll be a big help to have him back — we need the extra hands with the girls. And I really need to balance out my time more with my other business."

"The feed company?"

He glanced down at her, one dark eyebrow raised in question.

She laughed. "Jayde looked you up."

"Did she then? What did she find out?"

"Not much." She wasn't going to tell him that she'd looked him up online herself — that seemed a bit too much like stalking. "There was a bit about you winning an award."

"Oh yes — last year." He grinned. "All dressed up in my penguin suit and playing the successful entrepreneur."

"There was a picture. You looked very smart."

"I felt like a prat."

"Oh, go on — you must have been proud. It's quite an achievement."

"I suppose." But the quirk of his lips betrayed that he really was.

"When did you set it up?"

"About six years ago. Our neighbour, Harry, died. His kids had moved away, neither of them were interested in the farm. His fields ran alongside ours and were organic too — we were concerned that if they were taken over by someone who'd convert them out of organic it could affect the quality of ours."

He stooped and picked up a pebble and hurled it down the beach. Rufus raced after it, though he could have absolutely no idea where it had fallen among all the others. He ran around in circles for a bit, nose to the ground, then forgot about it and raced off into the sea again.

"So you bought them out?"

"It was the obvious thing to do. My grandmother had left me some money, and I got a business loan. It started out just selling the excess feed from Harry's land, but the market for organic's increasing. A few more farms wanted to convert too, so I did deals with them to buy their produce, and it just grew from there. Organically."

Vicky rolled her eyes at the dreadful pun. "How have you been managing to run it and the farm while your dad was away?"

"Ah, the farm always comes first. But depot's only up the road, on that old industrial estate just past Haytor Avenue. I've got a good bloke in charge there for the day-to-day stuff, and I've always done a lot of the trading online. But with Dad back it'll definitely be easier."

"Have they enjoyed the trip, your mum and dad?"

"It sounds like it." He laughed dryly. "Dad was a bit envious of Uncle Frank's spread — it's measured in square miles, not acres. Makes ours look like a pocket handkerchief. Mind you, then he thought about managing a herd that size and changed his mind."

"I bet."

He glanced down at her. "Why don't you come over to dinner next week?"

She hesitated, startled. "Oh, I . . ."

"Dad remembers you from when you were little. He'd love to see you again. Ollie and Lisa are coming too."

What to make of that? *Come to dinner and meet my family* . . . Wasn't it a bit too soon? And yet . . . it wasn't really like that. She had known his parents when she was a child — and besides, Lisa and Ollie would be there.

"I'd like to see them." She struggled for a casual tone. "But your mum'll be tired from the long journey home — she won't want to be cooking for guests."

He laughed. "I thought you knew my mother."

"Well . . . um . . . if you're sure it'll be okay . . . I'd like to come."

"Good." He slid his arm around her shoulders and turned her against him, and his mouth came down to hers in a long, lingering kiss. She closed her eyes, letting time drift away like the breeze from the sea . . .

A larger wave skimmed up the sand, soaking their ankles, and Rufus barked in protest, running up to scrabble at Tom's knees to suggest that it was time to go home.

He bent and tickled the little dog in his favourite spot behind his ear. "Okay, okay — we're going." He smiled down at Vicky, that smile that sent her pulse into instant overdrive.

"Are you going to invite me in for coffee?"

Her mouth curved in a flirtatious smile. "Oh, I think so."

CHAPTER SEVENTEEN

The farmhouse had changed little in sixteen years — homely, but spotlessly clean, with polished wooden floors and comfortably upholstered furniture. A heavy antique silver punchbowl stood on the gleaming mahogany sideboard, and on the wall above was a fascinating display of photographs of some of the previous generations who had farmed this land, back to a solid-looking Victorian family in a proudly formal pose.

Tom's parents had changed little too. Vicky had wondered if she would feel awkward, knowing that they knew that their son didn't spend his nights in his own bed. But they were as warm and welcoming as they had always been.

"Ah, thank you, my dear." Tom's mother beamed as Vicky gave her the wine she had brought.

"Thank you for inviting me, Mrs Cullen."

"Ah, now, call us Jack and Pam," she insisted. "That's what you used to call us when you were a little girl — Uncle Jack and Auntie Pam."

"Oh, yes — I remember!"

She could feel the warmth of Tom's hand resting lightly on the small of her back. It had been almost a week since that first night together, and she was fathoms deep in love with him — so deep it scared her.

"Why, it's little Vicky Marston." Jack Cullen strolled through from the kitchen. His eyes twinkled as he bent to kiss her cheek. As tall as Tom, his hair grizzled with grey, his skin weathered brown by years in the open air. "Last time I saw you, you were all skinny arms and legs like a newborn calf — and now you've grown into a beauty! And you've brought wine — that's a good girl. I like a nice drop of wine. I brought back a few bottles with me from Oz — would you like to try one?"

She smiled warmly. "Yes, please."

"Don't suppose you'll say no either, will you, Tom?" He beamed at his son. "Come on through to the dining room."

"Did I hear someone mention wine? I thought you were never going to offer."

Vicky recognised the tall, rangy man in glasses coming down the stairs — the scorekeeper at the cricket.

Lisa followed him. "Hi, Vicky." She gave her a warm hug. "You've sort of met Ollie before, haven't you?"

"Well, only from a distance."

"Ah — then it's nice to meet you properly." He extended his hand to grasp hers. "Though I've heard all about you from Arthur. You've been very kind to him."

"He's a lovely old man."

"Oh, ah — he is that." He grinned at Tom, exchanging a high five. "Evening, mate. Everything okay?"

"Fine. Yourself?"

"Better when Uncle Jack gets round to opening the wine."

"Now then, it has to breathe," Jack protested. "You can't hurry a good red wine. Here we go."

He filled the glasses waiting on the sideboard, and passed them round. In the soft rays of the setting sun streaming in through the window, they glowed like rubies.

"It's a Shiraz from Hunter Valley." His eyes danced with mischievous laughter. "It's a lively little wine, with a touch of berries and spice."

"Oh, get along with you." His wife shook her head in fond exasperation. "Mr Connoisseur."

Vicky took a sip of the wine. "It's delicious," she approved.

"There now!" He shot Pam a look of happy triumph. "She knows her stuff, this one."

"Is the little one asleep?" Pam asked as Lisa set the baby monitor on the sideboard.

"Fast asleep. She won't wake for a couple of hours yet."

"Good. Well, sit down, everyone. Dinner's ready."

Tom held out a chair for Vicky. She glanced up at him as she sat down, and he smiled — that smile that made her heart skip. It was a reaction she couldn't control — every time he looked at her she felt as if she was going a little crazy.

The dinner was delicious — cool cucumber soup, followed by pork-and-apple pie with vegetables, which Vicky guessed were homegrown.

"Tuck in," Jack urged. "I like to see a lass with a good healthy appetite."

Tom's glance flickered towards her, smiling with a secret amusement, and she felt that faint blush of pink rise to her cheeks again. He appreciated her appetite too — though not necessarily her appetite for food.

"So how was Australia?" Ollie asked.

"Big! And they've got spiders you wouldn't believe. Every time you go to the dunny . . . !"

Pam rolled her eyes. "Thank you, Jack — we don't need to hear the details of your dunny adventures while we're eating."

He chuckled. "You had a few yourself. But it was an eye-opener, and no mistake. Running a herd that size, and coping with those conditions . . ."

"Is there still a drought problem?"

"There's always a drought problem."

Soon the men were deep in discussion of silage and carrying capacity and irrigation systems. Pam turned to Vicky.

"Tom tells me you've done some renovations to Molly's place. It certainly needed it."

"That's right." She smiled. "You must come over and have a look."

"I'd like that."

214

"Can I come?" Lisa asked eagerly.

"Of course." She turned back to Pam. "You knew Aunt Molly well, didn't you?"

"Oh yes — I knew her for nearly forty years." Pam laughed. "She was quite a character."

"So I've heard. I've found out quite a bit about her that I never knew. Dancing at the Moulin Rouge, modelling for a top Parisian fashion house. And I found a medal she was given for working with the Resistance in the Second World War."

Lisa's eyes widened. "But wouldn't she have been just a teenager then?"

Vicky nodded. "Yes, she was. But Mr Digby's friend, the one who found out about the medal for me, said there were quite a few teenagers who helped. The youngest child who was involved was only six years old."

"Six!" Lisa looked shocked. "That's not much older than my Noah!"

"It's true — I looked him up. His father was a Resistance leader, and he carried letters between groups in his schoolbag. Molly ran messages for the Resistance too, and sometimes she carried weapons for them. And Mr Kovacs, the medal expert, told me that she'd helped with the lifeline for airmen who'd been shot down, and escaped prisoners of war, guiding them between safe houses on their way to Spain."

"That's right — that was how she came to be left the cottage." Pam had finished her dinner and took a sip of her wine. "There was a pilot who'd broken his leg when he'd bailed out — he couldn't be moved for a couple of months. Molly took care of him — nursed him, took him food. His wife and baby daughter had been killed in the Blitz, and he never married again. When he died he left the cottage to Molly, in gratitude."

"Oh — that's so sad." Vicky sighed.

"And that wasn't all," Pam went on. "Molly told me that she had spent several years in East Berlin during the Cold War, running a nightclub and cabaret. Then when they closed the border she began smuggling defectors to the West."

"Wow!"

"She was allowed to go backwards and forwards into West Berlin every few weeks, to buy the good wines and spirits the senior party members preferred to the stuff you could mostly get in the East. The border guards never even thought of stopping her or searching her van — she was too friendly with the higher-ups."

Vicky listened to the story, fascinated.

"She had a secret compartment behind the passenger seat where a person could hide. She brought out several disaffected military and party members, but most of them were just ordinary people who wanted freedom and a better life. That was how she met Juan."

"She helped him escape?"

Pam shook her head. "No. There was another artist, who'd been blacklisted by the Russians — they didn't approve of his work. He'd been labelled a dissident and warned he was in danger of being arrested. By that time things were getting a bit too hot for her in Berlin, so she fled with him to Spain. There was a group of other artists living there, and that was where she and Juan met."

"Oh, yes — Mr Loughton, the auctioneer, told me she and Juan lived in an artists' colony near Barcelona. Molly modelled for several of the artists, but it was Juan she fell in love with. Did you ever meet him?"

"No — he died a few years before I married Jack. She didn't speak about him much."

"There was nothing of his in the cottage, except for the portrait, and a poem he'd written. I wonder why she got rid of everything?"

Pam's eyes softened. "She once told me that she didn't need anything to remember him by. She sold everything but the portrait, and sent the money to an orphanage in Spain."

"Oh . . ."

"That's lovely." Lisa sighed. "So romantic."

"Why did they come and settle in England?" Vicky asked.

"I don't know the details. It was something to do with his brother and an assassination attempt on some politician. They lived here for . . . oh, it must have been about fifteen years. Then Juan got sick — lung cancer. It was quite quick in the end."

"He wrote a poem for her?" Lisa asked, a wistful note in her voice. "And he'd painted that portrait of her, too."

"Yes — I found the poem in one of her books. And he did the sketch of Arthur's wife, and a few others." Vicky took a sip of her wine. "They're all in that same weird style — not quite surrealist, not quite cubist. I don't know what you'd call it — it was unique. Mr Loughton at the auction house said it was closest to Expressionism."

"He did one of my grandmother," Lisa recalled. "Mum thought it was rubbish — she kept threatening to throw it away. But I think she's still got it. She'd probably be quite keen to sell it, if it was worth anything."

"He did one of Jack's mother too," Pam added. "It's upstairs."

"That old thing?" From the other end of the table Jack laughed raucously. "It's hideous. If these auction people think they can sell it, let 'em! Be glad to see the back of it — gives me the heebie-jeebies."

"You're going to sell the portrait of Molly?" Pam asked.

Vicky nodded. "Yes. I'd like to keep it, but I need the money to pay the inheritance tax on the cottage. And besides . . . well, if it goes to an art gallery, more people will be able to see it."

"So you're going to stay here?"

"Yes." Vicky glanced briefly at Tom. "I love it here — the beach, the village, the countryside. It's so beautiful."

"It is. So we'll be neighbours. That's nice." She stood up to collect the empty plates, waving Vicky and Lisa back to their seats when they rose to help her. "No, sit down, you two. It won't take a tick to put these things in the dishwasher. Coffee, everyone?"

* * *

Vicky sighed in well-fed contentment. "That was a lovely evening."

They were strolling up the lane to the cottage, Tom's arm resting casually around her shoulders, Rufus running at their side and dodging in and out of the hedges. "You enjoyed it?"

"It was really nice to see your mum and dad again. They've hardly changed a bit. Though I suppose they must be in their sixties now."

"Dad's sixty-seven."

"So he'll be retiring soon?"

He laughed, shaking his head. "Farmers don't retire."

"The farm always comes first?"

"You've got it." He hesitated briefly. "Sometimes . . . outsiders don't understand how it is. I was engaged once, but . . . She didn't want to stay buried away down here." There was a tension in his voice. "So it didn't work out."

They walked in silence for a few moments. Vicky didn't want to tell him that she knew about Nyree — it didn't feel like something to discuss. She crossed her fingers behind her back as they reached her gate. "So . . . would you like to come in for a coffee?"

He smiled down at her, that smile that always sent her pulse into overdrive. "I like your thinking. Anyway, it looks like Rufus has already decided." The pup had raced up the front garden and was scrabbling excitedly at the door. "He's going to be asking me to move his basket up here."

He spoke lightly, but Vicky felt her heart skip. Could she dare hope that he was suggesting . . . ?

No — she mustn't let herself read too much into it. It had been less than a week . . . But the dream had lodged obstinately in her brain, and it wouldn't go away.

* * *

"Yes, you can get to Dartmoor very easily from here. It's only about a twenty-minute drive, at most." Vicky picked up one of the leaflets from the reception desk and handed it to the

218

couple who had enquired. "This will show you the easiest paths for walking."

Saturdays were always busy at the hotel, with guests leaving and new guests arriving. But she didn't mind — she enjoyed it. Even when, as tonight, it meant working late.

It was after nine o'clock when she left. A soft breeze was drifting in from the sea as she strolled up the hill, the air tinted gold by the last long rays of the sun as it slid down behind the hills to the west of the bay.

She had a lamb tagine cooking in the slow pot — if Tom was held up by the calving, she could put his share in the freezer. She turned into the lane — and stopped dead. Dammit. There was only one grey BMW that would be parked on her drive. What on earth was Jeremy doing here?

He was sitting in the front seat, absorbed by his phone. He didn't even notice her until she tapped on the window. His face was taut with annoyance as he climbed out of the car.

"Where the hell have you been?" he demanded.

"What do you mean, where have I been?" she retorted. "What are you doing here?"

"I came down to see you, since you aren't answering my calls. I've been sitting here for two hours."

"I've been to work. You could have texted to let me know you were coming."

"Work? What work?"

Vicky sighed impatiently. "Assistant manager at the hotel."

He frowned. "You're a qualified estate agent. What do you want with a job as an assistant manager in some crappy little three-star hotel?"

"Four star." She stepped past the car and stalked up the drive. "We can't stand here arguing — I suppose you'd better come in."

"That's not a very warm welcome."

"What do you expect?" She opened the door and left him to follow her into the kitchen.

He glanced around, his professional eye evaluating the changes. "Well, this is certainly an improvement. Though

219

you've spent rather too much on it — you'll be lucky to recoup the cost."

"Doesn't matter. I'm not selling."

"Not . . . ? Well, what are you going to do with it?"

"Live in it. Would you like a coffee?"

"Live in it? Don't be ridiculous. What would you want to do that for?"

"I like it. It's a nice cottage, a nice village. I have a job, friends." She chose not to mention that she had a boyfriend.

"You had a job and friends, until you walked away."

"The job wasn't really all that, and my friends were mostly your friends. I can't say I miss any of them. Was that a yes to the coffee?"

He sat down at the kitchen table. "You've changed."

She returned him a bland smile. "Yes, I expect I have. I don't see that as a problem."

She turned her back on him to fill the coffee machine.

Had he always been so annoying? As if he had the right to just walk in here and question her decisions. Breaking off her engagement had been the best thing she had ever done — perhaps her stepsister had inadvertently done her a favour by hardening her determination not to back down.

She glanced at the clock. Tom would usually come over around this time in the evening. But she knew that some of the cows were due to calf, and there was one that they had been a little concerned about, so he could be up with them all night.

The coffee was ready. She added more cream to hers than she had usually allowed herself when she had been with Jeremy, and carried the two mugs over to the table.

"So what are you doing here?" she asked again.

"We need to talk." He gestured impatiently with his hand. "That day . . . I just came home and found your ring, and that stupid note. No explanation. How could you just end it like that, with no warning?"

Vicky sipped her coffee slowly, contemplating what to tell him. "How's Jayde?"

A flicker of his eyes told her that she had hit home. "Jayde? Your stepsister? Why ask me that?"

"Have you come back to me because things didn't work out with her?"

"What things? Don't be silly, Vicky. Whatever would I have to do with Jayde?"

"You tell me."

"Oh, really, this is ridiculous! Have you got some stupid idea in your head that I was having an affair with her?" Too much bluster — he was giving himself away. "Of course she's pretty enough, if you like that sort. But frankly she's a bit of an airhead. I don't think she's got two brain cells to rub together."

"You don't need brain cells in bed."

"Oh, come on, Vicky." Indignant now. "You're imagining things — letting jealousy get the better of you. Don't you trust me?"

"Er . . . no." She took another sip of her coffee and put down the mug. "You see, I came home earlier that day — it must have been around one o'clock. I let myself in, and, gosh, what a surprise! Jayde's leather jacket, hanging in the hall. You know, the red one."

"Well, I . . ." He couldn't quite look her in the eye. "She must have left it there sometime when she came round."

"I might have assumed that. But then I heard giggling from the bedroom." She raised one hand to stop him speaking. "Please don't try to tell me it was the radio. I know her voice, and yours, well enough. And just to clinch it, I stopped for a bite of lunch in the café downstairs — you know the one. And guess who I saw coming out of the block, and sharing a touching farewell at the bus stop?"

It was almost amusing to watch Jeremy slowly deflating. His only response was a weak, "Oh." He dropped his head in his hands, twisting his fingers into his hair. "It was a mistake. She came on to me. I admit it — I was weak. I shouldn't have done it. But she came up to the flat and . . . we had a couple of glasses of Prosecco . . ."

"In the middle of the day?"

"Yes . . . well . . . she'd brought it with her — she wanted to celebrate getting to a thousand followers on her TikTok. And, well, one thing led to another. It was only the once."

"Once?" She arched one eyebrow in sardonic enquiry.

He hesitated. "Well . . . maybe a few times."

She laughed. "Oh, you're such a liar, Jeremy. I suppose that patter works well enough when you're trying to convince some poor unsuspecting stooge to sign up to the insurance company that pays you the best commission. But I'm not impressed."

His face darkened with annoyance. "You really have changed."

She sighed, shaking her head. "Okay, maybe that was a bit mean. But you can't say you didn't deserve it."

He managed a crooked smile. "Yes, well . . . I suppose I do."

Vicky watched him, surprised at what was almost an apology.

"So, you're really sure that's what you want? An end to everything we had, to call off the wedding, to throw in your job?"

"That's what I want."

"I see." His shoulders slumped. "But . . . look, can we at least still be friends?"

Vicky sighed. As infuriating as she found him, she couldn't quite bring herself to knock him back — she had thought that she was in love with him, once.

"Okay, yes, we can be friends," she conceded reluctantly. She glanced discreetly up at the clock again. It looked as if Tom wouldn't be coming tonight. She hoped the calf would arrive safely.

Jeremy smiled, and sniffed the air. "Is that your lamb tagine I smell cooking? That's always been my favourite."

"Have you eaten?" The words were out of her mouth before she could stop them. Damn her mother for bringing her up to always be so polite!

Jeremy looked delighted. "I had something in a ser-vice station on the way down, but I suspect it was made of cardboard."

She laughed, in spite of herself. Well, if he was going to stay for dinner, at least he'd brought his sense of humour. She'd feed him, and then with luck he'd be gone.

* * *

"That was delicious." Jeremy downed his second glass of wine and poured himself another. Vicky declined his offer of a refill. "This is nice. Like old times."

"I suppose so." As the evening wore on, she was begin-ning to ask herself why she had taken so long to break off their engagement — in fact why she had let herself get engaged to him in the first place.

"Vicky, I can't tell you how sorry I am. Jayde . . . it didn't mean anything. I still love you."

"Jeremy, don't—"

"No, hear me out," he pleaded. "I've done a lot of think-ing these past few weeks, and I realise I'd been letting things drift. I was taking you for granted. But it can be different now — *I* can be different. I promise . . ."

"Jeremy—"

"Can't we get back together again? We were good together — we had some good times, didn't we? We've always said we'd go to Paris — we could do that. A long weekend — it'll be great. What do you say?"

"No, Jeremy."

"Don't answer at once. Think about it."

"I don't need to think about it."

"Vicky, please." He reached across the table and tried to take her hand. "Don't throw it all away, what we had. I mean it when I say I love you."

"I'm sure you do — or at least you think you do." She drew her hand back out of reach. "But it's over, Jeremy. I'm not going to change my mind."

His mouth thinned, and for a moment she thought he was going to persist with the argument. Instead he smiled suddenly, and poured himself another large glass of wine. "This is a particularly fine Merlot, don't you think? I got a whole crate from Freddie Lester, at quite a decent price."

"That's good." Hmm — change of subject. She knew him well enough to recognise his usual tactic — divert the conversation from the bone of contention, then come back to it later.

He had quickly regained his usual easy confidence. "I always get a good deal. I always get what I want, in the end."

She returned him a level look.

"Well, I mean . . . most things. I wasn't referring to us getting back together. I wouldn't expect . . . I wouldn't take that for granted. I just hope . . . well, just think about it."

"Jeremy, I told you — I don't need to think about it. I've made up my mind — in fact I'd decided before finding out about you and Jayde. I realised we were going in different directions — we want different things. Let's just accept that, and settle for being friends."

His eyes flashed with anger and he drained his wine glass in one gulp, and poured himself another.

"That's your fifth glass. You're not going to be able to drive anywhere tonight." Her voice was taut with impatience. "You'd better stay."

The glint of triumph in his eyes fuelled her suspicion that he had deliberately drunk too much so that she would be forced to let him stay. As he said, he usually got what he wanted.

But if he thought he was going to share her bed, he would learn his mistake. "I'll make up the bed for you in the spare room. I won't be a minute."

She slipped away upstairs. It was late — well past eleven o'clock. It was unlikely that Tom would come now. But she would see him tomorrow. That thought gave her a warm feeling in her heart.

Tomorrow . . .

* * *

224

But Tom didn't come.

Vicky had seen a hungover Jeremy off after breakfast, hoping he wasn't still over the limit from last night's wine. She had filled the dishwasher and done some laundry, then gone down to Debbie's for lunch before heading to the hotel for her afternoon shift.

She was singing as she pottered around the kitchen preparing a Thai curry for dinner — Tom's favourite. But as the evening ticked by he didn't appear. Eventually she ate her curry alone at the kitchen table, then sat down to watch some television — alone.

It was odd — she hadn't minded being alone those first few weeks after she had come down here. She had enjoyed being able to pick any film she liked from Netflix or being able to concentrate on her writing.

But even in the short time since that first night with Tom, she had got used to him being there, to snuggle up with on the sofa or in bed.

The film ended, and she checked her phone again — no messages. Should she ring him? No — she had promised herself that she wouldn't be the needy girlfriend. Besides, he might be busy — there could be more than one of the cows having a difficult birth, or new calves needing a lot of attention.

Instead she settled in her workroom and turned on her computer to crack on with the chapter she was working on. But somehow she couldn't concentrate. She was too conscious of the slow movement of the hands of the clock on the wall above her desk.

She stayed up until almost one o'clock in the morning — but he didn't come.

The next morning she woke alone. That in itself wasn't unusual — Tom often left for milking before she woke. But there would be a warm dent in the pillow beside her, the unique male scent of his skin lingering on the sheets.

But today there was nothing — and the scent was fading.

Maybe she should walk up to the farm and see if he was there. On the pretext of a casual visit to Pam. No — maybe not. He'd see right through that. Just be patient — be sensible.

Or . . . maybe he didn't want to see her today. Maybe the initial gloss of their relationship was wearing off already and he wanted 'space'.

She rolled out of bed, impatiently brushing a tear from her eye. Maybe she was the one moving too quickly. But would he really have dumped her like that, without a word? Even if she had just been a stopgap, a temporary bandage over the wound in his heart inflicted by the beautiful Nyree Donovan?

Surely he would have been upfront about it, told her honestly . . . wouldn't he? She didn't know — she really didn't know him that well.

In the bathroom she gazed bleakly at her reflection in the mirror. She'd watched some more episodes of that detective series. It was a stupid thing to do, but they had taunted her, sitting there on her screen, prompting her to 'continue watching' the box set every time she opened it.

As Debbie had said, Nyree was stunning — flawless features, the loveliest smile, laughing blue eyes. And though it might be just the role she was playing, she seemed to be sweet-natured and charming.

How could she follow that?

Well, if it was over, it was over. She'd been in relationships before that had ended, and she'd survived — she'd survive this time.

But first she'd sit down on the edge of the bath and let herself have a really good cry.

* * *

An hour later she was on her way to Exeter. She wasn't going to hang around waiting for Tom Cullen to deign to drop by — that would just be pathetic. Anyway she needed to pick up a few things for the cottage — new curtains for the spare bedroom, a good office chair for her workroom. Some perfumed candles.

She had lunch in the sunshine on the pavement beside Cathedral Green, browsed in a bookshop, thought about treating herself to a pretty necklace in a quaint little jewellers near the art gallery.

But when she got home there was still no sign of Tom. No missed calls. No messages. Just a long, empty silence.

Why? Had she done something wrong? Said the wrong thing? Almost obsessively she picked over the memories of their last time together, but she couldn't find anything that might account for him ending things like this.

Could he be ill, maybe had an accident? No — he would have let her know, or his mum would. At the least, Debbie would certainly have known.

Oh for goodness' sake — why couldn't she work up the courage to just call him? This was the twenty-first century. Women didn't have to sit at home waiting for the phone to ring.

Had he seen Jeremy's car parked outside and jumped to the wrong conclusion? Without even giving her a chance to explain? If that was it, then she'd be damned if she'd go running to him, begging, apologising.

She'd done too much apologising with Jeremy — for putting the cutlery the wrong way up in the dishwasher or not ironing his shirts exactly as he liked them. No more.

She made herself toast for dinner — she didn't feel like eating much. There was nothing on television she wanted to watch, and she had come to the conclusion that the novel she was trying to write was the most boring rubbish anyone had ever committed to print.

She went to bed early, but lay awake, alternately staring at the ceiling and sobbing into her pillow. There was no denying it — she'd been dumped in the most unceremonious way since the demise of the fax machine.

* * *

The days passed in a cloud of dull misery. Even the news from the auction house of the date of the sale of Molly's portrait couldn't lighten her mood. She avoided going down to Debbie's, afraid her friend would be sympathetic and she'd end up crying in public.

It was made far worse when she was out weeding around the roses in the front garden, and saw Tom drive past in his silver-grey SUV. He didn't even glance in her direction. So — not ill, not in an accident. Just very clearly not interested.

Ambling up the hill after work on Friday evening, she was even beginning to wonder if she should sell the cottage after all, move away, start again somewhere else. But the thought was painful. She had been happy here, before she had been stupid enough to fall in love with Tom Cullen. She loved the village, she had friends . . .

Turning in through her front gate, she was startled by a blast of excited barking and Rufus hurtling towards her.

"Well, hello, you." She laughed, bending to tickle his ear. "Have you run away again?"

The little dog raced off to zoom round the garden at top speed, then came back to her for another ear-tickle.

"You'd better go home. Your master will be looking for you."

His response was to roll on his back, suggesting that she might like to tickle his pink tummy.

"Go on, go home." She pointed towards the farm. "Go! Shoo!"

A pair of liquid brown eyes regarded her, filled with canine mischief, then a flea was found, which required immediate attention from a flicking paw. A passing bumblebee had to be chased, and there was a very interesting smell to be investigated behind the water-butt.

Vicky sighed. "Am I going to have to catch you and drag you home?"

The enquiry was ignored as Rufus snuffled off down the side of the cottage to the back garden. It was clear that she didn't stand a chance of catching him, at least not without resorting to bribery.

Armed with a couple of biscuits from the kitchen, she set off in pursuit. She found him bouncing around happily in the long grass. He regarded the proffered biscuit with suspicion.

"Here, boy — look. Come and get it."

The little dog crept closer then darted away, inviting her with a play-bow to join in his game. As she reached to grab him he darted to one side, barking happily and setting off to zoom around the garden again.

"Oh, for goodness' sake . . ."

"Ah. I thought this was where I'd find you."

She turned sharply. Tom was standing there. He spared her the briefest glance, then hunkered down on his haunches to call to Rufus.

Vicky felt her heart racing, her mouth too dry to utter a word. He was here — but in seconds he would be gone, while her mind was still spinning between the pain of losing him and boiling anger at the way he had dumped her so casually.

He clipped on Rufus's lead and stood up, his eyes unreadable. "So you're still here then?"

She blinked, startled by the question. "Where else would I be?"

"Aren't you selling the cottage and going back to London?"

"You know I'm not. Why would you think that?"

He arched one dark eyebrow. "Your fiancé told me."

"*Jeremy* told you?"

"I came over after we'd delivered Violet's calf — and what a surprise, there was your fiancé's car on your drive. I knocked, and there he was, in his shirtsleeves, very much at home, the remains of your cosy supper for two on the table. And delighted to tell me that you were together again, all nice and cosy. He said that you were upstairs getting ready for bed."

Vicky stared at him, appalled. "He . . . ? Of all the . . . it wasn't true! I had no idea he was coming down."

"Oh?"

"I'd broken off my engagement weeks ago. I'd already decided I was going to do that when I found out he'd been screwing my stepsister, the dirty lying scumbag — I actually caught them at it. There was no way I'd ever take him back after that."

His dark gaze levelled on hers. Did he believe her? He had to believe her . . .

"And I was upstairs making up the bed for him in the spare room. He'd had too much to drink — he did that deliberately so he couldn't drive home." She drew in a long, deep breath and let it go. "I didn't sleep with him."

"You didn't?" The start of a smile was lifting the corner of his mouth.

"Of course I didn't. How could you even think that?"

"Oh." The smile widened, warm with relief. "It looks like I jumped to the wrong conclusion — again. We both seem to make a habit of that."

She laughed a little unsteadily. "We do, don't we?"

"I'm sorry. Will you forgive me?"

Something was constricting her throat, but she forced her voice past it.

"I . . . might."

"Please?"

He opened his arms, and she walked straight into them. Happiness was bubbling up inside her like champagne, and she wrapped her arms tightly around his waist, resting her cheek against his hard chest.

She wanted to tell him that she loved him, but it still felt a bit precarious. She would tell him — soon. But for now . . . She lifted her face, smiling up at him as his mouth came down to hers in a long, deep, tender kiss.

CHAPTER EIGHTEEN

The buzz in the auction room was electric. Every seat was occupied and the bidding for the previous lots had been lively, with prices for all the paintings exceeding expectations.

Vicky was sitting at the end of the front row with Tom, unconsciously gripping his hand as the auctioneer announced the next lot — the five charcoal sketches Juan-Jorge had made of his neighbours in Sturcombe.

They were to be sold as a single lot. The porters in their white coats and gloves paraded solemnly across the front of the room to prop them on the display easels, and their images flashed up on the two big screens beside the auctioneer's head.

Bez's blog, with the story of the portraits and Juan-Jorge's final years in a quiet seaside village in South Devon, and Molly's amazing life, had gone viral. It had caught the interest of the media — the news of the sale had even made some of the national papers. Which was amazing for an artist who wasn't well known in the UK.

"This is it," she whispered to Tom as the bidding started. "I hope they get a decent amount."

The bids were clocking up on the screen beside the images of the sketches, showing the running tally in half

231

a dozen currencies. Along each side of the auditorium, the raised walkways were lined with assistants taking phone bids and internet bids.

The auctioneer had started the bidding at ten thousand pounds. Vicky had been staggered when Mr Loughton had suggested that sum, but he had been proved right — the numbers were mounting rapidly by the thousands. Forty thousand . . . Forty-five . . .

"How on earth does he keep up with it?" She was swivelling her head, trying to see who was bidding. "Just don't sneeze or we could find ourselves buying them back!"

Tom laughed. "It doesn't work like that. You don't even have a bidding paddle."

"Is it the same as how livestock auctions work?"

"Pretty much. Though livestock auctions are smellier."

She bit back a bubble of laughter. This was like some crazy dream — she felt as if she was drunk. The bidding had passed fifty-five thousand, but at last it was slowing.

"To you, sir. Fifty-eight thousand? Thank you."

A woman in a smart scarlet blazer sitting in the second row raised her numbered paddle — Vicky had noticed that she had just watched until the bidding passed forty-five thousand before joining in.

The auctioneer pointed at her. "Fifty-nine thousand — it's with you." He glanced back at the previous bidder. "Do you want to raise, sir? I'll take five hundred."

The man hesitated briefly, then shook his head.

"Very well. Are there any more bids? Then once . . . twice . . ."

The gavel came down with a sharp clack, and Vicky let go her breath.

"Oh, wow! That's going to be . . . heavens, nearly ten thousand pounds each after commission. Debbie's mum's going to be able to buy a very big freezer!"

The room relaxed, with a general buzz of conversation, rustling of papers, a few people leaving their seats, more crowding into the back. The porters came in to remove the sketches from their easels and convey them through to the back room.

Slowly the noise subsided into a silence filled with anticipation. The porters returned, carrying Molly's portrait as if it was a goblet of pure gold. They set it up on the easel, and its image appeared on the screens to a collective, "Oooh," around the room.

"I can't believe this," Vicky whispered. "I never thought it could be worth much." She laughed edgily. "Goes to show how much I know about art."

Tom squeezed her hand. "Well, you're about to find out how much it's worth."

"I know. I'm going to have to close my eyes — I can't watch."

He laughed softly. "That's no good. You'll still be able to hear."

The auctioneer raised his hands for silence. "Ladies and gentlemen, I'm pleased to present our final lot of the day. This was the last piece that Juan-Jorge Conejero painted before his death — a portrait of his lover, Meline Marston. Unknown for over forty years, it has a full provenance and has been fully authenticated by three experts. I have online bids and can start the bidding at three million pounds."

Vicky drew in a sharp breath. "That's more than the reserve!" she whispered to Tom.

The elegant room, with its pale-grey walls and crystal chandeliers swinging from the high ceiling, seemed to be swaying like a ship at sea. The bids were racking up even faster than for the sketches. Paddles were being raised all round the room, the heat and the electric tension were soaring. The numbers the auctioneer was calling sounded like a jumble in her ears . . .

She flinched when the gavel came down.

There was a collective release of breath, a round of applause, a few cheers. Tom whistled softly.

"How much?" she whispered.

"Seven million, three hundred and fifty thousand."

He had to repeat the figure slowly before she could take it in. She closed her eyes for a moment, trying to breathe slowly. Seven million . . .

People had gathered round to congratulate her.

"That was a very good sale."

"A record for a Conejero."

"The Pradera will be delighted to have got it for their collection."

"Yes . . . yes, thank you." She was gripping Tom's hand tightly, her heart thumping, her mouth dry. Seven million . . .

The room was emptying slowly as people drifted away. A newspaper photographer wanted a picture of her beside the portrait, the reporter with him wanted to ask questions. She obliged in a blur, not even sure what she was saying.

There was champagne to be sipped with Mr Loughton and the representative from the Pradera, and several other bigwigs of the art world, then paperwork to be attended to. But at last they were able to step out into the early evening bustle of London's trendy heartland.

"Dinner?" Tom suggested.

"I don't think I could eat a thing."

"Let's see if you can be tempted."

* * *

The restaurant was just round the corner from the auction house. Leafy fig trees in copper pots, their branches laced with golden fairy lights, were dotted between circular tables with scarlet tablecloths — the impression was of intimacy, though they were surrounded by other diners.

The head waiter showed them to a corner table and presented the leather-bound menus. Vicky barely noticed what she was ordering — she didn't even realise that Tom had ordered champagne until the waiter filled her glass.

"Oh . . . !"

Tom's eyes lit with amusement. "It's a champagne moment, don't you think?" He raised his glass in a toast. "To Juan-Jorge — and Molly."

"To Molly." She took a sip, letting the bubbles sparkle on her tongue. "I'm still in shock. That woman, the one in the red jacket — she was from the Pradera, wasn't she?"

"That's right. I spoke to her briefly while you were doing the interview. You'll be invited over to see the portrait once it's on exhibition there."

"They bought the sketches too, didn't they? Won't everyone be gobsmacked when they find out how much they've made!"

He smiled. "I suspect there's going to be a very big party."

Vicky nodded — yes, a party. A housewarming and a celebration of Aunt Molly's legacy.

The waiter had brought their starter — a cool salmon mousse. Vicky found that her appetite had returned — she had been too excited to eat any lunch and she was starving. The main course — tender lamb cutlets with julienne vegetables — was just as delicious.

"So what happens now?" Tom asked as the waiter came to clear their plates.

"Dessert?"

He laughed. "I thought you weren't hungry."

"I thought I wasn't. But they've got tiramisu — my favourite."

"I'll just have coffee," he told the waiter. He picked up the champagne bottle and refilled their glasses. "What I meant was, are you really going to stay in Sturcombe?"

She glanced across the table at him. Did he really think she would want to go back to London? "Of course."

The warm gleam in his eyes suggested that he had liked her response. "So what are you going to do with your money? I heard you tell Debbie you didn't fancy a world cruise."

She laughed at that. "No, I don't — I can't think of anything I'd dislike more. But all that money . . . even after I've paid the commission to the auction house and the inheritance tax, I'll have plenty to live on — I'll be able to concentrate on writing my novel."

"That'll be good."

He sounded sincere. Not like Jeremy, who had dismissed her dream of being a writer as childish nonsense.

"I almost deleted it at one point," she confessed. "But when I went back to it . . . the break seemed to have worked. It all started to flow; new ideas kept popping into my head. I don't know if it'll be any good, or if it'll ever get published. But I've dreamed about it for a long time. And . . . I have another idea."

"Oh?"

"I thought I might buy some houses in Sturcombe, and let them just to local people at affordable rents. When I thought the painting might make a couple of million I was thinking of just one or two, but now I could buy maybe half a dozen. And then I could put the income from the rents to buying more. What do you think?"

He smiled with instant approval. "I think it's a great idea."

She laughed again. "I know I said I didn't want to be an estate agent, but this would be different. I wouldn't be working for Charlotte Thorington, for a start! It would be mine. And it would be about helping people have a home, not making some greedy landlord rich." She picked up her champagne glass and raised it in another toast. "Sturcombe Properties."

"Sturcombe Properties." Tom smiled as he clinked his glass against hers. "And I have something else we might drink to."

He put his hand in his pocket and took out a small box, which he laid on the table in front of her. A jeweller's box. Dark blue velvet, inscribed in gold — Digby's. She lifted her gaze to his.

"Open it," he urged softly.

Her hand was shaking as she lifted the lid. A glint of emeralds, rich green, reflecting the fairy lights above her head in pinpricks of fire.

"Aunt Molly's ring . . ."

"Your ring."

"But . . . how did you get it?"

"I went into Digby's to get a new strap for my watch, the day after you went in to sell Molly's jewellery. We were chatting while old Cyril was fitting the strap, and he showed it to me, told me how you'd loved it. He'd decided to keep it back in case you changed your mind about selling it."

"Oh . . . what a lovely man!"

"He is. I asked if he'd sell it to me, and he said only if I gave it to you. I think he must be psychic."

Vicky felt her heart pounding. She didn't want to jump to conclusions about his intentions, but . . . there was usually only one reason why a man would give a woman a ring like this.

"But . . . you didn't even like me then," she protested, laughing unsteadily.

"Didn't I?" He smiled, a slow, enigmatic smile that left her even more confused.

"Well, I . . ."

He took the ring from the box and picked up her left hand. "I needed to know that you really are going to stay, that it's what you really want, for yourself, without any pressure from me. I love you, Vicky Marston. Will you marry me?"

And breathe . . . "I . . . don't think I'd make a very good farmer's wife."

He laughed, shaking his head. "You'll make this farmer an excellent wife. It's you I want, just as you are."

She looked at the ring, and his hand holding hers. He was waiting for an answer. It had been a day for dreams to come true, but this . . . to marry him . . .

But . . . could he really be in love with her? Could skinny and not-quite blonde really replace that gorgeous redhead? Would she always be second best, even though she wore his ring?

Or should she take the chance, trust her dreams . . . ?

"Yes." The answer came before her mind had consciously framed it. All the breath seemed to have left her lungs as he slid the ring onto her third finger. "Oh, yes."

* * *

"Great party, Vicky."

"Thank you." She smiled at Brenda. How things had turned around since the first time they'd met! She'd been a stranger then. Now she had a whole crowd of new friends, all of them here tonight for a combined housewarming party and engagement party and celebration of the sale of Juan-Jorge's portraits.

The French windows in the sitting room stood open and many people had drifted out into the back garden to enjoy the warm evening. Tom was out there chatting to Arthur Crocombe's son, Simon; her stepfather and Jack Cullen were discussing wines, and Debbie and Bill were dancing on the lawn to the music pouring out from her stereo.

She had even spotted Bez in the shadows round the corner of the cottage, heavily snogging Wayne, Tom's apprentice at the farm.

She felt a small glow of satisfaction as she wandered around the room picking up a few empty glasses. The ring on her finger sparkled with green fire every time it caught the light.

She had taken the chance, chased her dreams — whatever the outcome, it had to be worth the risk.

Carrying the glasses through to the kitchen she found her mother at the sink, washing up. "Hey, there's no need to do that, Mum," she protested. "They can all go in the dishwasher later."

"Oh, these few bits won't take a minute." She set the glasses down on the draining board in a neat row and wiped her hands on a towel. "You've made this very nice." She glanced approvingly around the kitchen. "Very practical."

"Thanks." Vicky managed not to roll her eyes — 'practical' was second only to 'sensible' in her mother's lexicon.

"So you're really going to stay here now?"

"Of course. I love it."

"Well, you do seem to have made lots of friends." Her mother still sounded slightly puzzled by it all.

"Yes." Vicky smiled reassuringly. "They're really nice people."

"And your Tom seems to have grown into a very nice young man. Though it's a shame about Jeremy."

Vicky laughed dryly. "Not really."

Her mother sighed. "Well, I suppose you know your own mind."

Vicky smiled to herself. She had been anticipating the word 'sensible' but she suspected that her mother didn't think she was being sensible at all.

She hadn't told her mother the whole story of what had happened — she didn't want to create a problem in the family.

It had been a relief that Jayde hadn't accompanied their parents on this visit. She had spoken to her only once since that fateful weekend.

She wouldn't have spoken to her at all, but she had rung on someone else's phone and Vicky had answered it because she hadn't recognised the number.

Jayde had been full of indignant self-justification. "You were going to break up with him anyway, so why are you so pissed off?"

"Jayde, you were sleeping with him while I was still engaged to him."

"Well, I—"

"*While I was still engaged to him!*"

"So that's it? I suppose you're never going to speak to me again, even though we're sisters?"

"Ah, you remembered that now?" Vicky sighed. "Of course I'm going to speak to you again, but it's not like borrowing a pair of shoes without asking. He was my fiancé — sisters don't do that to each other."

"Even though . . . ?"

"Even though. Goodbye, Jayde. I'll call you . . . sometime."

"Goodbye."

At least by the end of the call Jayde had had the grace to sound a little contrite. Though they hadn't been close for a long time Vicky had always been fond of her sister. She hoped that somehow they could rebuild that bond, for her mother and stepfather's sake.

And she had felt better for saying what had needed to be said.

Her mother picked up a plate of pizza fingers. "I'll just take these through."

Vicky began to load some more mini sausage rolls onto a plate, but turned as Lisa came into the kitchen. "Hi — just came to get some more wine."

"Here." Vicky gestured towards the row of bottles on the worktop. "There's plenty."

Lisa selected a bottle of red and one of white. "It's a really good party. Everyone's saying that."

"It's certainly a lot more fun than the ones we used to have with Jeremy's friends." Now she did roll her eyes. "All terribly sophisticated, *dahling*, with everyone standing around sipping wine and claiming they could detect a hint of dried cherries, sandalwood and tar."

Lisa laughed. "Sounds like you had a lucky escape."

"I certainly did."

Lisa leaned her hip against the worktop. "I never met him, and I might be biased — being related by marriage and all — but I'd say Tom's a much better catch."

Vicky glanced down at her ring. "He is." Her mouth quirked into a crooked smile. "I can't believe Nyree Donovan tossed him back in the pool, even for a part in a big TV series."

Lisa returned her a look of quizzical surprise. "That's not quite how it was."

"Oh?"

"I thought you'd come in here to get more wine?" They both turned as Tom appeared in the doorway. "People are dying of thirst out there."

"Just going." Lisa's eyes danced, and impulsively she wrapped her arms around Vicky in a warm hug. "Ask him about it!"

He smiled that heart-bumping smile as he strolled across the kitchen to Vicky. "Great party."

"So people keep telling me."

He glanced at the glasses on the draining board. "Have you been washing up?"

"No — that was my mum."

"Being sensible?"

"And practical."

"Ask me about what?"

Damn — she was hoping he hadn't heard that. But if she was ever going to resolve all the questions lurking in her mind she had to ask him. "We were talking about Nyree."

"Nyree?"

"Your ex-fiancée."

He laughed without humour. "Yes, I know who she is." His gaze flickered away from hers, then returned. "She's an actress — she was down here filming for a television series." His voice was cool, almost detached. "She's beautiful — absolutely stunning. Hit me like a ton of bricks — and she seemed to feel the same. We were engaged inside of a month."

He reached out to filch one of the sausage rolls.

"At first it was . . . She seemed to be really enthusiastic about living down here. She was talking about starting up her own theatre company, having people come down for holidays and theatre workshops, as well as performances. It was going to be a really big thing."

Vicky could feel a knot of tension coiling in her stomach.

"But . . . I don't know. It was like she was just playing a role, starring in her own miniseries. It wasn't long before the novelty began to wear off. She began to grumble about being buried down here in the wilds of Devon, missing all the parties and premieres. She started trying to persuade me to move up to London with her."

Vicky's eyes widened in surprise. "But surely she should have known you'd never do that. You'd never leave the farm."

"Quite." His mouth thinned. "For a while I did consider selling the organics business, splitting my time between here and London. But it was never going to work — Dad's not getting any younger, and he couldn't manage the farm without me. Besides, Nyree wouldn't be satisfied with that sort of arrangement. She was used to getting her own way, and when she found out it wasn't going to happen, she . . . wasn't very happy."

Vicky didn't need the translation — 'wasn't very happy' was probably a very big understatement.

"Then she got an offer of a part in some big TV series in America. I'm not going to lie — by then it was nothing but a relief."

She put her hand up to his cheek. "So you didn't mind her going?"

He smiled crookedly. "She left scars. She didn't break my heart, but she made me . . . wary. Wary of getting involved again — wary of outsiders."

"Like me."

"That was what I thought at first. That's why I was a bit off with you."

"A *bit*?"

He laughed. "Okay — more than a bit. I was trying not to be attracted to you — which was difficult, as I *was* attracted to you. But then I realised that in teaching me a hard lesson about when to be wary, she'd taught me something even more important — how to recognise the right one when she came along." He slid his arms around her and drew her close. "Which I did." He dropped a kiss on the top of her head. "By the way, have I told you this evening that I love you?"

"I think you might have mentioned it once or twice. Um . . . remind me. Have I told you that I love you?"

"You did say something along those lines, but I don't mind hearing it again." He took both her hands, lacing his fingers in hers. "Come and dance with me."

Her heart was already dancing. *The right one* . . . Not second best.

Instead of leading her out through the sitting room to the back garden, he drew her out to the front. Here it was quiet, private. A soft breeze was blowing in from the sea, rustling through the leaves of the trees and stirring the lingering fragrance of jasmine and roses from the flowerbeds. A million stars glittered in the inky sky — the moon was a thin silver crescent like the imprint of a thumbnail.

The grass was soft and springy beneath their feet as he drew her into his arms, and they danced slowly to the music that was spilling out through the open windows. His mouth came down to claim hers in a long, sweet, tender kiss.

Love is the stars and the summer breeze
Love is the silence in a kiss

At last she could let herself believe that he really was in love with her. And as she lifted her arms to wrap them around his neck, her hands came together and her fingers brushed against the ring on her finger. Aunt Molly's ring — entwined hearts.

Molly had had the courage to love, and to follow her dreams. Maybe her own dreams hadn't been quite as dramatic, but she had found out how important it was to follow them.

And 'sensible' be damned!

THE END

ACKNOWLEDGEMENTS

My thanks to Emma and all the lovely people at Choc Lit and Joffe Books who have helped pull this book into shape. Their attention to detail is incredible.

THE CHOC LIT STORY

Established in 2009, Choc Lit is an independent, award-winning publisher dedicated to creating a delicious selection of quality women's fiction.

We have won 18 awards, including Publisher of the Year and the Romantic Novel of the Year, and have been shortlisted for countless others. In 2023, we were shortlisted for Publisher of the Year by the Romantic Novelists' Association.

All our novels are selected by genuine readers. We are proud to publish talented first-time authors, as well as established writers whose books we love introducing to a new generation of readers.

In 2023, we became a Joffe Books company. Best known for publishing a wide range of commercial fiction, Joffe Books has its roots in women's fiction. Today it is one of the largest independent publishers in the UK.

We love to hear from you, so please email us about absolutely anything bookish at choc-lit@joffebooks.com

If you want to hear about all our bargain new releases, join our mailing list: www.choc-lit.com/contact

Milton Keynes UK
Ingram Content Group UK Ltd.
UKHW020804130524
442628UK00004B/253

9 781781 897041